I was almost to the foot of the ship's ramp, when I screamed and stopped dead in my tracks. A man who looked just like Len was there, but it was a Len I had never known. He was unbelievably big and well-muscled, wearing not a single stitch of clothing. I screamed again and cringed away from him, but he was on me in a flash. He threw me to the ground and over on my face, then bound my hands behind my back. I screamed for help, pleaded for mercy, but it was all wasted breath. *I was lifted to a wide, brawny shoulder, and carried against my will into that dread, brooding forest. . . .*

SHARON GREEN writes: "I've been reading science fiction since the age of twelve, began writing even before then, but never got serious about writing science fiction until five years ago. I read a speech of Robert Heinlein's that said, "Don't talk about it, do it!" So I did. Once turned on, it hasn't stopped yet. In my youth, I studied archery, fencing and horseback riding; taught archery at summer camp, rode in the drill team, and fenced at college. In the present I've studied belly dancing for two years and karate for one, and will probably go for further advancement in karate this spring. I sell steel for a living, and sometimes say to myself, "Bar steel by day, edged steel by night."

The Warrior Within

Sharon Green

DAW BOOKS, INC.
Donald A. Wollheim, Publisher

1633 Broadway, New York, N.Y. 10019

DEDICATION
For Moishe, who started it all,
and for my father, who left too soon.

FIRST PRINTING, FEBRUARY 1982

1 2 3 4 5 6 7 8 9

 DAW TRADEMARK REGISTERED
U.S. PAT. OFF. MARCA
REGISTRADA. HECHO EN U.S.A.

PRINTED IN U.S.A.

★ 1 ★

The infernal banging had no trouble breaking through my sleep. I wrapped the pillow around my head and that drowned out most of it, but as soon as I drifted off to sleep again my grip loosened, and the pillow was pushed aside by the din.

"Fatherless son of a female trajg!" I snarled in Baldochi, struggling out of the covers and to my feet. I didn't know what time it was, but as far as I'm concerned, a racket like that is a challenge day or night. I made it out of my bedroom and down the ramp to the first floor, then headed for the front door.

I caught a glimpse of myself as I passed the hall mirror, and would have turned back if I hadn't been in such a foul humor. My hair, unfashionably long and unfashionably dark brown, was hanging every which way, including over my eyes. My yellow sleep suit was brief enough to earn me a citation from any peaceman alive, and I wasn't even wearing any makeup. All in all a pretty outrageous sight, but I didn't give a damn. I'd needed the sleep I'd lost, and somebody was going to pay for it.

I was out into the sunshine before I realized it was there, and I had to squeeze my eyes nearly shut to keep from being blinded. The banging started again from my left, and I knew I'd been right. Sandy Kemper was at it again, but this time he wasn't going to get away with it. Tinkering belongs in the privacy of your workshop, not in the public nervous system.

With my eyes opened to mere slits, I stalked through the bright, windless sunshine across the grass to the verge of

5

Sandy's landing circle. Sandy was there, in a dark green one-piece, leaning into the guts of his deep blue quadriwagon, and the banging was coming from the inside of the access breach. I was vaguely aware of someone or something stretched out under a nearby tree, but I paid no attention. Sandy was my target, and a very tempting target he made.

I stopped about a foot away from him, dutifully restraining myself as I called out his name, but the noise he was making drowned me out. I shrugged a little with what I knew was an evil grin, stepped a bit closer, then booted him in the behind with my bare right foot.

The banging stopped with a muffled, "Hey!" then there was a hollow-sounding clank, followed by Sandy twisting himself out of the quadriwagon. He straightened up with one hand on his head and a pained expression on his face, but he went wide-eyed at the sight of me.

"Terry," he said weakly and for some reason nervously. "What are you doing here?"

"I heard your summons so I came right over," I answered, folding my arms. "Or maybe I was mistaken and it was supposed to be a mating call. I've never heard the mating call of a quadriwagon."

"It won't envelop," he explained apologetically, gesturing vaguely toward the 'wagon. "What good is a quadriwagon that won't envelop?"

"What good indeed," I agreed pleasantly. "All you can do with it then is take ground trips. Long, *distant* ground trips. Why the hell don't you try it!"

He flinched a little at my almost-shrill roar, then pushed his palms placatingly at me. "Now, Terry, no need to lose your temper. I had no idea you were home yet, or I would have. . . ."

"Well, now you know!" I snapped. "It isn't bad enough that I had to spend four months straightening out that mess in Dremmler's sector, just to get back in time for the Nervous Nellies' Annual Hysterics and Fit-Throwing Convention. Oh, no! After fourteen solid hours of diplomatically assuring every neurotic xenophobe on the planet that we are *not* in imminent danger of being invaded by the nearest alien barbarian horde, I really needed your symphonic rendition of 'When Worlds Collide'! Sandy, you may be a colleague of sorts, but so help me if I hear even one more tinkle out of you, I'll call the peacemen and activate an action against you for fire, flood, pestilence and rape! Do you read me?"

"Loud and clear," he groaned, covering his eyes with one hand. "Very, very loud and perfectly clear."

"You'd better," I told him flatly. "Your XD-5 rating will be as worthless as that quadriwagon if *I* press charges. Just remember that."

I gave his tall, thin form a last glare, turned to go back to my house, and promptly bounced off a brick wall instead. I "oofed" and went down, my hair obligingly covering my entire face.

"Terry, are you all right?" Sandy asked anxiously as I pawed the hair out of my eyes. He reached down fast to help me to my feet, but I ignored his outstretched hands in favor of the brick wall I'd collided with.

The man who stood there looked ten feet tall from where I sat in the grass. He also seemed about six feet wide, and every inch of his deeply tanned body was hard-muscled and trim. He had brilliant, light blue eyes, a mane of thick, light blond hair, and a grin pasted on his broad, rugged face. He stood easily relaxed with his brawny arms folded across his enormous chest, and all he wore was a pair of brief, dark gray swim trunks. I frowned as I looked at him, seeing something very out-of-place about him, there in the suburbs of Tallion City. For some reason, he did not belong.

"Here, let me help you up." Sandy fidgeted next to me, but I'd already decided to try out a theory that had just occurred to me. I raised my knees a little and leaned on them with my forearms, then smiled sweetly at Sandy.

"I think I'll add assault to that list of charges," I told him, and watched his face go pasty yellow. "Who's your co-assailant?"

"Terry, please be reasonable," Sandy begged, beads of sweat forming on his forehead. "This is just a friend of mine from Ashton who's visiting me for a week or two. You don't really want to make trouble for him, do you?"

"Why not?" I asked mildly. "What's his name?"

"It's—ah—Fred. Fred O'Herlihy," Sandy stuttered. "Fred O'Herlihy from Overton."

"I thought he was from Ashton," I commented, staring at a Sandy who looked like he was about to faint.

"That's right, that's right, Ashton. He moved from Overton to Ashton."

"Or vice versa," I said disgustedly and got to my feet unaided. "Sandy, who do you think you're kidding? That story wouldn't have got past a retarded seven-year-old, let alone a Prime XenoMediator. Come on, now, give. Who is he and what's he doing here?"

"I can't tell you," Sandy said in agony, just about wringing his hands. "Terry, please. Just go back to your house and forget all about this. You have my word that I won't make another sound."

"I'll bet you won't," I drawled, staring at "Fred O'Herlihy." Good old Fred still looked ten feet tall, but his grin had widened. "Sandy, I have a hunch that Murdock McKenzie has another lark going. How's my hunch quotient?"

"As high as ever," Sandy acknowledged miserably, his shoulders sagging. "I'm sorry, Terry, but I'm afraid I'll have to ask you to come into my house. Murdock will want to know about this."

"Not as much as Jack will want to." I grinned. "I can't wait to see the fur flying between those two again. This time Murdock will lose his ears. Let's see whose call gets through first."

I started back toward my house again, gleefully eager to pass on the word, and half-heard Sandy say something like, "Tammad!" It meant absolutely nothing to me, so I ignored it, but three steps later I got a very strong hint about what it might mean. A giant hand covered half my upper arm, and I was pulled definitely and firmly to a halt.

"Let go of my arm, Fred," I said in exasperation to the still grinning giant. "I have a top-priority call waiting to be made, and you're wasting my time."

"Terry, you must understand," Sandy said pitiably as he came up. "Murdock is depending on me and I can't let him down. You can call Jack after Murdock speaks to him, but you can't call Jack first."

"Oh, can't I?" I asked, tapping a bare foot in the grass. "In case you didn't know, Sandy, harboring an unregistered alien is against the law on this planet. For a member of the Xeno-Diplomacy Bureau to do it—on orders, yet!—is even worse, but the real kicker is the nature of the alien in question. I dare you to deny that whatever planet he comes from, he's of the warrior-equivalent caste. Go ahead, deny it!"

Sandy's long jaw dropped, and the look in his eyes was almost wild. "How can you possibly know all these things?" he demanded in near hysteria. "I can almost believe some of the rumors that are whispered about Prime XenoMediators. Terry, are you a telepath, too?"

"Don't be ridiculous!" I snorted. "It isn't telepathy when you use your eyes and head. Sandy, you're already in over your ears. Do yourself a favor and tell him to let me go."

"I can't," he agonized. "I *must* call Murdock. Tammad, bring her along to the house, please."

Sandy hurried on ahead, and his pal Tammad followed leisurely after him. Since I was still firmly attached to the giant's hand, I ended up going in that direction, too. The lawn stretched out quiet and green from house to house as far as I could see, but there wasn't a single person in view on it anywhere. That lack made me decide on a course of action I normally would never even have considered.

"Peacemen!" I shouted at the Neighborhood in general, trying to be loud enough to be heard. "Somebody call a—mmf!"

My yell cut off when the giant's hand slid firmly across my mouth and stayed there. I struggled against him, trying to pull his hand away with both of mine, but it was a waste of time. I'm slightly above average in height, but my head didn't even reach his chin. With his right hand over my mouth, he reached his left arm around my waist and lifted me off the ground, then continued on toward Sandy's house.

The trip ended in Sandy's inner study. The room was as flat and unimaginative as Sandy himself, done in various shades of brown and tan. It had a long, wide couch of dark brown leather against the back wall, four lighter brown leather chairs scattered here and there across the tan carpeting, a very neat and totally outdated light brown rembowood desk and chair on the wall to the left of the door, and matching floor-to-ceiling bookshelves on the wall to the right of the door. Brown and tan woodland scenes set in limited-frame movement squares hung on the walls above the couch and desk, but none of that was of any help to me. I'd been beating my heels against Tammad's right leg, hoping to make him shift his grip and thereby give me a chance to break loose, but I'd had no luck. Tammad ignored the kicks as if they were happening to somebody else, carried me down the hall and into the study, finally dumping me on the room's wide couch. I landed on my hands and knees on the soft leather pillows, and took a minute to flex my jaw before sitting straight. Tammad was in an easy crouch not three feet away from me, his arms resting on his broad thighs, the same idiotic grin on his face.

"The next time you try that you'll lose a finger," I snarled, pushing my hair back out of my eyes. "And what the hell are you staring at?"

"You," he answered in a deep, strong voice that matched the rest of him. "The thought has come that should you brush your hair, you would not be unattractive."

"You can't afford to talk," I countered, pulling my hand away from my hair. "Your hair looks like it was hacked off with a knife. And unless I'm mistaken, that's a nice, thick Rimilian accent you've got there. What are you doing so far from home?"

"Green eyes," he mused, ignoring my question as he looked me over in a way I'd never experienced before. "Such eyes are highly prized on my world. Most have eyes like mine, blue as the skies when no storms blow, but some very few have eyes green as the seas. I am pleased to see a woman with green eyes."

That insolent grin was getting me angrier and angrier, and his attitude wasn't doing much to help matters, so I decided to see how easily he might be reached.

"*L'lenda banarad*," I told him distinctly and watched as his blue eyes hardened with anger, then immediately changed back with his laughter.

"You place me well." He grinned in amusement. "I am indeed *l'lenda*—a warrior. But it is not wise to order a warrior not to overstep himself unless you carry sword in hand. I do not believe you could easily lift a sword."

"I'm stronger than I look," I said, eyeing the still open door. The inner study didn't have a window, but it did have that nice, open door. "Now why, I wonder, would Murdock McKenzie be hiding a Rimilian barbarian *here*?" I mused, shifting slightly to get my legs out from under me. "Because he plans on doing something with you? But why, then, doesn't he do it? Possibly because the time isn't right. Does he have to wait for something? Do *you* know what Murdock is waiting for, *l'lenda*? Or is he just using you, as a poor, helpless pawn? Poor barbarian, being used by others."

"No man uses me!" the barbarian growled, rising again to his full height. He was angry, and that's what I'd been trying for. I quickly flipped a couch pillow at his face and dived for the doorway, but as fast as I'd moved, he moved even faster. His hand went up, knocking the pillow aside, and he caught me with his other arm before I'd taken two full steps. He casually tossed me back onto the couch, and stood studying me.

"Neither am I to be used by a woman," he told me, and then the grin was back stronger than ever. "Now do I see why the Sandy Kemper regarded your presence as he did. He is not man enough to hold you in place."

"And you are?" I asked, my hands curled into fists as I fought to keep my temper. I had to get out of there!

"I am what I am," he answered, still amused. "Deeds may speak where words stand mute."

"That has all the earmarks of an ancient adage," I said in disgust, putting my arm up on the back of the couch. "How long are you going to keep me here?"

"Only until the Sandy Kemper has spoken with the Murdock McKenzie." He grinned, folding his arms as he looked me over in that exasperating way again. "The Sandy Kemper has then given you leave to go. I will not be pleased to see you go."

"You won't be pleased to see me come back, either!" I snapped. "When my boss hears about this, he'll have all of you locked up for kidnapping! I can't wait to see the peacemen take you away in force binders!"

"Perhaps such will occur," he agreed with a sober nod. "I, too, am a man of peace. Should your men of peace be greater warriors than I, then I will surely be taken."

I tucked my legs under me and turned away from him, determined not to waste my breath any further. Peripherally, I saw him fold into that easy crouch again, showing all the patience of a big cat on the hunt.

About fifteen minutes later, Sandy appeared in the doorway. He was still drawn and nervous looking, and he glanced uneasily at Tammad, then turned worried eyes to me.

"Terry, I'm afraid I have bad news," he apologized hurriedly. "Murdock asks that you stay here until he arrives to settle the matter. Unfortunately, he'll be tied up for some time yet, but will come as soon as possible. I'm sure that if you'll just be patient. . . ."

"About thirty years, I'd say, Sandy," I interrupted thoughtfully. "That's how long you can expect to be in compulsive rehabilitation for kidnapping a PXM. What would you like me to bring you on the days they allow you to be free of pain?"

Sandy swallowed hard and began trembling slightly, but he was made of sterner stuff than I'd thought. "I'm sorry, Terry, I truly am," he said miserably. "I should stay, but I must have that 'wagon repaired. I can have it done and be back before Murdock arrives if I go right now. Since I won't be here, I give you into Tammad's care. He'll see to your needs."

He closed the door fast, to keep from hearing the next thing I had to say, I suppose, but I wasn't saying anything. I stared at the door with my mouth and eyes wide open, then moved my head a little to look at Tammad. The barbarian warrior was laughing softly and slowly rising up out of the crouch.

"What you're thinking isn't true!" I said quickly, feeling my heart starting to pound. "He didn't give me to you because he can't. I'm not his to give."

"You know our language and our customs," he observed, coming toward me. "Also you must know that a host does not give what belongs to another. Do you belong to another?"

"Women on this world are free to belong to themselves," I said desperately, trying to edge away from him. "You can't just. . . ."

"Generous indeed is the host of my journey." He grinned, grabbing my ankle to pull me back. "No man of my world would be foolish enough to give a woman with green eyes as house-gift. I shall have to gift him well in return."

His hand left my ankle as he lay down on the couch next to me and pulled me to him. I was close enough to see the tanned skin beneath the thick blond hair on his chest, close enough to smell the strange, musky odor of him. His hands were warm against my suddenly clammy skin, and I didn't want to believe that this was really happening.

"Tammad, you must believe me," I yelled, struggling against those impossible arms. "I don't belong to Sandy Kemper!"

"That is quite true." He nodded, slowly moving his hands over me. "You now belong to me. Remove these coverings."

I swallowed hard looking at him, but swallowing didn't alter the situation. He was exploring me with his hands as he pressed me up against the couch back, but my sleep suit, brief as it was, was interfering. Now he wanted it off and had said so.

"I don't belong to you, either," I announced as firmly as I could. "And my clothes will stay on!"

He smiled slightly and pulled twice, and my halter and mini bottom were gone so fast that the discs barely had time to release. I grabbed at the suit, trying to get it back, but he just tossed it to the floor behind him and went on with his exploration.

I'd be lying if I said I felt nothing from his touch, but I was much too nervous to really enjoy it. I was hardly inexperienced where men were concerned, but he was so damned *big*! And I didn't have any choice, either. When I continued to struggle against his efforts, he pinned my wrists with one giant paw, then ignored me.

When it was all over, I lay curled up on the couch, trying not to groan. I'd been right in worrying about his size, and he was in no danger of being described as a "gentle lover." I was sore all over, from his fingers and teeth as much as anything else, and I felt totally spent. The barbarian had left the couch when he was through with me, and his sense of satisfaction was almost tangible.

"You struggle well," he grinned from the center of the room as he put his swim trunks back on. "It was long since I last had the use of a woman. I shall use you often."

"Over my dead body," I got out, not trying to be funny. If he ever touched me again, it would probably kill me.

"You seem disturbed," he mused, studying me with a curious expression. "Was the struggle not enjoyable to you as well?"

Talk about your barefaced gall! "How the hell could it be?" I snarled in outrage. "Do you think I enjoy being raped?"

"But you were not virgin," he protested mildly, as if that were the only excuse he could accept as reasonable. "Is it not a woman's purpose to be used by men?"

Talking to a barbarian like him was absolutely impossible and a total waste of time, but getting mad was even more useless. He was much too ignorant to understand even basic explanations, but I felt a need to say *something*.

"Some women have other purposes," I told him, forcing myself to sit up in spite of the aches. "I am a Prime Xeno-Mediator, the very best of the best. I was trained for years to function at the highest levels, not to be used beneath a hulking barbarian. Do you mind if I get my clothes back now?"

"Your coverings *must* be replaced," he answered, watching me retrieve my sleep suit. "The others may arrive soon, and it is not fitting to show a man that which cannot be his. I shall not be so foolish as to gift you to another."

I resisted the urge to close my eyes in frustration as I climbed into my things. "You'd better get it through your head that I don't belong to you," I said, after resetting the discs of my sleep suit. "Murdock will have enough to answer for without adding slavery to the list."

"Murdock usually has all the answers he needs," a voice rasped from the suddenly open door. I turned my head to see Murdock himself standing there, with Sandy hovering nervously behind him. Murdock got his twisted body moving again, dragged himself over to a chair and sat, leaning heavily on his cane.

"This time you're going to be a few short," I snapped, not waiting until he had himself settled. "Harboring a dangerous alien, kidnap, assault—oh, Jack will just love this!"

"Alas, my dear Terrillian, Jackson Randall did *not* love it," Murdock commented, moving his eyes to me. "He'll be joining us shortly, so you will see for yourself. Just now I'm more concerned with the vexations *you've* caused me. When are you ever going to learn to mind your own infernal business?"

"As a PXM it *is* my business," I countered, putting my fists on my hips. "Do you think I'm aching to mediate a riot between all of Central and its own XenoDiplomacy Bureau? Considering the XD personnel involved, I'd find impartiality rather hard to come by."

"I've often wondered about your impartiality," he came back dryly, leaning slowly back in the chair. "Nevertheless, this is a Diplomacy matter, and has nothing to do with Mediation. How in the name of problematical inquiry did you stumble on it to begin with?"

"With Sandy involved, it wasn't very difficult," I answered, glancing at my lovable neighbor where he perched nervously on the edge of the rembowood desk. "Only he would leave an illegal alien lying about while he was hand-destroying his quadriwagon—and then tell me his name was Fred O'Herlihy."

Murdock glanced sadly at a totally defeated Sandy, then

shook his head. "Sandros, Sandros, I despair of you," he sighed. "How are you to make your way in the world of diplomacy when even the most childishly simple dissembling is beyond you? You and I will have to talk."

Sandy just nodded miserably, so I took the opportunity to ask, "What specific event are you waiting for, Murdock? Why can't you complete your plans with your little friend now? And how long a wait are you going to be forced to endure?"

Murdock's expression went totally blank, and I had to admire his ability in spite of his poisonous personality. His narrow, sunken face gave no information whatsoever, and his faded grey eyes were as innocent as his unaccented grey hair.

"You seem to have picked up rather more than Sandros believed, Terrillian," he murmured, his attention squarely on me again. "Have you been plying Tammad with your all too obvious attributes? I warn you now that that is not the safest of endeavors."

"How sweet of you to warn me, Murdock," I answered with barely a quiver. "In turn let me inform you that active hostility does little to protect, either. When the hell are you going to learn how to teach your people about extra-planetary customs?"

The sharpness in my tone reached him immediately. "Why?" he asked. "What happened?"

"Sandy happened!" I snapped, running a hand through the tangle of my hair. "He very kindly gave me as a house-gift to his guest—who didn't hesitate to make use of the gift."

"What's a house-gift?" Sandy asked faintly, his face paling again as he stood straight from the desk. "How could I have. . . ."

"Sandros," Murdock interrupted quietly. "A house-gift on Rimilia is a gift given by a host to his guest, thanking him for the honor of his presence. It can be an article of clothing, of furniture, a decoration—or a woman. In any event, the gift, once given, is the property of the guest. Correct, Tammad?"

"Completely correct," Tammad answered, almost smugly. He was standing at ease with his arms folded, and he grinned at me. "I thank my host for the gift of a green-eyed woman. I shall gift him well in return."

"But—but—I knew nothing about this!" Sandy stuttered, staring at Tammad in horror. "All those sheets of information—I barely had time to skim them. With the alien here, and my 'wagon needing fixing. . . ." He trailed off on his own, stared at me guiltily, then turned abruptly and left the room.

Murdock watched him go, then tactfully cleared his throat. "Choosing Sandros was obviously a mistake, Terrillian. You have his apologies."

"Fat lot of good they'll do me now," I snorted, pleased that Murdock seemed to be uncomfortable. It was a reaction I hadn't expected, and it might turn out to be useful. "Why all the secrecy, Murdock? I'd like the answer to that, at least."

"And so would I," said a voice I knew very well. I turned my head and saw Jack standing in the doorway, leaning casually against the door jamb. The sight of his six-foot-two, dark-haired good looks let me know immediately that I was no longer alone.

"I believe the Bureaus Chairman had a word with you, Jackson," Murdock said smoothly, the discomfort suddenly and completely gone. "What did he have to say?"

"You know very well what he said," Jack returned angrily, coming away from the door. "He told me that this was your show, and Mediation was requested to cooperate with you. Cooperate, hell! Take orders, he meant."

"I'm pleased to see that you understand the true situation." Murdock smiled with barely veiled spitefulness. "Your Bureau is indeed subject to my orders, and I believe I've just solved my largest problem. If you will make yourselves comfortable, I'll tell you a story."

"I'll listen to it from right here," Jack said from the middle of the room. "Possibly I'll soon have something to speak to the Bureaus Chairman about, myself."

"As you wish," Murdock conceded, then waited until I'd stretched out on the couch again. There was no telling how long it would take, and my lack of sleep had long since caught up with me. Not to mention other things.

"On a certain day, beneath a certain sun," Murdock began, as if he were telling a story to children, "it was discovered that a once unimportant planet was no longer unimportant. The people of the planet, backward, primitive people, had no awareness of this importance, but those about them had no doubts. The planet was rich in not one, but many of the ores that are sought by the peoples of the Central Amalgamation. They had furs and silks lovely enough to adorn the highest of the high. They had herbs that, once properly processed, could cure the ills of untold numbers of people. All these things they had, but there was yet a greater importance.

"The planet lies, in its starry setting, in a most unique position. The stars and clusters of the Amalgamation are almost all the same travel time away from it. No being would find it necessary to travel twice the time of another to attend a conference there. It owed allegiance to none of the members of the Amalgamation, as its volume of space had been claimed by none. It was a neutral meeting place without equal."

Jack was still standing in the middle of the floor, his arms crossed in annoyance, resentment strong in his expression. He hadn't even glanced at Tammad, who was again folded into his easy cat-crouch.

"The leaders of the Central Amalgamation," Murdock continued, his eyes imperturbable, "wanted very much to build a complex on this unique planet that would house representatives of all of its members, but, to their dismay, found that they could not. The people of the planet allowed but a single embassy, and that only because they desired certain off-planet articles of manufacture. They refused to join the Amalgamation, and they refused to allow mining, exporting, or building.

"Military advisers to these leaders suggested that the barbarians' wishes be ignored, that the complex be built anyway, and troops be used to protect it. Political advisers agreed that the barbarians should be ignored, but suggested that the complex be built in some inaccessible spot that would keep them away without the need for troops. These two factions argued bitterly until diplomacy advisers informed them that neither suggestion could be followed.

"The men of diplomacy pointed out to the leaders that Amalgamation Covenants prohibited the use of planetary territory without the explicit consent of the planet's leaders. Although this supposedly applied only to member planets of the Amalgamation, it would not be wise to ignore it. A large number of the member planets were of such a turn of mind that they would wonder if the Covenants would some day be ignored if *their* planet was discovered to hold a unique prize. Forceful acquisition of a site for the complex could well result in a dissolution of the Amalgamation.

"The Central leaders were at a loss. What, then, could they do to acquire their complex? They finally decided to send certain of the men of diplomacy to make their way among

the barbarians, to see if they could find a ray of hope. The
chosen men went forth as directed, and found more than they
had expected to—not all of the barbarians were opposed to
Amalgamation membership. A large number of them were
for it, but the leaders of the majority were opposed, so the
rest followed.

"The men of diplomacy looked about themselves, and discovered a leader who desired for his people all that a
profitable trade membership could provide for them. He was,
however, a minority leader, and could not persuade the other
leaders to agree with him. The leader spoke with the men of
diplomacy, and asked if they could provide skilled assistance
for the Great Meeting that took place yearly. The leader was
a man of deeds, not words, but only words could be used at
the Great Meeting. His followers were not many enough to
force agreement from the rest.

"The men of diplomacy agreed to aid the leader, and
secretly brought him back with them to Central. It was
thought best that no one know of his mission, so no one was
informed of his presence. When the proper moment comes,
he will be returned to his people so that he may lead things on
to their fullest destiny."

Murdock's voice had almost put me to sleep where I lay on
the soft leather couch, but a dreamy understanding had somehow reached me. He hadn't told his story like a child's fairy
tale just to be irritating. He'd told it that way so that Tammad would understand everything he said. If Murdock had
used Bureau jargon, which he would normally have done
with Jack and me, Tammad would have been left miles behind.

"Is that all of it?" Jack asked Murdock from where he still
stood, his belligerence still obvious. "You're harboring an unregistered alien for the sake of the entire Amalgamation?
Nothing more important than that?"

"Spare me, Jackson." Murdock grimaced, shifting slightly
in the chair. "Sarcasm suits you not at all. Our efforts are
indeed on behalf of the Amalgamation, whether you choose
to believe it or not. Tammad needs someone to read his opponents for him, to dig out their weaknesses and insecurities,
to develop telling counterstrokes to their arguments—and to
find a point of compromise which they will accept. I've been
searching my entire Bureau, but haven't found anyone
suitable for the position—until now."

"So the masquerade will soon be over," Jack said with a slow nod. "I assume you want our word that we won't mention what's been happening. I'm willing to agree—for certain considerations."

"Always the negotiator," Murdock snorted, looking at Jack with contempt. "It's a pity you haven't the intelligence to understand that you have nothing to negotiate with. You'll keep silent on the matter because you are ordered to do so, and you will cooperate with the needs of my Bureau."

"What needs?" Jack choked out, white-faced with fury at Murdock's words. "What could our miserable, insignificant Bureau give you that you could possibly have a use for?"

"That, too, should be obvious," Murdock said, his tone going flat. "I told you the sort of person Tammad needs. Don't you think the description fits a XenoMediator?"

A light of understanding filled Jack's eyes, and the fury evaporated as a grim pleasure replaced it.

"Possibly," Jack agreed without letting the pleasure show in his voice. "It's a shame all of my Mediators are already committed elsewhere. Too bad, Murdock, but we carry heavy schedules."

"I'm sure the disappointment is shattering for you," Murdock returned, the dryness in his voice more pronounced than usual. "However, you do have one Mediator available, and I am requesting a priority assignment. The Bureau's Chairman will join me in my request, as this matter is serious enough to merit the attention of a Prime."

Murdock was looking at me possessively, so I stretched and gave him a lazy laugh. "It really *is* a shame, Murdock, but I'm not available either. I'm on a class-one vacation leave, and can't be reassigned unless I allow it. I don't allow it."

"She earned the class-one during her last assignment," Jack put in, looking at me fondly. "The Bureaus Chairman himself insisted that she have it, so don't expect any support from him. As I said, Murdock—a shame."

"I agree," Murdock said with a wintry smile. "But not for the same reasons. Terrillian will be taking the assignment in spite of any views the Bureaus Chairman has to the contrary. Rathmore will insist."

Jack looked startled, and I wasn't feeling sleepy any longer. Rathmore Hellman was the supreme leader of Centran in everything but name. His political power was such that no one dared oppose him on governmental matters of any sort.

Murdock had the most powerful ally he could wish for. Jack ran his hand through his hair and avoided my eyes, and that annoyed me.

"Will Rathmore publicly rescind my class-one?" I demanded of Murdock as I sat up on the couch. "If he does, he'll have to admit complicity in this thing. If he doesn't, I still refuse to allow it."

"My dear Terrillian—" Murdock chuckled, some slight humor creasing his narrow face— "you bolster my faith in my judgment. You realize immediately that Rathmore's support is unnecessary to you as a Prime, so you feel free to oppose him. You have no unskilled career position that may be taken from you, as it may be taken from others, so you consider yourself safe." His eyes flicked to an expressionless Jack, then returned to me. "However, you too are vulnerable to persuasion."

"In what way?" I asked. "Primes are too hard to come by for Rathmore to be foolish enough to fire me. He'll still use my skill no matter how annoyed he gets at me."

"Assuming you are available, yes." Murdock nodded. "In that you are quite correct. But should you no longer be available, Rathmore will not mourn your loss."

"And how am I to be made unavailable?" I asked in amusement. "Rathmore detests waste, and will never stand for my being put out of the way—in any manner."

"There is one way in which it may be accomplished," Murdock answered comfortably. "Rathmore is more than anxious to establish relations with Rimilia. A small gesture would be completely supported by him."

"What sort of gesture?" I asked with suspicion. It seemed to me that Murdock looked much too comfortable.

Murdock smiled slightly and turned his attention to Tammad. "You've been given a lovely house-gift, my friend. Is it your intention to take your gift home with you?"

"Of course." Tammad grinned. "A man would be foolish indeed were he to leave behind him so lovely a gift. And one so little used."

They both turned to look at me, and I began feeling pale. "Don't be ridiculous!" I said shakily to Murdock. "All I have to do is refuse to go with him. The port authorities would never allow him to. . . ."

"Which port authorities?" Murdock interrupted, his voice soft. "He wasn't seen when he arrived, and he won't be seen when he leaves. If there are two of you not to be seen, it won't be immeasurably more difficult."

"But you can't do that!" I protested, staring at a grinning Tammad. "Murdock, that's slavery!"

"Not at all," Murdock corrected, his face completely sober now. "It is merely political expedience. The altar of expedience has seen many such sacrifices in its time. Have you anything else to say?"

I looked down at the floor, unwilling to admit he had me in a trap. The thought crossed my mind that I could pretend to agree and then go to the peacemen as soon as I was released, but it was only wishful thinking. If I deliberately brought the matter to light, Rathmore would wait until the furor died down, then would personally see to my delivery to Rimilia. Rathmore had more patience than most, but he never forgot a disservice, and repaid it in the exact measure of his own disaccommodation.

I glanced over at Jack, but he still stood stonily silent. His entire career had been threatened, and I knew he'd never jeopardize his career just to help me. His career meant everything to him, much more than a Prime he had occasionally slept with.

Murdock sat quietly in his chair, his eyes fixed on my face. He was waiting patiently for an answer because he knew what that answer had to be.

"And how do I get back here once it's all over?" I asked with barely suppressed fury. "That—that—friend of yours will still have me!"

Murdock took my question for the acknowledgment of defeat that it was, and turned back to Tammad.

"Tammad, I'm sure you realize that Terrillian is the one I mean to send to your aid," he said in that uncomplicated but not condescending manner he seemed to prefer when speaking to the barbarian. "She is most skilled in her profession, and cannot be bettered even though she is a woman. Are you willing to accept her help, listen to her suggestions, give her the knowledge that will enable her to assist you to victory?"

Tammad rose to his feet and grinned slightly at Murdock. "I have known for some moments that that was the thought of the Murdock McKenzie," he answered. "I have myself seen something of the ability of this woman, and am not reluctant to accept her aid. When the deed is done, she will be returned to your embassy on Rimilia. For this you have my word."

"Does that satisfy you?" Murdock asked, twisting around to look at me. "You ought to know that the word of a Rimilian is not easily given."

"I do know it," I answered, and stood up from the couch. "I suppose it will have to do. Right now I'm going home and to bed."

I started across the room, but Murdock wasn't through with me. "One other thing," he called, and I stopped near Jack to look back at him. "It will be some days yet before your transportation to Rimilia will be available. As you so kindly pointed out, Sandros is not the one to be host to Tammad. He will stay with you until departure time."

"Haven't you done enough to her?" Jack demanded from next to me as I simply stared at Murdock. "Asking her to house that barbarian is unreasonable. If he can't stay with Sandy, take him home yourself."

"Considering that I live at State House, that would be most unwieldly," Murdock answered pleasantly. "Tammad will stay with Terrillian."

Jack frowned at that, then turned to me. "Terry, don't let this bother you yet," he said with some small part of his old confidence. "I still have a few contacts, and I'll see what I can do." Then he lifted his right hand and put it around the back of my neck. "Meanwhile, how about taking in a real with me tonight? You've been gone a long time and I missed you."

I opened my mouth to answer him, but didn't get the chance. Tammad was suddenly there behind me, his left hand gripping Jack's right wrist and lifting it from my neck.

"It is not fitting for a man to touch unbidden the belongings of another," he told Jack evenly in that deep voice of his. "I will now have your apology."

"Belongings?" Jack echoed in confusion while trying to get his wrist loose. "What belongings? What are you talking about?"

"I do *not* belong to you," I hissed at the great hulking beast, but he paid no attention to me.

"The green-eyed woman was my house-gift," he explained in the mildest of tones, watching as Jack struggled uselessly against his grip. "She will belong to me until her mission is done and she is returned to your embassy. I will have your apology for touching that which belongs to me."

Jack stared at him in disbelief, his face pale, beads of sweat on his forehead. He also had to look up, which couldn't have been a very familiar experience for him. Finally, his eyes dropped and he cleared his throat.

"I apologize," he muttered tonelessly. "I didn't know."

Tammad immediately released his wrist, and I looked at Jackson Randall with disgust. "You make me sick!" I snapped, but he just turned away, rubbing at his now free wrist. I moved past him without another word, went through the doorway to Sandy's central hall, flung the front door open, then headed home.

What was left of the beautiful day didn't reach me at all, and I was almost to my own front door when I realized that Tammad was right behind me. I could feel my lips draw into a thin, hard line, but I controlled my temper and simply ignored him. I swung through the door without caring who it hit on the way back, and went directly up the ramp to my bedroom and on through to my bathroom, slamming that door closed behind me. When the lock was firmly in place, I dialed a nice, hot bath, then got out a towel and a clean sleep suit.

The bath began relaxing me as soon as I was in it. I leaned back on the tub's headrest and closed my eyes, letting my hair be gently washed and dried. I'd looked at myself before getting in the tub, and the bruises weren't as bad as I'd thought they'd be—but they were still there.

Among all the men I knew, there had never been one like the barbarian. So self-assured, so easygoing, so—confident! As if everything within his reach could be his if he decided to take it. And he'd decided to take *me!*

I had to force myself to relax again, force myself to open my clenched fists. I was helpless to do anything about it, helpless to avoid it. I'd thought that Jackson Randall might have been able to stand up to him, but Jack had been as useless as Sandy had been damaging. How could a man stand to be shamed like that? I'd always thought that it was part of a man to defend his pride as well as his life, but one look from Tammad and Jack had folded like a quadriwagon partition. I wondered if the action would haunt him, or if he would put it out of his mind as if it had never happened. I splashed some water over my shoulders and thought about it for a minute, then decided that it would be both.

And Murdock McKenzie! The man was a fiend of the nether regions, just as I'd always known. He'd trapped me into doing what those of his own Bureau weren't able to do, and he didn't care what I had to go through as long as the job was done. He didn't care that that barbarian would hold me down and use me until he was satisfied, bruise me with fingers of steel, bite me like the animal he was. If Murdock McKenzie could experience *that*, just once, then *I* would be satisfied.

I promised myself the pleasure of revenge on Murdock McKenzie, and that helped to slow my breathing a little. I was still too upset to really relax as I should have, so I thumbed the switch that transparented the wall in front of me, and looked out at a darkening sky. The pink and purple streaks of the sky told me that it would soon be night, soon be time for people to go to their variously earned rest. I watched the trees wave gently against the pink and purple, remembering that I was still at least one night's rest short. The warmth of the bath water reached through to my muscles; the peace of the sky reached through to my mind; I lost myself in thoughts of elsewhen.

I jerked awake and just caught myself from sliding under the water. I climbed wearily from the tub, feeling the inner strands of my once-dry hair clinging to the wetness of my back, then toweled myself off well enough to be able to put on the sleep suit. Body lotions and powders would have to wait for my next bath. I plodded past the view of an all-dark sky, fumbled through the door into my bedroom, found my bed with half-shut eyes, then slid beneath inviting covers. My eyes closed the rest of the way, but I was already asleep.

★ 2 ★

I woke from the strange dream, still faintly annoyed. I'd
been called in to mediate a disagreement between Murdock
McKenzie and a giant, and I'd been determined to do the
best I could. I'd felt the hostility between them as soon as I
sat at the table, and I'd begun speaking soothingly, projecting
peace and harmony. Suddenly, the hostility had disappeared
as if it had never been, and Murdock and the giant were
grinning at each other in a brotherly way, ignoring me completely. Feeling slightly put out that I'd wasted my time, I'd
tried to leave, but the two of them turned quickly and
grabbed my arms, forcing me back down in my seat. They
turned away from me again and began talking, ignoring me
as long as I stayed where I was. Then my annoyance had
started to build. . . .

The dream was stupid and meaningless, and it made me
mad. I would not have mediated a dispute that Murdock
McKenzie was involved in for anything imaginable. In the
hopes that he would be destroyed in the resulting war, I
would lift not a single finger to help. Pleased with the idea of
Murdock McKenzie destroyed, I turned away from the cobalt
blue, flounced lace of my bedroom wall dress—directly into
Tammad!

"What are you doing in my bed?" I demanded furiously as
his arms started to go around me. "Get out of here this
minute!"

"The bed is of *my* belonging," he answered, grinning
faintly at my useless pushing against his chest. "What belongs

25

to what belongs to me is also of my belonging. Have you had your rest?"

"Get out of here!" I repeated desperately, suddenly realizing that I was no longer wearing the sleep suit, and his swim trunks were gone, too. . . .

"Your hair is long and fine," he mused, stroking it where it lay down my back. "The other women of your world that I have seen have not such hair. They wear it short so that a man would have difficulty enjoying it. I am pleased that you are not one such."

"I didn't do it for you," I told him, trying to slide down and out of his grasp. "Most of the beings I deal with prefer long hair on a female. It makes my job easier."

"And your long legs and full breasts and small waist?" he pursued, grabbing a handful of my hair to keep me from sliding down any farther. "Do these, too, make your burdens lighter?"

"At one point, the answer to that would have been yes!" I snarled, doing my best to resist the slow but determined tug on my hair that was pulling me back up to him. "I have a lot of things to see to before I can leave with you, so you'd better let me go. If I don't see to them, I won't be able to leave on time!"

"All things are done when they are destined to be done," he murmured, starting to nuzzle me. "A woman must always see first to him to whom she belongs. It is her place to do so."

"My place is out of this bed!" I insisted, using every ounce of strength trying to get away from him, but his arms seemed to be muscled with steel. He had no trouble holding me where he wanted me, just grinned as he put his hand on me, then laughed at my gasp.

"Your body desires the presence of mine," he teased, proving the point easily. "Your body speaks more truly than your words. It is often thus with a woman, and a man must learn to see beneath the words."

This time I tried desperately to move his hand away, but he pinned my wrists above my head as he'd done the day before, then proceeded to drive me insane with his fingers. I moaned and squirmed in spite of myself, hating myself for reacting to him, cursing my body for betraying me. No matter what *I* wanted, my idiot body was obviously aching for his touch. I'd never been that way with a man before, and it made no sense! Didn't my body know that a civilized man was preferable to a barbarian? That a civilized man would never rape it, never take from it what he wanted? A civilized man would wait to be given, and never simply *take!*

Tammad the barbarian did not wait to be given. By the time he took me, I would have gladly given him anything, but it wasn't in his nature to allow that. He took me with strength and sureness, aware that he possessed what was rightfully his. I raged at that thought as my body eagerly accepted his, and then I was drowned beneath a tide of maleness the likes of which I'd known only once before. I floated on the tide an unbelievably long time, but when it rolled out again, I lay panting and abandoned, the sheets rumpled under me, sweat soaking my body. Tammad stretched out beside me, completely satisfied, completely relaxed, and lazily toyed with my hair.

When I'd regained some of my strength, I looked over at him bitterly. He'd gotten what he wanted, and what I wanted simply didn't matter. He grinned and tugged at my hair and I turned away from him, shame flooding my cheeks. He turned me back to him with little effort, and forced my face up toward his.

"Why does unhappiness continue to find you?" he asked, his voice gentle as his big hand held my face. "I know that this time you had pleasure at my touch, and I do not understand."

"It's not in you to understand," I muttered, unable to move my face away from the sight of him. "I'm not like the women of *your* world! I'm an individual, a Prime! You have no right to treat me like this!"

"I have the right," he answered in amusement. "Here—do to me that which I have done to you."

He let go of me and lay back on the blue and white lace of the pillow cover, tucking his hands behind his head. I stared at him, at the trim, muscled, immovable bulk of him, and snorted.

"How the hell could I?" I demanded, sitting up and brushing my hair back over my shoulders. "Even you could see the difference between us."

"Then you understand my right," he said, continuing to lie stretched out. "I am able to do to you that which you cannot do to me. Ability provides the right."

"I've heard that one before," I said in disgust. "I still don't subscribe to it, but I'm sure the people of your world do. Especially the men."

"When was the time you visited my world?" he asked, eyeing me curiously. "Which were the areas you traveled through?"

"I've never been to your world," I answered, swallowing the urge to jam the heels of my hands into his unguarded stomach. "If I had the choice, I still wouldn't be going."

"But how, then, do you know my language?" He raised up on one elbow to study me. "Also, the customs of my world are familiar to you. Why should this be so?"

"It's so because it's part of my job," I said, looking past him. "I know the languages and customs of every world known to the Amalgamation. When my services are required, there usually isn't enough time for me to stop for a session with a teaching machine. You probably learned Centran at the embassy on Rimilia while you were waiting for transportation here."

"You are correct." He nodded. "I did indeed gain your tongue at the embassy. But if you have never been to Rimilia, there is much left for you to learn. I shall have to teach you the taste of my world."

"I think the word you wanted was flavor, not taste," I said, taking my own turn to laugh at *him*. "But speaking of taste, I've just realized that I'm hollow clear to my toes. I'm going to get something to eat."

I scrambled over his legs to the white-carpeted floor, only then finding what had happened to my sleep suit. I picked it up and put it back on without looking at him, then left the bedroom. My private kitchen was just down the hall, and I got there as fast as I could. The last time I'd eaten was right after the Nervous Nellies Convention, and I'd had indigestion even before I'd started.

The chef, for some reason, was programed for a dinner meal, so I changed it fast to the breakfast section and pushed the proper buttons. The aroma of lightly fried meela eggs almost killed me as the plate was delivered to the table in front of me, and I followed them rapidly with chemin sandwiches and grilled flatmock. A tall, cold glass of swed washed it all down, and made some room for a wedge of gerite cake. I had almost finished the cake, when I noticed that Tammad stood in the doorway with his arms folded, watching me almost in annoyance.

"You know little of the proper actions of a host," he said when my eyes were on him. "A Rimilian host feeds guest before self. You have not even inquired as to my needs."

"You've been doing so well seeing to your own needs that it didn't occur to me," I answered, taking another bite of cake. "Did you really want something to eat?"

"I do," he said, not moving from his place at the door. He hadn't dressed again, but it didn't seem to bother him.

"Then, by all means, help yourself." I grinned, waving at the chef which he probably didn't know how to operate. "I'll be through in a minute, and then I'll be going to dress. You'll be able to eat completely undisturbed."

"It was necessary to do so at the end of the last sun," he said, coming closer to stand over me. "I felt your anger and your need for solitude and did not intrude upon it. Now the need is no longer with you, and I will have my *dimral* from your hands."

I could see his expression clearly, and there was no amusement left in his hard, blue eyes. I tried to take another bite of cake, but it wasn't possible—not with him staring at me like that. I put the eating prong down and cleared my throat.

"My chef's run out of *dimral*," I said with a faintness I found unnerving. "What's your second choice?"

"You know well enough that *dimral* is meat," he said stonily. "Any meat will do as well. Produce it now."

His voice was as low as it could be, he hadn't threatened me in the slightest, yet I hadn't the least desire to argue with him. I wet my lips with my tongue, turned to the chef, and dialed an extra large portion of roast pimond. The platter of pimond was on the table in no more than fifteen seconds, but Tammad didn't reach for it. It took another fifteen seconds before I understood, then lifted it in his direction without looking at him.

"Truly, you have much to learn," he said, taking the plate. "You may now leave to dress yourself."

I stood quickly, furious that he dared to dismiss me in my own home. He paid no further attention to me, but went to the far wall and crouched down near it with his back toward it, put the plate of pimond on the floor, then raised the meat to his mouth.

"You might try learning to use a *chair*, barbarian!" I snapped, longing to throw something at that blond, shaggy-haired head. "But have no fear. I'd never *think* of suggesting a knife and prong. They're obviously too far beyond you."

I turned my back on him and strode out, still seething. Slamming my bedroom door helped, and slamming the bathroom door helped even more, but it still wasn't enough. I walked back and forth a few times while the tub was filling, then climbed in and scrubbed myself briskly and quickly. I toweled down hard, slapped on body lotion, then put my face in the makeup applicator. The applicator was set for Alderanean accent styling, and I was in no mood to change it. I pulled my face out again, checked the black outlining, peach background, and three blood-red diagonal stripes on left cheek in the mirror, then moved to the hairstyler. The styler matched the makeup by piling and curling all of my hair to the right, pointing up the red stripes of high social position. Then, and only then, did I go for clothing.

The Alderanean day suit was a perfect match to my makeup and my mood. I wound the triple-stripe red legging around my right leg, then pulled on the peach and black tunic. The tunic came down to mid-thigh, showing off my figure with a pleasing number of pluses, the high-heeled ankle boots doing nothing to detract from it. I admired myself in the mirror a few moments, went to add filigreed loop earrings, then checked the picture again. This time it was perfect, so I strolled out of the room.

Tammad wasn't in sight on the upper floor, but I found him downramp in my central hall, apparently waiting for something. He rose from his crouch when he saw me, showing he had his swim trunks on again. He studied me intently for a good deal longer than a minute, and what began as a smile ended in a grin.

"Your *collat* is tempting, woman," he said, looking down at me with that annoying stare again. "Sorry I am that I must go now to the Sandy Kemper's house. The Murdock McKenzie has sent clothing for me such as that of your world's men. I shall take the clothing quickly and return to seek you. See that you do not leave until then."

He leered at me again then turned away to go through the front door, and I let him go without saying a word as I was totally beyond words. As soon as the door closed I continued down the hall past the front door to my speedster hangar, and climbed into the speedster to warm it up.

"*Collat* indeed!" I muttered, watching the dials and waiting for the necessary RPMs. As if I would dress myself for the express purpose of tempting *him!* He had too high an opinion of himself, and it was time he got taken down a peg. As soon as the RPMs met minim I released the hangar door, rolled out to the landing circle, and took off straight up.

Tallion City was only twenty minutes away, and that's where I was heading. I leaned back in my seat, piloting manually instead of on automatic, thinking about what Sandy's quadriwagon had done to the Neighborhood lawn. There had been two straight furrows all the way through the grass from Sandy's landing strip out in the direction of the service mall. I'd seen them clearly from the air, and the Neighborhood Chairman was bound to see them, too. Sandy would have his head beaten for destroying the lawn, and it couldn't happen to a more deserving fellow. If we'd wanted ground traffic in our Neighborhood, we would have put in roads and walkways.

I was blinked into the T.C. traffic pattern and ordered to automatize my destination. Manual flying in Tallion City was prohibited, and for good reason. Out of thousands of people going to hundreds of different places, it's not unreasonable to expect at least one to experience loss of control. Since even one flyer out of control can kill hundreds of people, flyers flew automatically or not at all. If the flyer itself failed, it was caught in the traffic net that was waiting for it. You can't expect a traffic control computer to provide for a failing flyer that isn't meshed into its network.

I was landed easily on my parking building in almost no time at all, took my shoulder bag and left the speedster to be put in its slot, then took the express drop to ground floor. I had a good deal of buying to catch up on, so I dove into it with enthusiasm, but the enthusiasm soon paled. The newest clothing styles were dull and colorless, this year's furniture was heavy and repelling, and even the jewelry was badly set and lustreless. After hours of wasting my time, I gave up and went to my Neighborhood eating center. I could have gone elsewhere, of course, but after the day I'd had, I was in no mood for inferior courses.

The green and brown room was dim and inviting after the crowds in the buying audiences. People sat companionably at small tables while soft music played, and as I stood still a moment to let my eyes adjust to the lower lighting, I heard my name being called. I peered around through the privacy shimmer-strands, and saw Lenham Phillips coming toward me.

"Terry!" He laughed as he reached me. "It's hard to believe you're finally home! Let me offer my table in appreciation of that breathtaking outfit. It will make the food taste so much better."

"Len Phillips." I smiled fondly. "As big a liar as ever, but welcome in spite of that. How have you been doing?"

"Not badly," he said, taking my arm and leading me to his table. "Not as well as you, my dear Prime, but not at all badly. How was Dremmler's sector?"

"Don't remind me!" I grimaced, taking a chair opposite his. His gray street suit fit well on his athletic body, his smile making his dark-blond handsomeness even more attractive. "Dremmler's sector probably has the hardest heads and densest minds in the entire Amalgamation. Just pray that *you* never have to mediate there. It isn't even worth a class-one vacation leave."

"That's a matter of opinion." He laughed, taking my hand in both of his. "From now on, we're going to have to do something about our timing. You just got back, and I have to leave tonight. All that gives us is this afternoon. Will you go to a real with me?"

At first the idea wasn't very appealing, but then I changed my mind. "Why not?" I asked lightly. "Being with a civilized man is just what I need."

"I should hope so," he said with raised eyebrows, watching as I chose my meal from the table's chef. "Have you been spending much time with any other sort?"

"Not really." I laughed. "It's just that being away from Central makes me colicky. I'll be fine as soon as I'm back in the swing of things."

"I'm sure of it." He smiled. "I saw Jan the other day, and she made a point of asking if I'd seen The Terror lately. She said if I did, I was to be sure to insist that you call her."

"With *her* temper, she has a nerve calling me The Terror," I muttered, moving in the gold, deep-cushioned chair in annoyance. "I don't know who she picked it up from."

"I do," he grinned, "but I think it would be more diplomatic if I kept it to myself. I don't want you walking out on me before we get to the real."

"I'd better not pursue that," I decided, watching the sautéed valmin I'd ordered being slid to the table in front of me. "In the mood I'm in, walking out would be more of a certainty than a risk."

He patted my hand in appreciation, then turned to his own food. We ate in companionable silence until we were through, then left to find a real.

"I know just the one," Len said as we moved down the slidewalk. "Guy and Vera experienced it, and couldn't rave about it enough. It's a double, or I would have gone on my own before this. How does that sound?"

"I suppose it'll do," I said grudgingly. "I have no preferences one way or the other."

"Fine," he said. "It's just off the walk at Bend Five. Looks like we're almost there."

We had just passed Bend Four, so we moved to the edge of the walk, then stepped off at Bend Five. A discreet "R" on the front of the building before us told us that we were in the right place, and a greeter opened the door for us with a welcoming smile.

"Step this way, please," he invited warmly, then closed the door behind us. "Do you prefer group or private experiencing?"

"Private," Len answered, handing over a large block of Earning Pluses. The E.P.'s were taken by the greeter, a guide was summoned, and we were led to a small cream-colored room with two light-gold couches.

"Gentleman to the left, lady to the right," the guide instructed us. "Press the contacts in place as soon as you're settled. If you need any assistance, activate the button on either couch. Have a pleasant experience."

He closed the door behind him, and Len smiled at me. "You seem to be right, as usual, Terry. I suppose it's my lot in life to be left. Shall we?"

"One more comment like that and you *will* be left." I winced as I followed him to the couches. "What's the title of this electrifying experience?"

"It's called, 'Tree World Adventure,'" Len said, leaning over the light-gold console in front of his couch. "You like trees, don't you, Terry?"

"I'm mad about them," I answered with a small, unvoiced groan, lying down on my couch. "I may never speak to Guy and Vera again."

"You won't be the only one," he agreed as he reached for his headset. "Now let's coordinate."

We made ourselves comfortable on the couches, prepared the contacts, then pressed the headsets in place on the count of three. All outside sensation cut off immediately, then *I found myself standing alone in a large clearing surrounded by giant trees. I knew I had just landed my disabled ship on the planet, expecting to find a research base where I might find help, but the only clearing where the base might have been found was entirely deserted.*

I looked around at the trees again, hoping for some sign of the base or its personnel, and suddenly felt that I wasn't alone. I was being watched from somewhere, and the thought made me shiver.

I turned to go back to my ship, running slightly to get there faster. I might not be able to fly the ship, but at least it was shelter. I'd close the airlock and stay inside, and hope that my S.O.S. reached someone before my supplies ran out. I knew I would never be able to go into that forest for food.

I was almost to the foot of the ship's ramp, when I screamed and stopped dead in my tracks. A man who looked just like Len was there, but it was a Len I had never known. He was unbelievably big and well muscled, wearing not a single stitch of clothing. I screamed again and cringed away from him, but he was on me in a flash. He threw me to the ground and over on my face, then bound my hands behind my back. I screamed for help, pleaded for mercy, but it was all wasted breath. I was lifted to a wide, brawny shoulder, and carried against my will into that dread, brooding forest.

We went a long way through the trees, and I was quickly disoriented. My captor seemed to know exactly where he was going, stopping at long last before one of the mile-high trees. There was very little light, but he had no difficulty in finding his way about. His arms worked past my dangling legs, and then I was completely frozen with fear—he was climbing a rope or something up into the tree!

I hardly dared breathe while he climbed, for fear he would drop me or lose his grip and plunge us both to the ground. I kept my eyes squeezed tightly shut, praying to my Maker that I would survive the climb, and eventually my prayers were answered. He stood at last on a wide, long branch, and then moved closer to the tree trunk. In another minute we were inside the tree trunk, and I looked around with shock at a hollowed out room. It wasn't very big, but it was shelter with-

out doubt, and the man threw me down near the wall at the very back of the room-cave.

He left me to go outside again, and I whimpered and pulled at the rope on my wrists. It was impossible to loosen it, but even if I had, there was nowhere for me to go. I'd never be able to climb down the way he had come up, and even if I miraculously found myself whole, untied, and on the ground, I would still be hopelessly lost. I was doomed to depend on the mercy of the man who had found me, and could only hope that he had mercy within him.

The man appeared again in the doorway, causing me to gasp with fright. He came closer to stare down at me as I lay shivering, then he bent and said something in a harsh, guttural, totally unintelligible language.

"I don't understand you," I whispered to him. "Please don't hurt me! Please have mercy!"

Anger creased his features, and he slapped me hard across the face, pulled my head back by the hair, and repeated his original demand.

"I don't know what you want!" I screamed, terror strong within me. My cheek blazed hot where he'd struck me, my hair was being torn from my head, and I was at the mercy of a man who had no mercy.

He snarled angrily and shook my head by the hair, then released my hair. My relief was very short-lived, though, as the next thing he did was pull at my clothes. I was so petrified I couldn't speak, but could only hope that my clothing would keep him from me. My hopes were as doomed as I, poor girl, for my clothing resisted being opened, but could not resist his tearing fingers. It was torn completely from me, and I lay before him, naked and entirely helpless.

I begged him not to take me, not to make me his body slave, but he would not have listened even had he understood. He was brutal in his pleasure, brutal and complete. He caused me agony with deliberation, and I could do nothing but—

I sat blinking on the couch, the contacts in my right hand, trying to shake off the last lingering effects of the real. I took a deep breath and looked over at Len, but he was still deep within the experience. His arms were bent at the elbows and his fingers were flexing, his body bumped up and down in a rhythm, and his face showed cruel, determined excitement.

I tossed the contacts back onto the console and stood up.

The totally alien emotions the real had forced me to feel had also enabled me to break out of the experience. I was furious with Len for having brought me there, but I knew exactly why he had done it. He wanted the experience of humbling me, of making me a cringing slave, expecting the experience to stay with me long enough for him to take me physically in a master-slave way after the real had ended. Chances are that he would have succeeded, too, since reals cling to you for some time after their completion. *If* they complete. I took my shoulder bag from the floor near the couch, then headed for the door. I'd joined Len long enough in the real for him to be able to complete on his own. His frustrations would begin when completion found him all alone in the room.

The greeter stared at me curiously as I left, but naturally made no move to stop me. I stood outside the building for a time, watching people go by on the sidewalk, feeling a deep dissatisfaction that I couldn't trace. All those months in the conference rooms in Dremmler's sector had made me eager to be back on Central, but now that I was here, I wondered what it was that I'd missed. I finally shrugged it off, really looked around me, then made for Verasten Hardy's place.

Vera enjoyed city life more than she cared for suburban living, so she had opted for an apartment in her original Neighborhood's residential area in Tallion City. Some people maintained both house and apartment, but Vera didn't want a house and I didn't want an apartment, so we generally called one another if either of us had need of the other's location. Vera's apartment was all on one level, with the private living quarters behind the visitors' rooms rather than above them, and Vera herself opened the door to me, then squealed in surprise.

"Terry, darling, I don't believe it!" she gushed. "You've been gone absolutely forever! Do come in and tell me all about your marvelous adventures, I'm just dying to hear."

I let her bustle me into her guest room, fighting back a grimace when I saw that her apartment had been redecorated with this year's furniture. There were five heavy, dark blue chairs, two heavy dark pink couches, three low, hideously carved tables, a monstrously large, overdecorated hutch, and acres of thick, blue and pink patterned drapes on the windows. It took something of an effort, but I sat on one of the couches and smiled at her.

"Vera, love, your taste is always up to the minute. Do be a dear and save my life for me. I'm just dying for I glass of port Winsen."

"Of course." She laughed over her shoulder as she crossed the room. "I'll have a glass with you. How long have you been back?"

"Only a few days," I answered, watching her pour two glasses of port at the hutch. She carried them back to the couch, handed me one, then sat down beside me. "Has anything exciting been happening, or is it all the same as it was?"

"Most things don't change." She shrugged, sipping her port. "Jan has taken up with Rodmil Holper, and you'll never guess why. But that reminds me. I'd better warn you before it's too late."

"Before what's too late?" I asked in amusement, drinking my own port as she put hers down. "Vera, you always sound like the warning before crisis."

"This time I am!" she insisted. "I just wish someone had warned *me*. There's a new real around that you have to avoid at all costs. I've never had such a shattering experience!"

"You couldn't possibly mean, 'Tree Planet Adventure'?" I asked with only a slight edge to my voice. "If so, you're a little late. I just left there, and as a matter of fact, Len said you and Guy recommended it."

"Maybe Guy did, but I never would," she stated, then lifted her glass again to drain it. "On second thought, I'm sure Guy recommended it. Terry, it was unbelievable! How is it you're here now if you just experienced it?"

"I didn't complete the experience." I grinned. "I'd like to see Len's face when he emerges and finds that I'm gone."

"So would I," she said savagely, her dark eyes lighting in a way that made me uneasy. "I'd also like to see Guy in the same fix. He trapped me into it, Terry, and I completed the experience. When it was over I tried to throw it off, but I couldn't. I spent three days at his place, serving him on my knees, kissing him for every slap, thanking him for abusing me, before I could break out of it. Rod took Jan a week ago, and she hasn't broken out of it yet. The thing should be declared illegal."

"It probably already has been," I assured her. "That was a real house I'd never been to before, and I'm sure it's temporary and restricted, but they just 'forgot' to ask if I was willing. The most that could happen would be a fine for the house, and a warning for its owner. It's too effective a real to be suppressed."

"I'll say it's effective." She grimaced, a hand to her throat. "I still quiver at the thought of Guy. I've managed to avoid him since I escaped from his apartment, but I have the awful feeling that if he walked in right now I'd go to my knees in front of him, let him tie my wrists behind me, then follow him back to his apartment. I've been afraid to go out since I got back."

Vera sat staring into space, her eyes wide and frightened, her left hand clenched in her lap. She was on the verge of losing herself to her fears, and it wasn't an attractive sight.

"Why don't you take a trip?" I suggested, pitying her more than I cared to show. "I'm sure that a month or two away from here will make all the difference, and you'll come back just as you used to be."

"That's a good idea," she agreed shakily, brushing at her lavender-tinted hair. She wore lavender and red makeup, off-setting a purple-shaded house suit that hung loosely on her, and then her suddenly visibly weary eyes were resting on me again. "You couldn't use a house guest for a while, could you?"

I was almost tempted to accept her partial plea, but then I remembered what I had left at home.

"Unfortunately, I already have one," I told her, emptying my glass. "A colleague from Dremmler's sector, visiting Central for the first time. He's unbelievably backward, but I'm stuck with him, at least until we leave for the mediation assignment I've just been given. He's coming along to see if he can learn anything."

Her expression changed then, and it was an expression I'd never seen before. "I really envy you," she said wistfully, staring at me with surprising longing. "Here you are, a PXM with a wonderful career, and here am I useless at everything. After serving my required year with Central central, I'd hoped they would ask me to continue, but they never did. I just wasn't good enough. I have everything I need now but a purpose in life."

She was staring down at her hands in a way that left me shaken, but it wasn't something I could show. "Come now, it's not that bad!" I encouraged heartily, patting her knee.

"There are many things to do if you look about you. We'll get together again before I leave, and I'll help you choose something. Right now, it's getting late and I'd better be on my way."

"Wouldn't you like another port?" she asked in a hopeful tone as I stood up. "We could talk about old times and who's doing what now."

I begged off and left as fast as possible, feeling worse than I had before I'd arrived. I'd never known that Vera was so unhappy, and it was very unsettling. I hated to admit it, but the only composed person on Central seemed to be Murdock McKenzie!

It was dusk before I was back in my speedster, heading for home. I put it on automatic and leaned back, thinking about what was waiting for me. After this long a time, the barbarian should have realized that I was an individual to be dealt with, not a servant to be ordered about. If he expected my help with his problem, he'd have to treat me with respect and consideration. I stirred in my seat harness, knowing how fine it was going to be pointing this out to him, watching him compose himself for a sincere apology. After a time, I might even forgive him. His problem was an interesting one, and the professional in me was attracted by it in spite of Murdock McKenzie's underhanded methods. I would handle the problem well, and never let Murdock forget that he'd had to come to Mediation for his solution.

In just a few minutes' time, I set down on my landing-circle and rolled inside the hangar. The door closed securely behind me as the engine whined down to the shut-off point, so I secured all controls, got out, then ambled into the house. The ground floor was deserted, and that was just as well. I hadn't had dinner yet, and I was beginning to be hungry. I went upramp to the living floor, intending to visit my kitchen, but Tammad suddenly stepped out of my bedroom into my path. I stopped short to keep from running into him, and gave him a pleasant smile.

"So there you are, *l'lenda*," I murmured as I brushed at my tunic skirt. "I trust you've had enough time to do an adequate amount of thinking?"

"Indeed I have," he answered with a nod, folding his arms. "The day has fled in the time of your absence."

His expression wasn't quite as anxious as it should have

been, but that was surely because I hadn't explained matters to him as yet.

"True enough," I agreed. "I'm sure you now realize that I'm not to be trifled with. If you expect me to. . . ."

"I expect you to obey my word," he snapped, rudely interrupting me. "On Rimilia, it could mean your life! I shall have to teach you proper respect for him to whom you belong, lest this ever happen again. In the room!"

His broad face showed anger as he pointed toward the bedroom, but I couldn't believe it. He was treating *me*, a Prime, as if I were a nobody!

"How dare you speak to me that way," I gasped, moving a small step backward. "Don't you realize . . . ?"

"Woman, in the room!" he repeated, taking me by the neck and propelling me through the doorway, then following behind. "Too long have you lived among these nonmen, these *darayse*. They know nothing of the training of women for their place, but I have not that lack. Should you ever think upon disobeying me again, your fate will be well known to you!"

I stumbled from the push, nearly losing my balance, and felt shocked as I never had been in my life. I didn't know what the barbarian was talking about, but I knew it wasn't right. Couldn't he see that he needed my help badly? That if he mistreated me, my help might not be forthcoming? I tried to explain that to him, but he refused to listen. He pushed me over to the bed, then picked up what looked like a long, thin tree branch.

"You were bidden not to leave the house," he explained in his calm, even way, the anger frighteningly showing behind the calm. "Because you were not aware of the consequences of disobedience, your punishment will be less harsh than it otherwise would be. You are not to disobey me again."

I was wide-eyed and confused, determined not to tremble before the likes of a barbarian, but then he pushed me face down on the bed, putting one of his knees in the small of my back. I struggled to get away from him, fought to squirm loose, but his weight held me in the place with no other effort necessary from him. He stripped the triple-red legging from me and threw it aside, then tucked up my tunic skirt. I was wild with the thought of what he would do to me, and then it happened! He brought the thin, springy branch down hard across my hips, leaving a streak of fire in its wake! I'd never felt *anything* like it before, and I screamed with the pain, but it was just the beginning. He beat me with the branch, across my hips and thighs, until I cried wildly for him to stop, but he continued on as if he intended destroying me. When my tears ran my makeup down to the bed in a stream, he finally stopped and took his knee from my back.

"Your place will become more familiar to you as time passes," he said over my sobs. "I shall do my best to teach you the—*flavor* of- my world. The Murdock McKenzie has sent you writings which you are to study. Do so now."

He stepped away, came back to drop a pile of report folders near me, then went to the other end of the bed and lay down. The sobs racked my body, the pain of the beating burned at me unceasingly, yet I took the first folder and opened it. If I hadn't, he might have beaten me again.

I was able to make out that the report dealt with the situation on Rimilia. Although I learned nothing I hadn't already known, I read it all the way through, then went to the second report. I ached even without trying to move, and felt bewildered and afraid and all alone. For the first time in my life I'd been beaten, and it had been a horrible, alien experience.

The second report contained the statements of those who had gone to Rimilia, and it was their unanimous opinion that Tammad needed nothing more than some expert help in negotiation in order to deal with the other barbarian leaders. The conclusion almost set me sniffling again, because he hadn't needed *any* help in dealing with *me!*

When I put the second report aside, Tammad abruptly stood up from the bed. "I would have my *dimral* now, woman," he said with that same, unruffled calm. "You may finish those others later."

I didn't look at him, but raised myself painfully from the bed and followed along behind him to my kitchen. He stood aside as I went to the chef and dialed another portion of pimond, then he took the plate I handed him. I turned back to the chef for my own dinner, but his hand was on my arm.

"The writings have not been completed," he told me. "Go you now and see to them."

I stared at him for a minute, seeing the unyielding decision on his face, then went miserably back to my bedroom. He wasn't angry any longer, but I wasn't to be allowed to eat until I had his permission. The tears started again even before I lay down, making the third report one large blur. I cried and tried to stop crying, peered and tried to begin reading, but it was all too much. I cried and cried, then cried myself to sleep.

★ 3 ★

I opened my eyes to the comfort of my bedcovers around me, but wasn't ready to get up yet. I shifted position onto my back—and gasped at the soreness. I remembered then what the barbarian had done to me, and I moved my head to look at him. He lay peacefully asleep beside me, his blond head unpillowed, just as though he were the most innocent being ever created. I realized that my clothes were gone again and my hair had been released from the clips that had held it in place, and knew whom I had to thank for the condition.

I shifted the other way, onto my side, trying to come up with a positive course of action. The night before I'd been too shocked to do anything more than react, but *something* had to be done. He couldn't be allowed to beat me and order me about as if I were his—belonging. I was a Prime, and had my pride to consider.

"Are you refreshed from your long sleep?" Tammad's voice came suddenly from behind me. "You did not even stir when I placed you beneath the coverings."

So he was awake now, too. "Beatings are well known for curing insomnia," I told him coldly, keeping my eyes on the lace wall dress. "Perhaps some day you'd care to try it yourself."

"What need have I of an aid to sleep?" He chuckled, then pulled me around to face him. When I stiffened in his arms, he frowned at me, almost as though he were confused. "I had thought you were now pleased by my touch," he said, looking down at me. "Why do you again resist me?"

"I haven't stopped resisting you!" I told him, hands flat

43

against his broad chest. "And how am I supposed to know what your mood is? Am I to welcome you with open arms, only to be greeted with that branch again?"

"You seem to learn very slowly." He sighed, moving me closer to him to stroke my hair. "You were beaten at the end of the last sun for disobeying my word. If you do not disobey me, you will not be beaten. Is this now clear to you?"

"No, it is not!" I answered hotly, squirming against that unreasonable giant-strength of his. "You have no right to beat me for any reason! I'm a grown woman and a Prime, and I needn't listen to anyone!"

"You must now listen to me." He grinned, putting his hand beneath my hair onto my back. "I do not wish to see you die upon Rimilia, which is all too likely to occur if you fail to obey my word. Beginning with you then would be too late; therefore I have begun with you now. The switch will remind you should you ever forget."

His hand on my back reached more than just my skin, making me frantic. Desperately I said, "If you ever touch me again—in any way—I won't help you!" He was a barbarian and I feared his strength, but more than that I feared that his body would call to mine again. I hated him, hated everything he said and did, but my body didn't hate his. He had bewitched me somehow, and I didn't know how to break the spell. I watched him closely, and his grin faded to a small smile.

"Then I will have the help of another," he murmured, pulling me so close I could barely breathe. "You will merely return with me as a green-eyed woman I shall keep—or gift to a friend. Rimilia will then truly be yours."

He wasn't joking—I could see he wasn't joking. I felt sick at the thought and closed my eyes to keep the tears from escaping, but they seeped out anyway and ran down my cheeks to his chest. I didn't want to obey him, didn't want to go to Rimilia with him, but if I didn't obey him he would beat me, if I didn't help him he would own me. It wasn't fair, and I began screaming it out loud, beating against him with my fists, over and over, until the rage had evaporated and the tears were left by themselves, then he held me close again and let me cry against him. I cried a long time in the circle of his arms, and he didn't begin to take me until the tears were gone, but then he took me so completely there was no longer opportunity for tears. His body gave mine what it so desperately wanted, but my exhaustion was so great afterward that I fell asleep again.

When I awoke the second time, I was alone in the bed. I squirmed comfortably in the wrinkled linen and thought about Tammad with a great deal of annoyance. He was so damned difficult to understand that it was almost more than one could be expected to bear. One minute he was beating me terribly, and the next minute he was comforting my tears. How was I supposed to deal with him if I didn't know what to expect from him next?

And the way he treated me in bed! My body had begun to enjoy such treatment, had begun to demand it! He answered my demands so perfectly that I would likely be ruined forever because of it. Where would I ever find another barbarian on Central?

I sighed at the absurdity of the thought, then got up. Considering that the soreness of the beating and the barbarian's "love-making" was still very much with me, I would never again seek the company of a barbarian for any reason. They were much too prone to wanting things their own way, which did *not* agree with my own outlook on life.

I waited for the tub to fill, then stepped into the water. My mirror had shown me my bruises, and I was not at all pleased. There were no breaks in the skin, but it hadn't been for want of trying. The beast had applied the switch with a will, and I still flinched at the thought of it. If ever I had the opportunity to repay the favor, I would be sure to do so.

"Should you continue to bathe so often, you soon will have no skin left," Tammad's amused voice came from the doorway. I jumped in surprise, then glared at him.

"Don't you ever make any noise when you walk?" I demanded. "And what are you doing in here? I'm accustomed to having privacy in my bath!"

"You must now accustom yourself to other ways," he commented as he looked around. "On Rimilia you will never bathe without a guard on shore, and the guard may be any of my warriors. For what reason are these things here?"

He stood at my dressing table, fingering the pure white wood and the matching white furred chair. Then he lifted a bottle of scent, turned it this way and that, and finally moved his finger over the tiny photocell area. A thick mist of the scent sprang immediately out of the nozzle, spreading itself

all over his chest. At the appalled look on his face, I lost all
control and laughed uproariously.

"Those things are for trapping the unwary," I gasped,
watching him trying to wipe the scent off. He was totally un-
successful, of course, as the scent was designed to penetrate
the skin immediately. He gave up trying with a sigh, and
looked at me ruefully.

"Truly have I forgotten that the unknown should be approached with caution. Now I, too, shall require a bath."

"About time, I'd say," I commented under my breath,
standing up to redial the tub. The dirty water was gone by
the time I stepped out and fresh water had replaced it by the
time I had my towel, so I waved a hand at it. "The tub is
now yours, barbarian, but don't complain about the fit. It was
never designed for someone of your proportions."

"I shall make do," he said, stepping carefully into the
water. When it didn't immediately dissolve him, he lowered
himself to a sitting position, then glanced at me. "When a
man relaxes in the *camtah* of his people," he mused, "often
his woman will dance for him. Do you now remove the covering and dance for me."

His eyes moved to study me in that way he had, but that
in itself wasn't enough to make me lose control.

"Sorry, but I don't dance," I told him, pulling the towel
more closely about me. "Dancing tends to disturb the mental
attitudes necessary for Mediating, so I must avoid it. I'm sure
you understand."

He continued to stare at me for a minute, then slowly
nodded his shaggy blond head. "Perhaps it is the truth," he
decided. "You dance well when lying down, but have no control of your *aman* then. It is your *aman* which will be needed
at the Great Meeting. Why have you not yet eaten? The bathing could have waited."

"I always bathe when I arise," I said, reflecting that bed
with him was the only time I had no control of my *aman*.
There was nothing wrong with my mental ability under other
circumstances. "And I didn't know I was to be allowed to
eat. I thought perhaps you had decided I was too fat."

"You've hardly enough flesh to lure a man's hands." He
grinned, leaning back and making the water slosh onto the
floor. "When you are not permitted to eat, you will be told
so. Go you now and see to it quickly. The remainder of the

writings of the Murdock McKenzie must also be seen to this day."

Being reminded about the reports annoyed me, but not as much as his automatic assumption of obedience. I shrugged a bit, as if resigned to my fate, then dropped the towel and went for my body lotion. I began spreading it slowly in long, sweeping curves, timing it so that I'd be through and gone before the barbarian could wash and dry himself. I'd teach him to order me around.

Suddenly, there was a great splash of water, and I was seized from behind and thrown to the carpeting. The barbarian was on me at once, his dripping body in possession of mine before I could gasp out my shock. He took me hard, forcing his hands below me so that I jerked my soreness from him, only to be hammered at by him from above. He dictated my movement with his hands, meeting it at just the right moment with his hips, and through it all I barely knew what was happening. When he had used me well, he stood straight above me and looked down at my dazed and battered form.

"Do not offer temptation when you do not care to have the offer accepted," he lectured, folding those massive arms. "The lesson will serve you well on Rimilia. Go you now for your sustenance, lest I decide to find other use for you."

I sat up and pulled my towel to me, thoroughly wide-eyed by what had happened, but I must not have moved quickly enough for him as he took a step toward me and began reaching out a hand. I gasped and jumped to my feet, then fled to my kitchen, trailing my towel and the sound of his laughter. The laughter infuriated me, and I would have broken something if my kitchen had had anything that was breakable. A lesson had been taught, all right, but when would I be able to teach one to him?

I dialed my meal, then wrapped the towel about me while it was being delivered. I had no interest in Murdock McKenzie's reports, but I knew I would read them anyway after I'd eaten. I was damp from the dripping wet barbarian, and also because of him needed another bath, but after I'd eaten, the reports would be seen to. I'd already had my orders.

I ate my food with very little appetite, cursing Murdock McKenzie all the while. If not for him, I would not be where I was, subject to the whims of a giant. I'd not had such restrictions even as a child, having been raised in a crèche for the gifted. We'd had such freedom there that my mother and father had found visiting painful. When their visits had stopped I hadn't even missed them, and I'd been surprised when they came to my formal appointment as XenoMediator. They'd shown pride and considerable shyness, but to me they'd been half-remembered strangers whom I'd avoided as soon as possible. They'd never tried seeing me again.

Annoyed with the turn my thoughts had taken, I began disposing of the dishes, but was interrupted by the signal of the call. I waved my hand in its direction, and was startled to see the features of Janverin Elliott.

"Terry!" she said at once. "I'm so glad I caught you in. How are you?"

"The question is, how are *you?*" I countered, studying her unmadeup but radiant face. "I saw Vera yesterday, and she seemed to think you were in a lot of difficulty."

"I know." Jan laughed, looking somehow both younger and older. Jan had always been a proud woman, almost larger than life, but there was nothing left of her former pride. "I spoke to her myself this morning. That's how I knew you were back. I haven't much time, so I'll get straight to the point. Rod is letting me have a party tonight, and I'd like you to come. Will you, Terry?"

"Why, you know I'd love to," I temporized, shocked at the change in her, "but I have a house guest now, and. . . ."

"Please, Terry, you *must* come!" she begged, her face now pleading. "I want you to see my new happiness and understand it. And Rod said I was to get you here if you were back. Vera will be here, and you can *bring* your house guest. Please, Terry, say yes."

"Jan, what's happened to you?" I demanded, staring as she brushed anxiously at her loose, black hair. "People used to beg *you* for invitations, and you would laugh at them. What has Rod done to you?"

"He's made me a fulfilled woman at last," she said, her eyes gazing glowingly on some faraway, promised land. "I've never been as happy as I am now, and I pray daily that he never tires of me." Her gaze, still shining, came back to me again. "Will you come to the party, Terry? For the sake of old friendship?"

"All right, Jan," I conceded, feeling more than just disturbed. "I'll be there. But what have you. . . ."

"Please forgive me," she interrupted, "but I have other

calls to make before Rod awakens from his nap. I'll see you tonight, and perhaps I'll be allowed to speak with you. I hope so. Clear."

"Clear," I repeated automatically to the already blank screen. I was shocked again to realize that Jan was no longer chatting for hours with each call she made. The changes in her were incredible, and I'd get to the bottom of it that night—whether Rod cared for the idea or not!

"You may serve me before going to the writings," Tammad said from behind me. I was tired of having him sneak up on me, but I had other thoughts to occupy me.

"Barbarian, we've been invited out tonight," I said as I dialed femmer stew for him. "Did you say Murdock McKenzie sent clothes for you?"

"He did." He nodded, keeping serious eyes on me. "The woman who called upon friendship—was it she who asked for our presence?"

"She's the one," I agreed. "I've already told people that you're a colleague of mine from Dremmler's sector, so they won't be expecting much from you. There's also very little risk since her crowd includes only two XM's—me and Len Phillips—and Len left the planet last night. If you feel you'd rather not take the chance, though, I can always go alone."

"I shall accompany you," he said, taking the plate I handed him. "The woman did not seem right, and you will not go alone."

"Your concern is touching," I told him with a snort. "Are you going to protect me from a feral Jan Elliott?"

"Your amusement is misplaced," he countered. "It is not the woman herself who bids caution, but the reason for her condition." He started toward the wall with his plate, hesitated, then turned back to the table. He put the plate down, then gingerly lowered himself into the chair. The chair creaked under his weight, causing him to grab for the table edge, but it held together in spite of the threat and he was able to glance at me again.

"Do you need the switch to remind you of that which you must do?" he demanded testily. "Get you gone!"

I swallowed a smirk, then turned and left the kitchen. Unless I was mistaken, he planned on trying to use a prong as well as a chair, and I was much better off not seeing that.

I took the opportunity to rinse off quickly in the tub before stretching out across the foot of my bed with the reports. The third one that I'd been unable to read the night before was nothing more than the explanation of Rimilian customs that Sandy had neglected. I glanced through it, sure that it held nothing I hadn't already learned, then picked up the final report. It was a thick one, filled with geographical exactitudes, approximations of barbarian populations, definitions of Centran aims, and more nonsense of the same sort. I began at the obvious point, bored with the thing already, and made my way through it.

I read for hours, mostly under the watchful eye of Tammad. He had come into the bedroom and stretched out on my bed, but hadn't said a word. He napped lightly for a while, opening his eyes each time I shifted my position, only to close them again immediately. Finally, he opened them and kept them open, reaching over to unwrap the towel from me so as to have what to look at. The action irritated me, but there was little I could do about it. I read the report, and ignored him completely.

When I finally finished the last page, I sighed and stretched, looked at the time, then stood up. "We'd better eat now if we're going to dress for the party," I said. "This is one party I have no intention of being late to."

"Will there not be food at this party?" he asked, snatching at the towel I'd wrapped around me again. I jumped back out of his reach, and tucked the flap firmly in place.

"The place to eat is at home," I lectured over my shoulder as I headed for the kitchen. "Parties are for socializing and nothing more. Don't tell me you eat at parties on Rimilia because I already know it and am shocked no end."

"We both eat and drink at gatherings on my home world," he answered lazily, following along behind me. "My brethren too would be shocked at such singular lack of hospitality. To invite a man to your roof and then fail to offer sustenance is a deadly insult."

"We're much more broad-minded on Central," I said, dialing two portions of matider in cream sauce. A nice, chilled wine also seemed to be called for, so I ordered a bottle, then added, "Deadly insult is a refined art here, and a game most of us enjoy playing. If your planet is ever civilized, you'll know what I mean."

"Such does not mean civilization to me," he muttered, lowering himself carefully into a chair. "Such are the ways of beings without a purpose in life."

"And I suppose *you* have a purpose?" I snapped, stung unreasonably by his backward, barbarian criticism.

"Indeed I do," he answered, taking the plate I handed him and sniffing at it. "For the moment, my purpose is to learn what manner of *dimral* this might be. Do you serve me poison, woman?"

"Poison?" I repeated in deep indignation. "I'll have you know, *barbarian*, that that dish is not kept in every home. Only those of the highest social position can even consider it, and. . . ."

"I shall be pleased to taste it after my host," he interrupted flatly, gesturing toward my plate. I glared at him, then took a good-sized prongful without further comment. He watched me chew and swallow, then tasted his own. The taste did not please him, but he began eating anyway. I controlled my outrage, and poured two glasses of wine.

"I'm sure you'll find this vintage much too bitter," I said, lifting my glass without really looking at him. "Don't bother if you aren't in the mood."

"It is discourteous to refuse the offerings of a host," he muttered, taking the glass with a singular lack of enthusiasm. He sipped at it, his brows went up, then he drained the glass in a single gulp. "The drink has no body, but it pleases me," he announced graciously. "You should have offered this sooner."

He took the entire bottle then, drinking half of it without using a glass. I rubbed my eyes for a moment, then turned my attention to my food. In future, I'd make a point of separate meals.

As soon as I finished eating, I went back to my bedroom, but my house guest was right behind me—with something to say.

"Do not dress as you did during the last sun," he ordered in an offhand manner, going toward a pile of boxes that was nothing of mine. "Should there be men at this party, such a display would be most improper."

I stopped where I was, and turned to stare at him in disbelief.

"You have more nerve than an aching tooth!" I said in outrage. "How many times have you stripped me naked in

the last few days? How many times have you raped me? How
many times have you. . . ."

"That has no bearing," he interrupted impatiently, waving
it all aside with a single gesture. "Will you never learn that
you are my belonging? Do as I bid you, and do not cover
your face as it was covered. A woman's beauty was not
meant to be hidden beneath the paint of savages."

"Savages!" I echoed weakly, realizing again that he was beyond belief. He, a barbarian, spoke to me, a woman of civilization, of savages! I closed my eyes in surrender, then
continued on to my bathroom.

I set my makeup applicator for the barest minimum possible, then studied the results in the mirror. I'd asked for the
barest minimum, and that's what I'd gotten. I hadn't even received cheekbone underlining.

Sighing deeply, I settled myself under the hair styler. I suppose I shouldn't have been surprised to have my hair parted
in the middle and combed straight down, but I still felt upset.
If I hadn't been so eager to see Jan, I would have gone
directly to bed.

Considering my mood, there was only one thing for me to
wear. I hadn't worn it since I'd Mediated a dispute on Garen-
dar, but it was absolutely perfect for the occasion. It was a
sheer, gauzy material of brilliant green, wrapping so many
times around me that it covered me tightly from neck to
ankles, winding one extra time around my shoulders and half
my upper arms. Nothing could be seen of me but my face,
and naturally I went barefoot. I examined myself in the mirror with a very deep sigh, then returned to the bedroom.

Tammad was there, but I almost didn't recognize him. He
wore a dark gold formal suit, one-piece and form-fitting, with
a light blue ascot at his throat that matched his eyes. His feet
were encased in short gold boots that gave him unnecessary
extra height, and his blond hair had been combed. When he
heard me he turned, and a small smile touched his lips.

"*Collat* indeed," he murmured, coming close to stare down
at me. "Should the men of your world prove to be other than
darayse, I will have to fight for you this night. Gladly will I
do so."

"The men of my world don't fight for women," I said, ignoring the feeling that I sounded apologetic. "They offer
themselves, and then wait for a woman to choose them."

"More fools, they." He grinned, stepping back again. "We had best be on our way now, lest we find the need to redress. You tempt me sorely, and I am but a man."

I didn't have to be told that twice, and hurriedly led the way to my hangar. I opened the door of my speedster and tried to step up to the hatch, but found that it was impossible—the windings of the cloth were much too tight. I stood there, wondering what to do, and the problem was solved for me. Tammad picked me up without the least effort, then put me in through the hatch; I got to the controls as quickly as possible—he had put his face to my stomach before setting me back on my feet.

The safety harness of the second seat closed around Tammad, but only on the last notch, and at that, just barely. I got us airborne and set the course for Jan's place, then put it on automatic. It was a twenty-five minute flight, and I didn't care for the thought of accidents, but I needn't have bothered. Tammad sat stiff and straight in the seat, his jaw set, no expression on his face. He was obviously afraid of flying, and that confused me. If he was that afraid, why had he come?

We eventually reached Jan's house, where I landed among dozens of other speedsters and quadriwagons. It was barely past the earliest party time, but most of the other guests had already arrived. Obviously, I wasn't the only one who was curious about the new Jan.

Tammad unstrapped with a great deal of relief, led the way out of the speedster, then lifted me down; I took over the lead to Jan's front door and walked right in. The short hall into Jan's party room was deserted, but the party room itself was beginning to be well filled.

Jan had decorated floor, walls and ceiling with dimmed pinpoint glows, giving the effect of jewels scattered about all over. She had resisted this year's furniture choice, wisely staying with last year's long, low, plain look. People stood or sat about, chatting around the soft music, but Jan was nowhere in sight. I caught a glimpse of someone coming toward me, and turned to see Vera. She wore a short, lilac party dress of plumed feathers, and nervously plucked at one of the feathers as she hurried over.

"Terry, I'm glad you came," she whispered. "I wanted to refuse the invitation, but Jan begged me. You must have spoken with her this morning. What did you think?"

"I didn't like it," I admitted, looking at the crowd again. "Hasn't she come down yet?"

"Not yet," Vera said. "And that isn't like her, either. Terry, you don't think she's—sick?"

"We'll find out once we talk to her," I said soothingly. "It isn't smart jumping to any. . . . What's the matter?"

Vera's glance had gone past me, and she'd suddenly paled and gasped. I looked around to see what had frightened her, but couldn't find a thing. I turned back, and she pointed a restrained finger behind me.

"Don't you see him?" she demanded in a whisper. "I've never seen a man that big! He makes me nervous just standing there."

It finally came through that she was talking about Tammad, so I smiled weakly. "As a matter of fact, Vera, he's the house guest I was telling you about. Do let me introduce you."

Vera had as little choice about going as I'd had about offering. We both turned reluctantly to Tammad, but I knew I was the more reluctant. I had no idea how he would acknowledge introductions.

"Vera, allow me to present Tammad sek L'lenda, my colleague from Dremmler's sector. Tammad, this is my friend, Verasten Hardy."

"I am honored, Verasten Hardy," Tammad said, his direct, blue eyes smiling at Vera. "Your presence makes the room glow more brightly."

"Why, thank you!" Vera simpered, forgetting all about how frightened she'd been. "You're going to be a wonderful new addition to Central. Terry, why have you been hiding him? He's absolutely delightful."

"I'm glad you think so," I muttered, and then kept quiet. It was a miracle that Tammad had said the right thing. He might just as easily have ripped off her clothes and raped her. But then in all honesty I had to admit that that wouldn't have been possible. Rimilian customs demanded courtesy from a man when dealing with a woman who wasn't his. He was only free to rip and rape after the woman was given to him.

Strangely enough, the other women in the room began drifting over, keeping me busy for a while with introductions. Then the women had Tammad surrounded, and *he* was busy being courteous. He seemed to be enjoying himself so much that I walked away from the throng to sit down.

"Terry, that wasn't very fair of you," Allynson Scoville scolded gently as he came up to me. "Bringing a man like that to a party almost guarantees that the other men will sit alone. Shame on you."

"I'm a ba-a-d girl," I answered unsympathetically. "How have you been doing, Allyn?"

"Well enough." He nodded amiably as he sat down near me. "I must compliment you on your outfit tonight, my dear. The stark simplicity of it is very stirring. Would you like to go to a real with me later on this week? I understand there are some good ones about these days."

"I think I've had enough of reals for a while," I answered, brushing at my hair. "Have you any idea about what's been happening with Jan? She called me this morning and I almost didn't know her."

"I haven't the faintest," he said, shaking his head. "Rod called me with the invitation, and he seemed a bit strange, too. I imagine that's why everyone is here so early—they want to hear about this magnificent revelation."

"Well, they'd better get down here soon," I muttered, looking back toward the party room's entrance door. "I've never been to Jan's private part of the house, but if they take much longer, that's just where I'm going."

"You'd better have patience, Terry," Allyn cautioned, bringing my attention back to him. "This is not a situation we've ever come across before. We'll all find out about it eventually, but right now the music is lovely. Would you care to dance?"

Allyn had always been a good dancer, and I almost accepted before remembering that Tammad was there, too. I enjoy dancing, and had no intentions of ruining that enjoyment by being forced to dance for a barbarian.

"Some other time, Allyn," I answered, shaking my head. "I'm too upset right now."

He nodded in understanding and sat back, and we continued to chat for a while. A few of the other men came over, asking who the stranger was, and I repeated my explanations. They nodded too and glanced over at the knot around Tammad, but made no move to join them.

A few more people showed up, two of the women going over to the others around Tammad. They'd urged Tammad into a chair out of respect for the cricks in their necks, and were taking turns trying to get his attention. Tammad himself had a slightly amused smile on his face, as if he were used to having women throw themselves at him. The whole thing irritated me, so I looked away and didn't look back.

The soft music that had been playing since I'd arrived trailed off and then stopped altogether. No one noticed it at first, but when they did the buzz of conversation grew louder. Music was rarely interrupted at a party until the party was over.

Vera appeared next to me and started to say something, but she was interrupted by the arrival of our host and hostess. Rod came in first, dressed in a deep blue formal suit with wine red ascot, and he paused in the doorway with fists on hips to look around. He was a big man, broad shouldered and hefty, but as a man, Rodmil Holper had never appealed to me. His narrow, dark eyes rested briefly on Vera, shifted slightly to me, and a hint of amusement showed on his lips. He glanced around at his silent guests again, then laughed shortly.

"I'm glad to see you're all here," he said in a superior way. "And so early, too. Well, you won't regret it. Jan."

At the flat-voiced summons, Janverin Elliott appeared, making me gasp along with everyone else. Jan was a big woman, taller and broader than either Vera or me, usually flaunting her size. She normally wore high heels, high-piled hair styles, wide, flowing outfits, matching them all with quick-tempered, sweeping gestures and moods. But the Janverin Elliott we all knew so well wasn't there. Instead, we saw a woman with nothing left of her former pride. Her black hair hung loosely above the thin, short, cut-out garments that was her only clothing, and when Rod said her name she hurried to kneel before him, pressing her forehead to the floor. We were all speechless at this terrible servility, and Rod laughed again.

"As you can see, friends, Jan has learned what will please me. Let's see how Jan feels about it." He reached down and pulled Jan up by her hair, then slapped her face so hard that blood appeared in the corner of her mouth. "What do you say, Jan? Do you want me to turn you loose?"

"No, Rod, please!" she begged, quivering with emotion, but seeming to be afraid to touch the man who held her so cruelly. "Please keep me as your woman. I've never known such happiness as that which I've known as your woman. You've taught me what being a woman really means, and I'll devote my life to you if you'll let me."

Rod let go of her hair and she slid down to grasp his ankles, kissing them and pressing her face on them. Vera was very quiet beside me, but I felt sick to my stomach.

"You see?" Rod asked the other men smugly. "She knows when she's well off. And the same can be accomplished with any woman if you just bother to try. Watch."

He looked toward the doorway and we all followed his gaze to see Guylor Sutton standing there. Guy wasn't as big as Rod, but they both had the same narrow-eyed look and were close friends. Beside me, Vera began shivering.

Guy entered the room and stopped about five feet from Vera, his eyes angry as though he had been deeply insulted.

"Verasten Hardy, your time has come," he said in an ugly voice. "Place yourself before me in the correct manner."

Vera shuddered, her eyes and fists closed tight, and I quickly put my arms around her.

"Guylor Sutton, you leave her alone!" I snapped. "I don't know what sickness has gotten into all of you, but Vera wants no part of it. Leave her alone, I say!"

Guy's lips tightened, but Rod kicked Jan away from him and came to stand near Guy.

"Terrillian Reya," Rod said, looking me over in a way I didn't like. "You're another one who needs to be taught how to be a woman. You'll stay with us, and Jan will show you what to do to avoid the lash—or usually avoid it. Whipping you will be a pleasure."

He was nearly drooling as he discussed his twisted expectations, and I had never been so repelled by anything or anyone.

"You *are* sick," I told him coldly, holding Vera even more tightly. "What's the matter, Rod, can't you cope with a woman who isn't a slave? Can't you face her if she isn't groveling at your feet? Can't you realize your masculinity without a whip in your hand? Treating Jan like that doesn't make you a man, Rod! It makes you a self-professed coward!"

Rod's face had twitched at everything I'd said to him, but the last word was more than he could stand. He snarled wordlessly and came forward to hit me the way he'd hit Jan. I put my arm up to ward off the blow, but it never reached me. Tammad was suddenly there between us, and he lifted Rodmil Holper by the front of his suit. He lifted the man clear off the floor and *threw* him, easily and without effort, into the wall ten feet away. Rod struck the wall with a thud, slid down to the floor, then looked up at Tammad with a dazed but fear-filled stare.

"She is correct," Tammad told Rod calmly, staring down at him without expression, but with a definite tinge of disgust to his voice. "Only *darayse* cause pain to women without reason. The woman learned nothing through the pain you gave her, and no true man could be tempted by a slave such as her. To raise your hands in such a manner to another man may gain you the name of warrior; to raise your hands in such a manner to a woman gains naught but shame. It is time to depart."

The other people in the room shook themselves, as if coming out of a daze. They began filing past Rod, who was still on the floor with Jan crying in a heap near him, and none of them said anything or looked at the couple on the floor. When I began urging Vera out of the room, Guy tried to get in our way, but Tammad just brushed him aside so that we could leave.

Once outside, I tried to talk Vera into coming home with me, but the night air seemed to have braced her. She straightened up, brushed at her hair, and smiled weakly.

"Thanks anyway, Terry," she said and patted my shoulder. "You've done enough, and believe me, it helped. I'm not afraid of Guy any longer, because now I know that he can't do that to me unless I let him. And I'm not going to let him! I'm going to stay with some friends for a while, and if Guylor Sutton shows up, I'll call the peacemen."

She ended with an emphatic nod of her head, marched to her speedster, climbed in, and flew away. I watched until she'd disappeared into the distance, then looked back at Jan's house.

"You cannot aid the other," Tammad said quietly, almost reading my thoughts. "She wishes to remain as she is, and will not allow you to help."

"But why?" I asked him, really needing an explanation. "Why should she want to live like that?"

"She does not care to direct her own destiny," he said, looking down at me and brushing the hair from my cheek. "She will accept the abuse of the non-man because she believes him to be stronger than she. If he were truly stronger, he would force her to do the right, not the pleasurable. Let us return home."

I looked away from him, back toward the house again, feeling very reluctant to leave Jan like that. She had been a friend of sorts for a long time, but the choice was taken from me. Tammad lifted me in his arms, carried me to my speedster, and thrust me into the hatch.

"You can do nothing further, so let us be gone," he directed, slapping my bottom to move me out of the way. "I would be beyond the necessity for flying through the air as quickly as possible."

"I'm calling the peacemen as soon as I get home," I decided as we both strapped in. "If they detain Rod, Jan will have a chance to. . . ."

"You shall not," he said, giving me a disapproving look. "The woman has chosen her lot in life, and cannot be taken from it save through her own will. If she does not feel death preferable to slavery, slavery is the proper place for her."

"You'd never say that if *you* were the slave!" I snapped. "Wouldn't you want someone to come and help *you?*"

"One cannot free a slave," he answered, still patient, but just barely. "Likewise, one cannot enslave a free man. The former may be unshackled, but will soon seek a new master to serve; the latter may be weighted down with chains, but can never be made to bend the knee. Think upon that, woman, as you take us home."

I started the speedster and got us airborne, but I still didn't care for what he'd said. Jan was no natural born slave; all she needed was a little help. The peacemen would help her, and she would be fine again.

By the time I rolled into my hangar, I'd long since made up my mind. A call to the peacemen would harm nothing, and Jan would one day be grateful. I followed Tammad to the speedster hatch, but instead of lifting me down, he took me by the waist, put me over his shoulder, and proceeded to carry me into the house.

"What are you doing?" I demanded of him. "Put me down immediately!"

"I shall not," he answered without even slowing. "I see by your face that you are determined to court a further switching. I shall save you from it by occupying your time with other things."

"Barbarian!" I screamed. "Let me go!" But he didn't. He carried me to my bedroom, stripped the wrappings from me, and showed me what other things he meant. By the time he was through with me, I hadn't the strength left to walk to the call.

★ 4 ★

I glared at Tammad over breakfast, but he just gazed back at me in amusement.

"Why do you thus look upon me?" he asked innocently. "Have I done something amiss?"

"*Everything* you do is amiss!" I countered, wishing looks could kill. "Don't even speak to me!"

"Words are not necessary between a man and his belonging," he murmured, stroking my arm with his finger. I pulled my arm away as if it had been burned, and he laughed out loud. "Woman, it is not me you fear, but yourself. Was it not clear, but moments ago, that the fire burned high in you? That I took you and cooled your fire should not make you angry."

"The only thing you take is advantage of me!" I said, trying to crumple the eating prong in my fist. "I never invited you into my bed, and a gentleman would know when he wasn't wanted. But, of course, I forgot. You don't even know the *meaning* of the word, 'gentleman'!"

"Exceedingly strange," he sighed, applying himself to his food. "Perhaps your actions will become understandable when we have reached Rimilia. On this world, many things are unclear to me."

I began to assure him that he would never understand me, when the visitor flash showed on the wall board. I left the food I had no real desire for, and went downramp to see who had come into my hall. Sandy Kemper stood there, an uncomfortable expression on his long, thin face.

61

"Well, well," I drawled, folding my arms as I stopped in front of him. "To what wondrous good fortune do I owe *this* visit? If you've come to take the barbarian back, please, be my guest!"

"Now, Terry, I'm sorry about what's happened," he mumbled, "but it wasn't really my fault. I did tell you to go home, you know. If you had, you would not have gotten involved."

"I wouldn't have gotten involved if I could have stayed asleep," I snapped. "Whose fault do you think *that* was?"

He looked even more uncomfortable, then glanced past my shoulder. "Ah, Tammad," he said in relief, "I came to give you a message from Murdock. Do you have a moment?"

"Of course," Tammad answered as he came up to us. I noticed that he had his swim trunks on again, but was eyeing my sleep suit with considerably more disfavor than he had been showing. "Go you back to your food, woman. This talk does not concern you."

"How would *you* know?" I countered. "You haven't even heard what he has to say."

"I do not need to hear," he answered. "Should some part of it concern you, you will be told."

"I'll just save you the trouble and stay around anyway," I said, feeling the itch of another hunch. "Go ahead, Sandy, get it said."

Sandy seemed upset, but Tammad didn't hesitate. He lifted me off the floor under one great arm, carried me back upramp, and found the switch where he'd left it. By the time he returned to Sandy, I was long since reduced to tears and sobbing. The switch is a painful instrument of teaching, and the barbarian's arm had reminded me that he would stand only so much of my disobedience before the lesson was taught again. The second switching was more painful than the first, and I had no curiosity about a possible third.

I had nearly made up my mind to run away no matter what the consequences, when Tammad came back. He stood over me as I lay face down on a bed that was damp from my tears, and studied me. At last, he shook his head.

"In truth, the beating should not have been yours," he said, almost in disgust. "Did your life not hinge upon your heeding of my word, I could not fault you for your actions. How else could you be, living your life among *darayse*?"

I sniffled and stared at him, and he crouched down to

smooth my hair. "The Sandy Kemper asked what I had done to you to make you scream so. When I explained what I had done, and why it was necessary, a rage filled him. None but a barbarian would treat a Prime so, he shouted. A Prime was to be spoken to gently and persuaded, he insisted. And what, asked I, if she cannot be persuaded? Is her life to be lost should my tongue fail to be glib enough? He refused to consider this, maintaining only that a Prime is not to be touched. When he spoke his message and left, I was pleased to see him go."

"What makes you so sure that *you're* right?" I demanded weakly with a sniff. "I've never been beaten before in my life, yet I've managed to survive!"

"You were not upon Rimilia," he said. "Therein lies the difference. But fear not, woman. I shall not save you from the lesser pain and allow you to be lost to the greater. I shall return you to your embassy as you will leave it. You may rest now until the soreness has passed."

He stood straight again and left the room, graciously allowing me to rest. He was so sure that *his* way was best, so sure that I'd never survive without him. He, who had knowledge of no more than his one, small world, knew that I, who had visited dozens, would never survive! I was furious at that, furious that he considered himself so much better than I, furious that in his imagined superiority he dared to beat me. I resolved to teach him that he was wrong, to shame him as he had shamed me. I didn't know when, but I knew I would do it.

He left me alone that day, coming for me only when it was time to eat. I served him first, but was unable to sit at the table with him, instead carrying my plate back to my bedroom to eat, belly down, like an animal.

I was about to leave the kitchen with the last meal of the day, when the call sounded. Without thinking, I waved my hand in acknowledgment, and Murdock McKenzie's face appeared on the screen.

"Ah, Terrillian," he said, his cold, narrow face wearing the faintest of smiles, "I'm pleased to see you looking so well."

I blushed in embarrassment even though I knew he could see nothing more than my head and shoulders. The barbarian had stripped off my sleep suit to beat me, and I hadn't dressed again.

"Sandros was most concerned about you," he continued

smoothly. "He insisted that you were being mistreated abominably, and that I was to do something at once. Tammad, my friend, have you been mistreating our Prime?"

"I have been teaching her obedience," Tammad answered in a neutral tone, looking straight at the call. "It is something that should have been done sooner."

"I'm afraid I'm forced to agree with you." Murdock nodded with a rueful smile. "She is a most disobedient child, and is sorely in need of strict guidance. For her sake, I wish you success."

"The Murdock McKenzie need have no fear," Tammad murmured, showing a faint grin, knowing then that he wasn't being criticized. "She shall be taught that which she needs to know."

"Good." Murdock nodded again. "And when you go tomorrow to register for the voyage, have her show you Tallion City. You may not have the opportunity to see it again."

"I shall do so," Tammad agreed. "The Sandy Kemper felt she knew the location of where we must go. Is this true?"

"It is," Murdock said. "Have you told her yet?"

"She will know when she must know," Tammad answered. "There is time yet for the telling."

"As you wish," Murdock agreed, then moved his eyes back to me. "Terrillian, you'd do well to be on your best behavior. Tammad is not to be gotten around as easily as Sandros—or Jackson. Perhaps you've already discovered this?"

"Instead of answering, I waved my hand and cleared the call without first announcing my intention. Murdock McKenzie was enjoying my torment, was gloating over my helplessness. When I returned from Rimilia a free woman again, I would have my revenge on him. Rathmore Hellman was keenly aware of all disservices done him, but also habitually acknowledged good turns. When I was successful, I would ask a favor.

I retired to my bedroom again to consider what I'd recently learned. There was only one "voyage" Tammad would be taking, so he was soon to return to his planet. If we were to register for the flight in Tallion City, he was no longer an unregistered alien to be hidden away. Also, the flight would take place within three days, reservations never being taken earlier. I was not unhappy at the thought of leaving Central; on the contrary, I wished the business over and done with.

Since we first had to leave before I would be free to return, I was anxious to be started.

The barbarian said nothing to me about our visit to Tallion City until the next day. At the first meal, he calmly announced our destination and handed me a sheet of paper.

"The writing contains your instructions," he said. "Read them well and dress yourself, for I would leave as soon as possible."

I glanced at the paper, confirming my guess that he was to continue as "my associate from Dremmler's sector," and also to see what flight we were to book on, then handed it back without comment. The barbarian narrowed his eyes at me.

"Have you no further need of it?" he asked with something like suspicion. "No questions on our destination?"

"We leave for your world within three days." I shrugged. "What more do I need to know?"

He stared briefly at me, then nodded his head. "It is no less than I would expect you to know. Dress yourself then, and let us be about it."

We both dressed, he in a casual, dark gray coverall, I in a knee-length, fitted smock, then went again to my speedster. The trip to Tallion City was of its usual length, and I had little difficulty in finding the flight reservations office. I had been there before, but not often and not lately. Prime assignments generally require special and immediate transportation.

Tammad and I were assured our cabins aboard a medium-sized transport that would leave Tallion City Outer Port late the following day, and I was then free to show the barbarian around the city. People come to rubberneck at Tallion City from all over Central, but why they do it is completely beyond me. There are very few Neighborhoods anywhere on the planet that don't think of Tallion City as purely, basically, evil, as most of Central is more backward than one would imagine possible. Our distant citizens want nothing whatever to do with people of other worlds, unless they, themselves, choose to do the traveling, and visiting citizens of other worlds have even found themselves locked up if they dared to venture beyond Tallion City and its immediate Neighborhoods. More than a few Neighborhood Chairmen have been chosen for their posts because of outspokenly firm stands against Tallion City and its "unnatural" practices, and once a year, representatives from most Neighborhoods descend on the city demanding to know what is being done to save our planet from the savages and barbarians who are lined up waiting to invade and pervert us. All planetary governmental offices were located in the city, and governmental employees tended to live in and around the city, just so they could live the sort of peaceful lives they prefer. Casual alliances between men and women aren't permitted in other Neighborhoods, and if a cohabitation agreement isn't firmly in evidence, the guilty couple is immediately ejected—if they're lucky. If they aren't lucky, they might find themselves the unwavering objects of Peacemen attentions, and thereafter find themselves explaining to a totally unsympathetic Neighborhood Chairman why they should not be punished in some way for their inexcusably heinous behavior. Natives of Tallion City tend to avoid non-natives, but it isn't always possible, especially when those non-natives come thronging to sightsee in total disapproval. Nothing about our city appeals to them, but they continue to come in their hundreds and thousands, frowning and shaking their heads and spending as few of their Earning Pluses as possible.

That day was no different from any other, and the barbarian and I spent hours fighting our way through the crowds. I was asked why this and why that so many times that I lost count, eventually taking to answering as mechanically and shortly as possible. Why were people given numbers when joining buying audiences? Why was merchandise displayed on a large screen in the center of each category buying room? Why were harmless animals kept behind force screens where people stared at them? Why were there no greetings exchanged between people? How did one buy things when no one seemed to have *dinga*? I answered in desperation that people were given numbers so that they would be identified when ordering merchandise, that the merchandise could be more easily seen by all when displayed on the screen, and still not be shopworn, that most of the animals behind the force screens were far from harmless, and even if they weren't, no one wanted them wandering around loose, that people exchanged greetings only with those whom they knew, and most of the people around us were strangers to each other, that one bought things with credit issued by the government, the same amount issued to all; the only time extra needed to be spent was when someone wanted something that wasn't considered a necessity, and then Earning Pluses, issued for necessary work done for Central central, were used. We went from place to place, and Tallion Central Exchange, two miles high and half a mile broad, impressed my guest no end, but I haven't much of the sightseer in my soul. Museums and art exhibits held no interest for him, and riding the various speed slidewalks is a necessity, not an entertainment. I finally purchased a late meal for us in an eating place open to anyone, then suggested that we return to my home.

"I would see more of this city first," Tammad decided with a shake of his head as he examined the multicolored decorations and listened to the loud, blaring music with what was obviously approval. "Never have I imagined such things could be. Also, I have seen no saddle animals about. For what reason, then, are those watering places in so many locations?"

"Those aren't watering places," I told him with a yawn. "They are decorative fountains, to be looked at and appreciated, not used and dirtied."

"The desert dwellers of Hamarda would use them well." He grinned, leaning his arms on the small table between us. "Their beasts would roll beneath the spray, as would the nomads themselves. They worship the fall of rain from the skies, reveling for days after such an occurrence. One may know the timing of such rains from the spate of nomad brats dropped at the end of their women's cycles."

"Fascinating," I commented, sipping at my wine. After a day of Seeing Tallion City, I'd needed the wine as never before.

"There is one thing you *must* show me," he continued, a little too casually. "I have twice now heard mention of that which are called 'reals.' The men who offered these to you seemed anxious that you accompany them—for a reason which I believe may be all too clearly seen."

He was rating me with his eyes again, but this time there was disapproval involved, perhaps at the idea that others found me attractive. I didn't understand his attitude, but that didn't stop me from resenting it.

"Well, whatever their reason," I said frostily, "at least they *asked*, not demanded. They don't consider a woman theirs for the taking."

"Perhaps they spend too much time in the asking," he murmured, staring at me from below half closed eyes. "I have not seen many children in this magnificent city of yours. Are the children kept elsewhere?"

"Some of them," I answered, looking away from him. "Having children is out of fashion these days, for the most part. People are too busy to be bothered with children."

"I see," he said quietly—and somehow I felt that he did see—and then changed subjects again. "Where are these reals kept and how does one use them?"

"You experience them, not use them!" I snapped, annoyed again by his superior manner. "And I don't know if you would be capable of experiencing them. Your mind may not be able to make the adjustment."

"We will soon know," he said, rising to his feet. "Take me there."

He stood there tall and strong, already having given his orders, now waiting only to be obeyed. Familiar fury rose in me, but I didn't let any of it show.

"If that's what you want," I said, "that's what you'll get." I finished my wine in a swallow, then led the way without objection to a slidewalk. The idea must have been growing in me for some time, as there was no need to stop and think it out. Unhesitatingly, I chose the slidewalk that would take us to Bend Five.

There was a different greeter at the door of the house, and that made matters considerably easier. I requested private accommodations, handed over a block of Earning Pluses, then followed the guide to the room. By thanking the guide quickly and closing the door in his face, I avoided any extraneous comments about who should sit where. Tammad looked about at the almost bare room and was not impressed.

"The couches are not comfortably wide enough for two," he observed. "There is little else to be done here."

"Appearances can be deceiving," I remarked with a small smile. "Take the couch on the right."

He stretched out carelessly on the couch, supremely confident that there was nothing there that could touch him or harm him; I lifted the headset of contacts and handed it to him.

"Place that on your head just as I gave it to you," I directed, picking up the other headset and sitting down with it. "As soon as it's on, close your eyes."

He glanced at the contacts, still suspecting nothing, then reached up to position them. I quickly separated out two of the contacts from my own headset and placed them to my head.

Although the real sprang immediately into my mind, I could still see Tammad on his couch. I had no intention of submerging myself in a man's role, and I wanted to see the barbarian's reactions. He lay on the couch, much too large for it, and frowned.

In my mind, *I watched from the anonymity of the giant trees as the big, blonde girl looked around hesitantly in the clearing. I knew myself to be bigger yet, big and male and all-powerful, and I knew that the helpless female soon would be mine.* Although I was not fully experiencing the real, the compulsion of it was almost overpowering.

The blonde female turned to go back to the strange thing she had emerged from, and I moved quickly to head her off. She looked around as she hurried, and I was able to put myself directly in her path before she saw me. She stopped abruptly with a scream, covering her mouth with her hand, and looked up into my eyes. She recoiled from what she saw there, cringing back, but I didn't wait any longer. I threw her immediately to the ground, shoved her over onto her face, then tied her wrists tightly behind her.

Tammad moved slightly on his couch, a deep frown on his face, flexing fists. He would be experiencing the helplessness and terror of a small female subjected to the brutality of a much larger male. He would know the reality of it, and later he would know the shame.

The blonde female screamed and cried out in an unknown tongue, but it made little difference. She was mine now, and I lifted her struggling but negligible weight to my shoulder, then returned to the home-forest. The presence of the great trees comforted me, telling me that I, too, was undefeatable and eternal. I found my way easily to the tree that sheltered me, then climbed to my limb in the usual manner.

My trunk dwelling was a welcome sight, and I put the female in a far corner of it. She had stopped screaming, but looked about herself in great fear. She was very beautiful, and her beauty drove me to hunger for her. I went again to the outer limb to pull up my vine and coil it, then returned to my blonde female. She gasped and quivered at the sight of me, and I knew a moment of curiosity.

"From which tree do you come?" I demanded of her. "Are there other such females in your tribe?"

*She responded in a low, fear-filled voice, but spoke nothing
I could understand. Anger touched me then, and I struck her,
taking her by the hair to force her to face me.*

*"From which tree do you come?" I demanded again.
"What of the other females in your tribe?"*

*She screamed out in the tongue I didn't know, and I could
smell the fear on her. She was worthless to tell me what I
wished to know, but she had other worth. I released her hair
and turned my attention to her covering, but could not discover the opening of it. Impatiently, I tore it from her, and
she lay before me, the swell of her breasts, the turn of her
hip, all calling to me and heating my blood.*

*As from a distance, I heard her unknown words again, but
cared nothing for them. Her body was mine to conquer and
use, mine to pleasure in, mine to do with as I wished. She
tried feebly to resist me, but her resistance was as nothing. I
vented my need upon her and forced her to my pleasure.*

I gripped the edges of the couch with tightened fingers,
watching Tammad. His expression was hopeless and wild,
and he writhed as if to escape from some unbearable sensation. I knew what he was feeling and I was glad he felt it,
glad that the mighty barbarian had been reduced to a whim-
pering pleasure toy. I withdrew most of myself from the real
and watched Tammad writhe.

When the brutal assault was complete, I removed the contacts from both of us. I had accomplished my aim, and had
no intentions of burning either of us out. It's possible to
switch sexes in reals, but it isn't recommended. It produces an
unnatural strain that I'd never understood until right then. I
felt drained in some strange, undefined way, and I didn't like
the lingering effects in my mind. I had no normal desire to
rape anyone, and the residual urge toward it was very unsettling.

In a number of minutes Tammad opened his eyes, but they
weren't focused. He groaned as if he still felt the pain of his
taking within him, and I wondered how it had seemed to
him. I'd had sex with men before him, and for me the difference was one of intensity and volition. For him, it was an entirely alien experience, a true virgin rape. What would it do
to a man to be taken like a woman?

I was beginning to think about Rathmore Hellman's dis-
pleasure when Tammad sat up and shook himself. He got un-
steadily to his feet and shook his head again, as if to clear

away the aftereffects of a nightmare, but when I looked up into his eyes, I could see that he wasn't entirely returned. I didn't relish the thought of taking him back to my speedster across the slidewalks, so I called for a guide, told him that my friend had taken suddenly ill, and asked for an emergency lift to my parking building.

The operator of the emergency lift helped me get Tammad settled in my speedster, and I flew directly back to my house. The greeter and guide at the real house had stared at us suspiciously as we'd left, but they could hardly ask any questions. They let us leave unmolested, and were probably hoping that nothing would come of the incident.

I rolled my speedster into the hangar, wondering how I was to get the barbarian into my house. Without the help of the lift operator, I never would have gotten the giant into my speedster to begin with. I turned the engine off, and only then noticed the three men standing near the door to my house. Two of them came forward immediately, entered the speedster, and went to the barbarian. I left the speedster to them and went to face the third man, a coldly furious Murdock McKenzie.

"What sort of woman are you?" he demanded as I came up to him. "What sort of woman would subject a man to conscienceless indignity? How could you have. . . ."

"Just as easily as you did!" I snapped, cutting off his tirade. "You gave me to him, to be beaten and used by him, and it didn't bother you a bit! But now that your—*friend*—has had a taste of the same thing, you're up in arms. Well, that's too bad about you, but it's too late to stop it. It's done and I'm glad!"

His face twisted even more at the venom in my words, and his cold, grey eyes seemed made out of stone.

"We shall see how glad you are if he can't be pulled out of it," he said in a low, deadly voice. "If I hadn't had you followed and watched, I would never have known about it. Stupid, vindictive woman!"

He turned away from me then, dismissing my presence as he watched the two strange men help Tammad out of the speedster. The barbarian moved as if in a dream, causing the men to struggle to direct him. They took him past me into the house and down the hall to my party room, Murdock McKenzie following painfully behind them with his twisted body. The door was closed, shutting me out, but I didn't care.

I didn't care if the barbarian *never* came back to himself! I ran upramp to my bathroom, bathed hurriedly, then went to bed.

I struggled out of the dream, bathed in a sweat I couldn't control. I'd been lying in bed in my dream, and Tammad had come to me. I'd felt the fury I usually did, thinking he would use me as always, without my permission, but I'd been wrong. He lay in the bed next to me, staring at me fearfully, and he'd quivered and moaned when I'd turned toward him. He lay stretched out flat, his hands behind his head, but he wasn't relaxed. He was tense and almost terror-stricken, his hands not resting behind his head but almost chained there. I'd put my hand out to him, feeling revulsion and a strong sense of wrongness, and he'd whimpered and turned his face away. I'd been sick then, knowing I'd destroyed the mighty barbarian forever. He'd never be the same, and it was my fault, my fault, my fault. . . .

The queasiness was too much to bear. I ran to my bathroom and threw up, guilt emptying me of everything within. I'd wanted to have vengeance on Murdock McKenzie, using the barbarian to strike at him as he had used Tammad to strike at me. But Tammad was the one who had been struck, for no other reason than being himself. He behaved as a barbarian because he was one, and it was no fault of his. If he had been raised on Central, he would have been different.

When the spasms passed, I leaned weakly against the tub, transparented the wall, and looked out. The sky was dark with the loneliness of night, empty of the life that day seemed to bring. I hadn't lighted the bathroom so I sat in the dark, in it but not part of it. My loneliness was a separate thing and I'd never be free of the guilt I felt.

"The sunless time is for sleep," a voice said. "Why do you sit here awake?"

I gasped at seeing Tammad in the doorway, then got quickly to my feet and ran to him. "Are you all right?" I demanded, my hands flat on his chest to prove to myself that he really was there. "How do you feel? Are you—changed in any way?"

"How would I be changed?" he asked in amusement. "I have spoken with Murdock McKenzie for a longer time than is usual, but such a thing has no power to change me."

"But the real!" I insisted. "Didn't it hurt you?"

"I remember nothing of the real," he murmured, folding his mighty arms around me. "The experience was of so little consequence that it is gone completely. When the next sun comes, you may remind me if you wish. For now, I have no desire for talk."

He picked me up and carried me to the bed, and my relief was so great that I barely resented his use of me.

★ 5 ★

I was annoyed, but I tried to control my annoyance. It wasn't Tammad's fault that he was a barbarian. I knew it was my place to try civilizing him, but the job wasn't going to be easy.

"You just can't, that's all," I said, trying to sound reasonable. "It isn't done on most of Central, and people will be offended."

"How will my action with you offend others?" Tammad asked patiently. "I may do as I wish with that which belongs to me."

"But that's just the point!" I said in exasperation. "I do *not* belong to you, and those people out there know it! If you try to make me sleep in your cabin, they'll complain to the captain."

We were aboard the *Central Starshine*, the transport that would take us to Rimilia, and we stood in my cabin. Tammad had had all memory of the real removed from his mind, and Murdock McKenzie had called before we'd left for the Port to tell me how lucky I was. I'd listened to the first of his words coldly, and then had cut the call the way I'd done the time before. Murdock McKenzie had nothing to say that I cared to hear.

My cabin was right next to Tammad's, one of twenty around the circle of the middle deck. The center of the middle deck was devoted to tables for eating and couches for socializing, and was spacious enough for a medium-sized transport. With the crews' quarters above on the control deck, and the cargo below on the lower deck, the passengers could spend their travel time undisturbed by anything other than minding everyone else's business.

"Of what will they complain?" Tammad the Innocent asked. "I do not take any women to my cabin but my own."

"It's not the men who will be doing the complaining," I said sharply, annoyed all over again that he still considered me his woman. "Didn't you see how that Paulamin Tumley looked at you? She's a Neighborhood Chairman in her district, and the other passengers look up to her. She already disapproves of you on general principles—the rest of Central is much more provincial than Tallion City. If she sees you taking me to your cabin, she'll explode."

"This is not clear to me," he insisted, shaking his head. "The woman can say nothing on the actions of a warrior. Is this captain a warrior that he will fight me for possession of you? Do you fear that I will lose you to him?"

I groaned feelingly, then threw myself on my bed. The legs of the bed were secured so tightly to the deck that the bed didn't even quiver. "You're a barbarian and can't be blamed for your lacks," I recited, trying to keep the thought firmly in mind. "You know nothing about the workings of civilization, and I haven't the time to teach them to you. We will each sleep in our own cabins, and do nothing to upset Paulamin Tumley. It will be hard staying inconspicuous if I have to use my Prime status to counter her narrowmindedness."

"Is this your word on the matter?" he asked in amusement, coming over to sit on the bed next to me. "Will you punish me if I fail to obey you?"

"You can't refuse to do as I say," I insisted, starting to sit up again, but I found my hair tight in his grasp, which kept me firmly in place. I reached up to see if I could loosen his fingers, and my wrists were abruptly held instead.

"No, *you* may not refuse to do as *I* say," he corrected softly, those blue eyes directly on me. "It is a warrior's place to say a word, a woman's place to obey that word. Do you again wish to disobey me?"

"You're impossible!" I snapped with resentment, completely out of patience. "I don't know why I bothered. If you want to tangle with Paulamin Tumley, go right ahead. People like her never learn anything, and they never change their minds. I hope you end up in the brig."

"Should that eventuate," he said, grinning, "you will yet be with me. I know not the meaning of 'brig,' but I will require my woman wherever I be. What is the meaning of that sound?"

He was talking about the gentle gonging that could be heard from the one-way on the wall. "It's to notify passengers that food will be available five minutes from now," I told him. "We can go out now and get a table."

"We may seek our table later," he said, stroking my side with his hand. "For now, I find that having discussed requiring a woman has given me hunger of a different sort. I shall deal with this hunger first."

He dealt with his hunger in the usual way, and I found myself wishing that at least some of the real had stayed with him. His appetites were beyond the bounds of belief, and could have done with a little trimming. Correction—a *lot* of trimming.

When my clothes were decently arranged once more, we went out to have our meal. As we stepped from the cabin, the eye of every person at every table turned to stare at us, and each of those eyes was accompanied by a frown. I ignored both frowns and stares and followed Tammad to the one empty table in the area, discovering that the barbarian wasn't even aware of being stared at. He sat himself with easy grace, not bothering to notice anyone in the circle. I sat too, feeling the red flush on my cheeks in spite of everything I could do.

The steward came and put our plates in front of us, then fetched a bottle of wine which he poured for us. Tammad bent to his food as if famished, but as soon as the steward was gone, Paulamin Tumley stood herself in his place. She was a nicely built woman, with a pretty face and hair as blond as Tammad's, but her brown eyes were cold and uncompromising, and her expression totally unforgiving.

"You eat as if you've done something to acquire an appetite," she said frostily to Tammad. "I'd better be wrong about what that something might be!"

The barbarian looked up as if noticing her for the first time, and examined her with his eyes just as if she hadn't introduced herself to us as soon as we'd come aboard. She flushed slightly at his frank appraisal, and her eyes flashed fire and destruction.

"Answer me!" she snapped. "What were you and that girl doing alone together in that cabin? We are all of us decent people here, and will not condone goings-on of a lewd and lecherous nature! Tallion City is a hotbed of licentiousness, but we here will not be contaminated! We demand to know about your conduct!"

Tammad snorted in amusement, then started to laugh. He threw his head back and laughed as if touched, and Paulamin Tumley really turned red. She stood with her fists clenched and her lips clamped tight, furious at being laughed at. I ate my steamed haldivar in silence, watching the proceedings with interest.

The irate Neighborhood Chairman finally grew tired of watching Tammad laugh, and turned on me. "I'll have my answer from you!" she said in a choked voice. "What went on between you and that—that—deficient?"

"Oh, I wouldn't *dream* of interfering with your conversation with him," I said around a mouthful of haldivar. "You and he are establishing such a lovely—rapport."

"I will be answered!" she screamed, shaking her fists in the air. "Come and stand with me, good people, and demand your right to know!"

At her urging, the other passengers came to stand behind her. There were three other women and fourteen men, and every one of them wore a grim, demanding expression. Tammad's laughter trailed off into chuckles, and then died altogether.

"At last!" Paulamin said in triumph. "He ceases his caterwauling and now, perhaps, will answer us. I repeat, man of iniquity—what were you doing in that cabin?"

Tammad was looking around at the men behind Paulamin, ignoring her completely, then suddenly he was on his feet, no longer looking amused.

"A foolish woman is to be laughed at and overlooked," he announced in a death-cold voice. "A foolish man is an entirely different matter. Do you men now step to me and ask what you will ask."

The men glanced at each other, shuffled their feet nervously, then backed away to return to their tables. The three women hesitated no longer than the men, having no intentions of standing there by themselves. In no more than a minute or two, Paulamin was alone again. She looked around herself in disbelief, then saw that Tammad was staring down at her.

"You don't scare *me!*" she said in a high, shrill voice. "Murder me if you will, but my voice will never be stilled!"

"Woman, you are exceedingly foolish," Tammad said in annoyance. "Take yourself from my sight, else your voice will be raised at the urging of the flat of my hand. Too long has the man to whom you belong neglected your punishment."

Paulamin turned pale and spluttered, trying, no doubt, to announce that never had anyone had the effrontery to speak to her like that. Tammad took a step toward her, and her spluttering turned into squeaking as she moved fast to avoid him. She scurried into the passage that led to the control deck, and Tammad came back to the table.

"Beautifully done," I commented as I took the last bite of my haldivar. "I wonder if you'll be as successful with the captain."

"Keep silent," he said irritably, his eyes on his plate. "I have had enough of foolish women."

I leaned back in my chair with a shrug, sipping my wine and watching him eat. He left his own wine standing where it was, not even tasted.

Tammad had just finished eating when Paulamin reappeared, leading the captain and two of his crewmen. The captain was also a big man and, although not of Tammad's giant proportions, still a good size. He had some grey in his dark, short-cut hair, but could not, by any means, be considered old. Paulamin led him to our table, and pointed an accusing finger at Tammad.

"He's the one!" she shrilled. "He threatened me and everyone heard it! Arrest him, Captain, arrest him at once!"

"Calm yourself, Chairman Tumley," the captain soothed. "I'll soon find out who should be arrested. May I ask your name, sir?"

"I am called Tammad sek L'lenda," Tammad answered with his eyes on the captain, looking as if he'd bitten into something sour. The name I'd given him meant, "Tammad, he who calls himself warrior," and it was something of an insult. He disliked saying it, but Murdock McKenzie had told him that it was necessary.

"I see," the captain nodded. "Am I correct in assuming that the lady with you is Terrillian Reya?"

"She is," Tammad said with raised eyebrows. "You know of us?"

"I have spoken with one Murdock McKenzie," the captain answered, his face still expressionless, but his eyes beginning to appear impressed. "It was requested that I give you and the Prime every consideration to make your trip a pleasant one. May I be of any service, sir?"

"I think not," Tammad chuckled, looking at a stricken Paulamin Tumley, but this time Paulamin was ignoring *him*. She stared at me with her mouth open until she finally found her voice.

"You're a Prime," she whispered, blushing furiously. "You're a Prime and I spoke to you as if you were a nobody. I've never been so embarrassed in my life."

"What matters if she be a Prime?" Tammad asked curiously. "Is a Prime unable to do that which you accused her of?"

"Don't be ridiculous!" Paulamin snapped, blushing even more deeply. "A Prime can do anything she wishes to do. No one has the right to direct her. You could have said she was a Prime. Oh, how I hate you."

She glared furiously at Tammad, then ran to the peace of her cabin. The captain took a deep breath as he watched her go, then turned back to us.

"If there's anything I can do for you, just let me know," he said with a formal bow in my direction. "I hope you enjoy the trip."

He led his men back toward the passage to the control deck, and I rose from the table, marched to my cabin, slammed the door, and locked it. I was furious with Murdock McKenzie, and would have strangled him if he'd been in reach. The nerve of him, protecting that barbarian with the prestige of *my* position as Prime! I hated Murdock McKenzie, I hated the barbarian, and I hated that stupid Paulamin Tumley for idolizing me. I ignored the ringing at my door, undressed, then went to bed *alone*.

★ 6 ★

I spent the balance of the four-day trip in my cabin, having my meals delivered to me through the service slot. My door rang constantly in spite of the fact that I never answered it, and the captain called on the two-way to inquire about my health. I informed the captain that I required time for meditation, cut off the two-way, then went back to brooding.

Everything that barbarian did turned out well for him. He was in control of every situation and, what was infinitely worse, he was in control of *me*. As Paulamin Tumley had said, a Prime should be free to do anything that pleased her, but the barbarian refused to see that. He stubbornly insisted that I obey him, that I serve his needs, whatever they were. That it did *not* please me was of no consequence to him. When we reached Rimilia he would undoubtedly beat me for locking him out, but I was beyond caring.

My small case of belongings was ready when the crewman came to carry it to the transport's transfer slip. I followed along behind him, holding myself with calm dignity even in the face of the fact that the barbarian would be waiting for me there. The other passengers hovered just out of reach, staring at me and waving slightly so that I might notice them and perhaps even nod. I nodded mechanically, too preoccupied to appreciate the attention, and then we reached the transfer slip.

The barbarian was already seated in the slip, and he looked up as I entered. I nodded calmly to him and took my own seat around the circle, a seat slightly removed from his.

As we were the only ones going to Rimilia, I had my choice of seats. I watched the pilot take his place in the center of the slip so I didn't have to look at the barbarian. The brief glimpse I'd gotten of him showed him looking not at all pleased.

We grounded gently on Rimilia in spite of the pouring rain to be seen in the pilot's screens. A lone figure stood beside a ground vehicle, staring up at the slip, waiting patiently for someone to emerge. Tammad was out of his seat immediately, standing impatiently in front of the door ramp that the pilot hadn't yet opened. I took my case and stood behind him, but somehow I had lost my calm and dignity.

As soon as the door ramp was activated, Tammad sprang out into the rain. I went more slowly, grasping my case tightly, reflecting that the warmth of the rain did little to compensate for its drenching aspect. I was soaked through almost as soon as I stepped out in it, my hair hanging in sopping strands down my back.

I stopped two or three steps past the foot of the ramp to see that Tammad had already reached the man at the ground vehicle, and they were pounding each other like long-lost brothers. The other man was considerably smaller than the barbarian, but he gave as good as he got. The door ramp to the slip retracted behind me, the slip lifted into the air, then it was gone in the grey of the sky and I stood alone in the downpour. There was little sense in just standing there, so I made my way through the mud to the ground vehicle.

The man gestured that we were to enter the vehicle, but as he and Tammad appropriated the front of it, I was relegated to the back. At that point it made little difference, as anything out of that rain was welcome. I got in and pulled the door closed behind me, then turned to wring out my hair.

"Terry!" said a deep voice I thought I recognized. "It can't really be you!"

"Why not?" I asked, looking into the amused eyes of Dennison Ambler. "If the infamous Denny Ambler, sweetheart of the Diplomacy Bureau, can be exiled to Rimilia, why should I be any different?"

"The same old Terry." He laughed, shaking his handsome, brown-haired head. "You haven't changed a bit. Tammad, my friend, your cause is won. With a Prime like Terry to help you, there's nothing you can't do."

"There's very little that he doesn't do now," I remarked,

throwing my soggy hair back over my shoulder. "I find it in-
conceivable that there could be more."

"Uh oh," Denny said, flinching a little at the coldness in
my tone. "Don't tell me you two don't get along? Tammad,
what happened to the old charm? I thought all women found
you irresistible?"

"All women save she who is my belonging," Tammad answered in a growl, his eyes examining the landscape through
the wide, front windshield. "House-gifts do not come properly
trained on your world of *darayse*."

"House-gifts?" Denny echoed. "How the hell was she—
never mind. You can tell me the story later. Let's get over to
the embassy and into some dry clothes first. Did I mention
that I almost didn't recognize you in that snappy Central leisure suit? I'm not used to seeing you dressed up."

Denny started the vehicle with a chuckle, and drove away
from the cleared landing area. We sloshed and splashed our
way a short distance to the outskirts of a dingy group of huts
that materialized out of the rain. A right turn and another
quarter of a mile took us to a large, two-story, typical embassy building. Denny drove the vehicle down a ramp,
causing a door to open in front of us. We entered the embassy's parking level, the door closed behind us, and the rain
was shut comfortably out.

"I'll find a couple of rooms for you," Denny said as he
turned the vehicle off. "Your things are just as you left them,
Tammad, all ready and waiting."

"Good." Tammad nodded, unfolding himself carefully
from the seat. "I am pleased to be home again, and will be
even more pleased to once again have room to move myself.
On your world, I always feared that something would break.
Have you *imad* and *caldin* for the woman?"

"Sure, she can have one of Asdir's," Denny answered amiably, stepping out of his own door. "Asdir won't mind in the
least since she'll then have an excuse to wheedle some new
ones out of me. So our Prime will be traveling as a native
woman, hm? What does *she* think about it?"

"*She* wasn't even consulted!" I snapped, getting out of the
vehicle, too. "I brought my own clothes with me. Why should
I have to wear someone else's blouse and skirt?"

"You will wear *imad* and *caldin* because you are instructed
to do so," Tammad said, his eyes on me with more than
slight annoyance. "Your lessons were incomplete on your

world, but we have now reached my world. Do you wish to disobey me?"

"Ah, let's go find those rooms," Denny interrupted hastily, taking my arm and leading off, but then he stopped suddenly, letting my arm go as if he thought I had something contagious. He turned back to Tammad, and his face had a slightly flushed look.

"Excuse me, my friend," he said quietly. "Old habits die hard. I didn't mean to touch your belonging without permission."

"My friend Dennison need have no fear," Tammad answered just as quietly as he moved to where Denny and I stood. "What is mine is his, and I would have him know it."

"I appreciate that," Denny said with obvious sincerity. "And I have a house-gift that's been awaiting your return. Come and let me show it to you."

Denny started for the ramp again, and Tammad followed behind him. The barbarian hadn't even taken his case of clothing from the transport, but then why should he have? He'd probably never wear civilized clothing again. I thought of my own case in the vehicle, then followed them up the ramp.

The embassy visiting level was bright with intricate chandeliers, vibrant wall and floor carpeting, luxurious furnishings, and well placed knickknacks. Denny kept his dripping form away from all that, leading the way directly upramp to his living quarters. Less luxury and more livability prevailed there, and he threw open the door of a room.

"Terry, this is yours," he said. "I'll be back with something for you to wear as soon as I get Tammad settled. Help yourself to the hot bathwater."

I nodded slightly and went on in, swinging the door shut behind me. The room was nice, but the yellow carpeting wasn't appreciating being dripped on, so I went through to the bathroom and stripped off my soggy clothes. I left them in a pile, stepped into the life-saving warm water in the tub, then transparented the wall. The rain was still coming down in a torrent, and there was nothing to see through it.

After a while, I wrapped a towel around me and went back to the bedroom. Surprisingly, Denny was there, sitting in a chair next to a table that held a pile of clothes and a tray of food.

"About time," Denny observed when he saw me. "Didn't you get enough of soaking outside?"

"It's not the same," I commented. "Is that supposed to be for me?"

"Nobody but." He grinned. "Something for both inside and out. I have to take care of my favorite Prime."

I pulled a chair closer with a sigh and started to eat, and Denny frowned at me.

"What's the matter with you?" he demanded, putting his forearms on the table. "You look like the living example of joy gone out of everything. It can't be *that* bad."

"Why can't it be?" I asked, poking at the food. "Is there some law against it?"

"Come on, Terry," he urged, "snap out of it! This is a great world and you'll love it! I doubt if I'll ever go back to Central even if I'm recalled."

"I'm glad somebody's pleased to be here," I muttered, still not looking at him. "How long do you think it will take?"

"There's less than two weeks until the Great Meeting," he sighed, leaning back in his chair. "Allow maybe another week for the meeting itself, plus your travel time back here. Terry, what's wrong between you and Tammad? I thought everyone would like him as much as I do."

"You enjoy being raped by him?" I asked with raised eyebrows, finally looking at him. "Well, each to his own."

"That's not what I meant," he protested, flushing a little. "And Tammad doesn't rape women—he just uses them the way they're made to be used."

"From my particular point of view, I fail to see the difference," I said, finishing the last of the food. It was strange, but oddly tasty. "And I also fail to appreciate being beaten. Your good friend Tammad is nothing but a barbarian, and I wish I were back on Central."

"Stop feeling so sorry for yourself," he said, a definite impatience in his tone. "You were never beaten in your life, and Tammad hasn't changed that. A simple switching or two is hardly likely to cripple you, and that man is used to having obedience from the people around him. Just because you can't antagonize him the way you do everyone else, doesn't mean it's the end of the world."

"A lot you know about it!" I snapped, standing up. "I'd love to see how *you'd* take to 'a simple switching or two'! And I don't antagonize *anyone*."

"The hell you don't!" he snorted, looking up at me with the large, brown eyes that most women found so compelling. "Why do you think Murdock McKenzie nicknamed you 'The Terror'? Everyone who knows you knows how fitting it is! Now that you're through eating, try these clothes on. I want to check the fit."

I pulled the clothes out of his hand and stormed into the bathroom, wordless with outrage. So that's where that nickname had come from. Murdock McKenzie. I should have known! That was something else I would owe him for!

The *imad* and *caldin* were like nothing in my entire wardrobe, and I didn't care for them. The *imad* slipped on over my head and was slit up the sides, then tied with a thin piece of leather at either side of my waist. The long sleeves of the thing were slit too, all the way to the armpit, and were tied at the wrists with more leather. The *caldin* was very full, but fell without pleats from my waist all the way down to my ankles. It was tied with a sash at my waist, and was made of the same thin material as the *imad*, although of a different color. The *imad* was a well-washed rose color, the *caldin* a dull gold. Nothing at all was worn under them, and I felt more undressed than in a sleep suit. I barely glanced at myself in the mirror, then went back to Denny.

"They don't fit at all," I told him as soon as I walked out. "If you don't have anything better, I'll wear my own things."

"You've got to be kidding," he grinned, getting up to walk all around me. "They look better on you than they do on Asdir. I've got half a mind to take Tammad up on his offer."

"What offer?" I frowned, turning around to keep him in view. "And you keep mentioning Asdir, but you haven't said who she is."

"She's my woman." Denny grinned. "A gift from her father who's head man in that village near here. He also gave me a switch to go along with her, but I haven't had to use it much. Her father trained her well."

"No wonder you like it here!" I said, putting my hands on my hips. "You've gone native. I never thought I'd live to see the day that Dennison Ambler went native."

"Don't knock it if you haven't tried it." He laughed. "And I haven't gone completely native, or you would be flat on your back now. When Tammad said that what was his was also mine, he meant *everything*. These buskins will fit well too, but you won't wear them until the rain stops. Tammad can pack them in with everything else. Now put on the bands."

"What bands?" I asked, looking around to keep from screaming. Denny had become perfect as a friend for the barbarian. They were more like brothers than I would have thought possible.

"Right here," Denny answered, picking up one of five, short, bronze-colored chains. "Tammad said you're to be five-banded, and I agree with him. Men will make offers for one-, two- and three-banded girls, and sometimes even for four-banded ones, but a five-banded girl has to be fought for. Not many men are willing to face Tammad, not even for a green-eyed, dark-haired woman like you."

"You've got to be wrong," I said, shaking my head firmly. "I know about the custom of banding, but I'm sure it's with ribbon or leather or some such. It can't be with chain!"

"But it is," he said patiently. "Here, this one goes on your ankle."

"Not on *my* ankle!" I balked, folding my arms. "I'm a Prime, not a slave! Take your chains somewhere else!"

"Terry, don't be difficult!" he said in exasperation. "You have to be banded if you're to travel as a native woman."

"I don't see the burning need for that, either," I countered. "What's wrong with my being a sightseer of sorts? A visitor on vacation or something?"

"This isn't Alderan," he snapped. "They don't have tourist bureaus and guided tours. And how close do you think a tourist would get to the Great Meeting? Use your head, will you?"

"That's what I'm supposedly here for," I snapped back. "To use my head, not to be chained."

He opened his mouth again, but whatever he would have said was lost as Tammad came in. I stood and stared, because the barbarian had gone through a transformation.

Gone was the leisure suit as if it had never been. The giant stood in nothing but some brown cloth wrapped around him from waist to upper thigh, his mighty chest bare. On his hips was a broad, plain, leather belt, from which a large, sheathed sword hung to the left and a long, sheathed dagger to the right, and when he turned slightly to close the door, I could see a second dagger wedged into the back of his swordbelt. He had leather wristbands, was as barefoot as I, and was altogether an unfamiliar sight.

He stopped briefly to examine me, then turned to Denny. "The *imad* and *caldin* suit her, my friend. If you can spare but one other of each, we will be on our way."

"That's no problem," Denny answered. "You're welcome to anything I have. The *seetar* is packed?"

"And the other saddled." Tammad nodded. "Some distance should be covered before dark. She has been fed?"

"She has," Denny confirmed, "but there's still one problem. She won't wear the *wenda* bands."

"The choice is not hers," the barbarian answered. "All seem much in awe of this woman who is called Prime, but here she is *wenda* and will wear the bands."

He picked up the chains and came toward me, so I turned and ran to the bathroom, quickly locking myself in. There was nowhere else to go from there, but that didn't matter. I was *not* going to be wearing chains.

I'd started toward my wet clothes to see if they were at all wearable, but there was a sudden crash behind me and the splintered door flew open. Tammad strode in through the wreckage, grabbed my arm, and forced me to the floor. In spite of my struggles the chains went on, one each on my ankles, one each on my wrists, and the last, to my absolute fury, around my neck!

When the last was closed, the barbarian pulled me to my feet again and dragged me by the arm out to a grinning Denny, who, with a folded bundle of cloth, was waiting in the corridor. We went down to the visitors level and along a wide hall to the back of the embassy, then paused by a door.

Denny and Tammad were saying good-bye to each other, but I paid no attention to the farewell. I was examining the band on my left wrist with a mixture of fury and despair. The chain was small-linked but strong, fitting too tightly to be slipped off. The ends of the chain had pieces that fit one inside the other, but there was no way to release the catch. I strained at it with every ounce of strength I possessed, and the inside part moved very slightly. It came to me then that someone with Tammad's strength could open it easily, but the accomplishment was far beyond the strength of a woman. I wore *wenda* bands because I was *wenda*—a mere female—and would continue to wear them until they were removed by *l'lenda*.

"Well, Terry, it was nice seeing you again," Denny said, taking me away from the bands to realize that Tammad was

no longer with him. The door stood open, and I could see the
rain falling beyond the overhang next to the building.

"But it's still raining," I said in confusion. "Aren't we going to wait until it stops?"

"The rain may fall for some days yet," the barbarian said,
coming back in time to hear my question. "We have a far
distance to travel, and will therefore start at once. Put this
on."

"This" was a smaller version of something he already
wore—a long rain cape of sorts in a grey material. It went on
over the head and was hooded, the hood being drawn closed
with a strip of leather. The body of the thing hung down
front and back, and was open at the sides where one's arms
came through. Mine had another strip of leather to close it
tightly around me, but his hung loose and billowing. I put it
on without comment and went toward the door, but Denny's
hand stopped me.

"Take care," he said softly, "and may the sun shine on
your undertakings. I'll see you when you get back."

I stared at him for a minute, then went out into the rain,
closing the door behind me. I had nothing to say to Dennison
Ambler.

Tammad stood about ten feet away near two monstrously
large animals. They were soft-hided rather than scaled, four-
legged rather than bipedal, maned, hoofed, and tailed rather
than feathered, and dead black in color. I'd never seen anything like them before, so a closer description-by-analogy is
impossible. One of them was piled high with a covered
mound, but the other had a large saddle and intricate bridle.
I walked closer to the barbarian who had swung up into the
saddle and was adjusting one of the stirrups. Even he looked
smaller on the back of the monster, and he glanced down at
me.

"There's only one saddle animal," I said against the roar of
the rain, closing my eyes most of the way to protect them
while my face angled up. "Where's one for me to ride?"

"You could not control a *seetar* even were it fitting for
wenda to ride one alone," he answered. "In clear weather you
will walk in my track, but for now you may ride behind me."

He put his arm down to me, and all I had to do was reach
up to be pulled into his saddle. I was being offered the generosity of sharing *l'lenda*'s saddle, the privilege of riding behind
a mighty warrior, even though I was nothing more than a

lowly female, mere *wenda*. I felt the symbolic weight of the five, bronze-colored bands on my body, and turned away to walk behind the *seetar*. I stood quietly then with my feet in the mud, saying nothing, waiting for him to get started.

The barbarian had watched me walk away from him, but he hadn't said a word, either. When I stopped behind the *seetar* he reached over to the other one, pulled on the leather lead to make sure it was secure to his saddle, then kicked his mount to get it moving. I waited until the second *seetar* had passed, then started moving, too.

We went along a pure mud road that circled the nearby village, and once we'd topped a small rise, even the embassy was gone from sight. Walking was hard in that downpour, through that mud, all alone, but I preferred it to riding. The barbarian pulled ahead at the pace I was forced to keep to, but I just kept walking.

The time went by, and my world narrowed down to the next step I had to take. There was a dripping forest to the left of the road, grey, empty fields to the right, but I could no longer see them. I felt the rain on my head, shoulders, and back, and let it drive me along the mud of the road. One foot in front of the other, put it down and watch the mud splash up, covering the rain cape and the very bottom of the *caldin*. Put the other foot down and watch it splash again, no patterns made or at least none seen.

It had gotten darker without my noticing it. Everything was wrapped in dingy, grey mist, and I might have been the only person in the world on the only road in the world. I'd long since pulled my arms in closer to my body, but I was beginning to shiver from the chill that crept into me in spite of the rain cape. I felt damp all over, damp and chilled and all alone. My feet were covered to the ankles with mud, and the bronze color of the bands was completely gone. The bands at my ankles were spattered with the mud, and I could almost pretend they weren't there.

I reached my last step before I knew it. I'd been moving more and more slowly, but that was only because I was tired, not because I intended to stop. I watched my foot take a step and waited for the next step to come, but it never did. My knees refused to keep stiffened and I went down in the mud, down on my knees and hands. I felt depressed then, knowing I would have to stand up again before I could go any farther.

I tried to stand up, tried to push myself out of the mud, but
it was just too hard. The mud pulled at me; it would be so
easy just to lie down and sleep. I knew I had to go on, but it
was much too hard. Better just to sink down into the mud
and let go.

Then I was out of the mud, lifted high in the air by two
arms that barely felt my weight. The barbarian carried me to
his *seetar* and mounted, placing me sideways on the saddle in
front of him. His left hand held the reins, but his right held
me tightly to him. I leaned on his chest, my cheek against his
rain cape, and the *seetar* started moving. Once, he muttered,
"Stubborn, foolish woman!" and held me tighter. I said nothing.

I must have slept briefly; when I opened my eyes we'd left
the road for the forest. The *seetar* moved calmly along between the trees, trampling down anything that got in its way.
I stirred against the barbarian, wanting to tell him to put me
down so I could walk the rest of the way, but his arm
tightened again, holding me still.

It was dark there, under the dripping trees. The roll and
creak of the *seetar*'s saddle kept putting me to sleep and waking me up again even though I tried to stay awake. The barbarian changed direction once or twice, following signs that
my eyes couldn't see, then abruptly we came to a stop in
front of a large, square, tent. The entire tent was roofed over
and floored, but the front face of it was open. Halfway back,
a full wall of leather closed off the inside, a veranda of sorts
being formed by the rest. I saw the other *seetar*, then, without
its load, hobbled and tied to a tree. My progress along the
road had been so rapid, then, that the barbarian had had time
to stop and put up his *camtah* before I'd come anywhere
near. I wanted to cry about that, but I was much too tired.

The barbarian dismounted, then carried me to the veranda
of the *camtah*. He had to bend over to get under the roof,
but he didn't put me down until we were inside the *camtah*.
He took the rain cape from me, then the *imad* and *caldin*; I
was beyond struggling, but struggling wasn't necessary. There
were large pieces of thick, luxuriant furs on the floor, and
once I was free of the mud-covered clothing, he put me on
one of them and covered me with another. Immediately I felt
warm and snug, and my eyes began closing in earnest.

"Before you sleep, *wenda*," he said softly, bending over

me, "there is a word I was told to say to you. The word means nothing to me, but perhaps it has meaning for you."

He said the word and I heard it, but it didn't register in my consciousness. Then I could fight the waves of exhaustion no longer and I slept.

When I opened my eyes, light streamed in from the *camtah*'s leather curtain, and I could see that I was alone. There was a vast excitement within me, and I dressed quickly in the clean yellow *imad* and blue *caldin* near my furs, then went outside.

The sky was still grey through the trees, but the rain had stopped falling. The barbarian was nowhere in sight, and one of the *seetarr* was gone, too. The other stood hobbled and tied to a tree, grumbling to itself in vague annoyance. There was a flying thing in the tree above it, waiting patiently for something, and another flying thing shied nervously in the air at the sight of the *seetar* below the tree.

The world was wonderful, and I gloried in being fully alive again. I strolled away from the *camtah*, reaching out to the living minds around me, feeling their emotions and experiencing them. The blindfold was gone, the earplugs were gone, and I was whole once more, free to be what I was.

The ground was still soggy underfoot, but I didn't care. I walked on for a few minutes, then finally stopped and leaned against the trunk of a tree, feeling the clean breeze on my face, the rough bark against my back. The night before, the barbarian had said the triggering word that released me from the repressive conditioning that kept me from using my gift, from even knowing that I had it. All XenoMediators had to have the gift of full empathy, the ability to read the emotions of others and also influence those emotions, but Primes were the strongest of all. Bitter misunderstandings and bruised sensibilities weren't possible with an awakened and alerted Prime in attendance, and agreements and treaties were easily reached.

Many, many years ago, it was decided that awakened empaths, no matter how valuable they were to Central, couldn't be allowed to move about freely on Central. Even if the government had permitted it, the population would have been too uneasy for peace to last very long. Riots would have started, and even the strongest of the Primes would have been unable to save himself from a mob that screamed for his blood. To avert such a disaster, empaths and Central government had made a pact: the empaths agreed to live half lives when on Central, and in return they received everything else that they wanted. In a carefully formulated program, the people were told from their first days of education that XM's, and especially Primes, were giving up the equivalent of sight and hearing just to live among them and serve them. The indoctrination produced pity and awe in the people, and they all did what they could to make the lot of an empath easier.

I moved away from the tree, smoothing the back of the *caldin* with a quick stroke so I could squat down without dipping it in the mud. There was a small, dirty pool of water near my feet, and I could almost see myself in it.

"Why do you keep going back there?" I asked my distorted reflection. "Why don't you live elsewhere so you can stay alive?"

My reflection didn't answer, but it didn't have to. I already knew that after every assignment was completed, someone came by with the countertrigger that took my gift away from me again, along with the very memory of it. You can't resent the loss of something you don't know you have, something you can't even wonder about, and you become dependent on the people who can give you your life back. We'd long since passed the need to fear the people of Central, but the government was much too fond of the leash it had on us to turn us loose again.

"What do you do so far from the *camtah*?" the barbarian demanded suddenly, wrenching my thoughts back to the present situation. I looked up at him, cursing myself for being so deep in thought that I hadn't felt his approach. He blazed with anger, but there was a residual of fear there, too. Had he been afraid that he'd lost his Prime?

"I felt like taking a walk," I told him, standing straight and brushing at the *caldin*. "You didn't say I couldn't."

"I do say so now," he growled, staring down at me with the anger cooling a bit. "You are not to leave the *camtah* save with me. These woods are not safe."

I opened my mouth to say that I would have warning of any danger, but was hit so hard with a solid wave of hunger and viciousness that I staggered as if I'd been struck physically. The barbarian took a step toward me, but I waved him away, pointing frantically in the direction that the emotion was coming from. He whirled around, sliding his mighty blade out of its sheath as he turned, bringing it up just barely in time to meet the charge of the beast I had felt.

The thing raced from the brush on four legs, but it was taller at the shoulders than the top of my head. It was a tawny gold in color, with short, bristly hair all over it, long, flexing claws on its legs, sharp, slavering teeth in its mouth. Its eyes and mind were mad with kill lust, and I backed away a few paces, trembling more from the mental onslaught than from its physical appearance. A gentle, intelligent being may be housed in the most grotesque of bodies, and it doesn't matter in the least. The mind is the thing that counts.

The barbarian swung his blade at the beast as it closed with him, cutting deeply into its shoulder. It screamed out its pain and turned briefly aside, then charged again in renewed rage. The wound was a serious one, but I knew from its mind that the berserk beast would not slow down until it was dead. The barbarian cut at its other shoulder then jumped aside, barely escaping the teeth and claws that hungered for his blood.

I forced calm and control over myself, then reached out toward the beast. As I'd suspected, there was a small node of fear behind the insane rage, a fear that in large part produced the rage. I touched the fear, encouraging it and causing it to grow larger, unpenning it from the beast's denial.

The beast had scrabbled around as Tammad backed up to a tree, preparing to launch itself at him in a desperate attack. The barbarian's sword was red with gore, his body so splattered with it that it was hard telling whether or not he was hurt. The animal took three short steps toward the man, then the fear flowed out into the beast's mind, causing it to howl in an agony that tore at me. It stopped still with its legs spread and its head back, howling its fear and pain, and the barbarian stepped forward and swung his sword, cutting the beast's throat and almost severing its head from its body. The howling cut off as the body collapsed, but the agony faded more slowly.

The barbarian paused to look down at the dead beast, then turned away from it and walked to me. There had been no fear in him during the battle, but only, I thought, because there had been no room for it. His emotions had been filled with the need to win, the determination to win. Fear is accompanied by doubt, and there had been no doubt in him either. He carried his bloody sword in his hand, and he walked slowly to where I stood.

"Your warning was timely," he said, staring down at me speculatively. "We are fortunate that you saw the beast as it attacked. I must have been distracted indeed not to have detected it myself. A strange *fazee* it was, insane as they all are, yet something more. Come, we will return to the *camtah*."

I went with him, walking slightly ahead as I followed the grumbling of the *seetarr* that was clearer than any trail. We reached the *camtah* without further incident, but the barbarian threw his sword down on the tent's veranda, then put his hands on my shoulders so that he could stare down into my eyes. I could feel his curiosity as if it were an itch as yet unscratched.

"There is much strangeness here," he said, narrowing his eyes somewhat. "You have never seen a *fazee* before, I know, yet you made no outcry and did not run. The *fazee* did not behave as it should have before it died, and you returned here to the *camtah* as if you knew the way well. I would hear what these things mean."

I considered telling him exactly what they meant, exactly what I was now. I would have told him, but telling that much, I would have had to tell him about my crippled life, too, and I couldn't face the pity he would feel for me. His hands were heavy on my shoulders, but not as heavy as the weight of his pity would be.

I said, "They mean that I won't be as much of a burden to you as you thought. Primes are Primes because of their ability, not because of someone's arbitrary order. You should be pleased with your bargain."

"Bargain?" he asked, raising his eyebrows. "Ah, you mean with my house-gift, my belonging. No, *wenda*, I am not quite pleased. Take that cloth and clean my sword."

He pointed to a piece of material sticking out of a partially open sack near the *camtah*, then went toward the *seetarr*. His curiosity was still with him, but he had taken all of his emotions tightly in hand, not allowing them to rule him, and they were too mixed together for me to read easily. My own emotions, though, were a different matter entirely.

Wenda he'd called me! My hand went to my banded throat and I grasped the chain he'd put there. I was nothing but *wenda* to him, to be closed in chains and given orders!

The *seetar* he'd been riding had the carcass of an animal strung across its neck. He pulled the carcass down to the ground, then unsaddled the *seetar*, rubbing it briefly before returning his attention to the carcass. He took the knife that was wedged in the back of his swordbelt, and began skinning the thing.

I glanced at his bloody sword, then got the material to wipe it with. Looking at the carcass had reminded me how hungry I was, but I couldn't ask him for food. I went back to the veranda and began to lift the sword—but it flatly refused to lift! I had to use two hands to get it off the ground, and then had to kneel down and lay it across my lap before I could begin cleaning it. It felt as if it had invisible roots anchoring it to the ground, and I wondered how the barbarian handled it so easily. The barbarian supposedly still had his eyes and attention on the carcass, but I felt his amusement and almost heard his chuckle. I ground my teeth together and rubbed at the sword.

The barbarian skinned the animal quickly, then took a large bag of what looked like ordinary wood, dumped some of it on a scarred place in the front corner of the veranda, and started a fire. When the fire was going well, he cut a slab of meat from the carcass, stuck a long, sharp stick through it, and brought it over to me.

"Do you hold this over the fire, turning it from side to side, until I say it is done," he directed, taking the clean sword from my lap and replacing it in its scabbard. I took the stick with the meat, and went to the fire.

The meat stick was too wet to burn, but that doesn't mean it didn't smoke nicely. I coughed as I held it, squeezing my watering eyes shut, wondering if the meat would take forever to cook. My arms felt like lead by the time the barbarian called me, my stomach was knotting in cramps from the delicious smell, and I was nearly drooling. I carried the meat to him where he was still cutting up the carcass; he took it and inspected it, nodded his head, then took a bite.

"True *dimral* at last," he said around the mouthful, chewing away at it. "A bit underdone, perhaps, but you will gain facility with experience."

He squatted down and took another bite, and I could feel his contentment as well as see it. Without being able to stop it, I blurted, "But what about me?"

"You?" he asked with a surprise he didn't feel, his eyes looking up at me. "You also have need of *dimral*? I hadn't considered such. You have my permission to seek in the woods for *dimral* of your own."

His tone was light and uncaring, but his mind was expectant, waiting for something to happen, and I knew what that something was. He was waiting for *wenda* to acknowledge him as the great warrior and hunter, to admit that she would starve without him, to beg him for something to eat. Well, a true *wenda* might, but despite the bands, I was still a Prime! I turned, grabbed up the knife he'd left in the carcass, and ran into the woods.

I listened hard as I ran through the bushes and between trees, both to avoid any other carnivores and to find something that would show I wasn't helpless. In a few minutes, I caught a wisp of shy thought, lost it, then caught it again. I sent reassurance ahead of me to the shy animal, changed course slightly, and slowed down.

I rounded a tree and saw the animal I had felt, a long-legged, big-eyed innocent of a beast. It was a dusty red in color, and it had taken the reassurance I'd sent and was clinging to it, grasping it eagerly and accepting it. It came up to me without hesitation, rubbing its soft nose gently on my arm, trust and affection clear in its mind.

I held the bloody knife behind me, telling myself that I *had* to do it, if I didn't, I would starve. I touched the silken neck with my fingers, feeling the pleasure the caress gave the beast, seeing the trust clear in its eyes, then laughed bitterly at myself. I could starve more easily than destroy that trust in me, die more easily than betray the confidence of a thing that was almost all emotion without defense. I let the knife slide out of my fingers and sank down into a crouch, giving myself over to hopelessness and despair.

The beast had been nuzzling me gently, but suddenly it turned and ran, radiating terror. I scrabbled after the knife

I'd dropped, searching for the terrible danger that had
frightened the beast, finding the barbarian staring at me from
beside a tree not three steps away. His mind was in a calm
turmoil, sharp questioning prevailing, his eyes unblinkingly
on me. I knew he'd seen me fail to kill the animal, and I
couldn't stand it. He'd make me admit that I was helpless,
make me beg to be protected. I got to my feet to run just as
the animal had.

I'd barely taken a step before his hand was on my arm,
pulling me around to face him. His blue eyes showed the dis-
turbance he felt, and I trembled, trying to hold my own emotions in.

"The *tenna* did not fear you," he said, more a statement
than a question. "The *tenna* cannot be approached, yet you
approached it. The *fazee*, too, was touched by something outside itself. What power do you have, woman, and why have I
not seen it before?"

I didn't answer him, but he nodded just as if I had. "The
word I spoke to you. I believe it woke the power within you,
did it not? That was the purpose of the word. You reach to
the beasts some way, healing them or destroying them at your
pleasure. Yet you could not slay where you had healed, and
this I understand. Is your power over beasts alone, or may
men also be touched?"

"Not as easily," I choked out, closing my eyes, but unable
to close out the calm control of him. "If I couldn't touch
men, I would be of little use as a Prime."

"Now do I understand the awe of your people," he said
slowly, letting my arm go. "And why my friend Dennison
spoke of you as he did. There is much yet I must learn of
this. Let us return to the *camtah* before the *dimral* grows
cold."

"*Your dimral*," I said as he started off wrapped in thought.
"I haven't caught mine yet."

He turned back to look at me, and annoyance flared in
him. "Enough, *wenda*!" he snapped. "Have you not yet
learned your lesson? Bring the knife and come!"

I tried to hold his commanding eyes, tried the way I'd tried
to kill the *tenna*—and failed just as miserably. I picked up
the knife and followed after him, hating myself because he
let me walk behind him with a knife in my hands. He knew
well enough that he had nothing to fear.

When we got back to the camp, I put the knife back into

the carcass while he went toward his meat. Without stopping, I hurried to the *camtah* and inside, unable to watch him eat. The furs I lay down on were soft and comfortable, but they did nothing to fill the belly. Feeling miserable, I stretched out and lay still.

"What do you do in here?" the barbarian asked, poking his head and shoulders in past the leather curtain. "Come outside and eat, so we may speak further about this power you possess."

I turned slightly in the furs so that I could look away from him. "I have nothing to eat," I answered, feeling my stomach roll around and knot. "What questions do you have?"

"You possess too much pride for a woman," he said, some strangely mixed emotion filling him. "I was merely returning to you the courtesy I received in your house. I did not bring you here to force you to hunt or starve, *wenda*, and you shall earn what you eat."

That word again! "Stop calling me that," I hissed furiously, jerking my head back to him, then shouted, "Stop calling me that name! And take these chains off! I can't think if I'm in chains!"

"Why do the bands disturb you so?" he asked curiously, unperturbed. "They merely show you to be a highly valued belonging. Would you prefer men to think you completely unprotected, and therefore free for the taking?"

"I don't care *what* men think!" I snapped, sitting up on one elbow. "I want these chains off!" Then I reached out to him, filling him with my desire to be free, forcing agreement on him.

Mechanically, woodenly, he came farther into the *camtah*, reaching for my ankle to free me, but then he stopped, frowned, and shook his head hard. He'd been about to do as I'd demanded, but then he drew his hand back again, and there was anger all through him.

"You will not again attempt to control me!" he ordered, cold-eyed, completely in possession of himself again. "You will wear the bands as long as you remain on this world. Too long have you been allowed to force others to your bidding. You care nothing of consequences, only of your own desires, but I shall teach you what others have not. Out of the *camtah*, *wenda*, and to your food!"

He grabbed me by the ankle and pulled me out, through the leather curtain and across the veranda to the very edge of it. I was drained by the projection I'd attempted, and I lay where he left me, astounded that he could resist me, appalled that he dragged me around, agonized in that I still wore the bands. I was a Prime, and couldn't be treated so!

"Eat this!" he ordered, coming back to hand me a piece of the meat I'd cooked. I sat up slowly, brushed the hair out of my face, then took the meat. It was cold and slightly gritty and not cooked all the way through, but the first bite was pure ambrosia. I chewed it, savoring its taste, and the barbarian crouched down near me with the rest of it.

"I do now see more fully how you touch men," he said around a bite of his own. "Had I not had some idea of your power, I would have been taken. I do not know if I care to have those who oppose me twisted in this manner. It is not a thing to do to a man."

"That's not what I'll be doing," I mumbled, looking only at my bit of meat. "I'll just be seeing that they listen to your arguments with an open mind, and finding arguments for you that will convince them. Forcing agreement on them isn't something I'm allowed to do."

"Ah!" He stirred, satisfaction strong in him. "Then how is it you attempted thus to twist me?"

"I don't want to be banded," I muttered, then looked up at him. "Nobody forces you to wear chains."

"They are free to make the attempt." He shrugged. "But who would wish to have a warrior in wenda bands? And would you have all women go without them, so a man cannot know which belongs to another? With the bands, a man's overfamiliarity with a woman belonging to another cannot be excused by ignorance. He either forfeits his life, or wins the woman for his own."

"And the woman has nothing to say about it," I returned heatedly, forgetting about the meat in my hand. "You men chain her and beat her, and hand her around as you please, and she's helpless to stop it."

"For what reason should she wish to stop it?" he asked mildly, feeling complete conviction for the nonsense he was spouting. "A woman is rarely dissatisfied with the man who chooses her. Her father seeks carefully before he gives agreement for another to band her. Should she so dislike her father's choice that she cannot accept him, she will not please him enough that he will band her further. A woman with a single band who has not been recently acquired may be bought for very little, all men knowing that she who does not belong with the man who possesses her may be the very one for whom he has been searching. A woman with one band may quickly acquire five with the proper man."

"So she literally has to work her tail off for the privilege of being chained," I summed up in disgust. "And you don't see anything wrong with that?"

"Where is the wrong?" He laughed, shaking his head. "Would a woman be happier if she were allowed to choose him to whom she will belong? I think not. Should she choose wrong, she would thereafter be unsure of herself, hesitant lest she make another mistake. Our women do not have this to plague them. They are free but for the word of him to whom they belong."

"Some freedom," I muttered, finishing off the last of my meat. "Free to be bartered and beaten. Hooray for liberty."

"A woman is not beaten without cause," he said, studying me carefully. "If a man protects her, hunts for her, clothes her, he has the right to demand obedience from her. Were he to obey *her*, he would be little more than her slave. But you shall learn the ways of a woman on this world, and shall grow with them. Too long have you been kept as a willful child, and it was no kindness. A child cannot truly be a woman."

I watched wide-eyed as he stood straight again and went back to carving up the carcass. He really believed everything he'd said, and he was completely confident that he could make *me* believe it, too! I didn't know what I should do, didn't even know if I *could* do anything! He'd decided to save me from a life that anyone would be crazy to want to leave, and I was to have no say in the matter. I thought about my house on Central, the ease with which I'd had anything I'd wished, and felt like crying.

As the day wore on, I had little time for crying. He had me feed the *seetarr* while he finished with the carcass, then we went together to a stream not far away. Instead of being allowed to bathe, though, I was made to wash the muddy *imad* and *caldin* of the day before while he stood guard. The wet clothing was then taken back to camp to be spread on the roof of our *camtah*, and we began cooking the rest of the meat. As each piece came out of the fire, he placed it carefully on a large leaf, wrapped it up, and put it away in a sack.

I was sweating and soot-covered when we stopped to eat
again, but my eyes weren't watering. Standing upwind of the
fire had helped. The sky stayed grey and threatening, but it
still hadn't rained when the last of the meat was sacked. I
thought I'd be able to rest a while then, but my tormentor
handed me a brush that was to be used on the *seetarr*. I
brushed *seetarr* until my arms ached, and was laughed at for
suggesting that the barbarian do some brushing, too. The
mighty warrior was too well occupied with oiling his sword to
be bothered with other things.

At long last, every acre of *seetar* had been brushed. Again
I thought I would rest, but again I was mistaken. I was taken,
along with the clean *imad* and *caldin* and a good half-dozen
waterskins, back to the stream. I carried the waterskins, and
the barbarian carried a long, thin spear.

After washing the *imad* and *caldin* that I'd been wearing, I
was finally allowed to wash myself. The water was delight-
fully refreshing, and the barbarian stripped himself so that
he, too, could bathe. When he entered the water, he handed
me his strip of brown cloth and told me to wash it for him. I
had the urge to let the stream current take it, but the thought
must have occurred to him, too. He watched me carefully until the cloth was safely back on the bank.

Although the barbarian had left his swordbelt on the bank,
he had taken the thin spear into the water with him. He
buried the blade in the streambed until he had bathed, then
he waded out farther with the spear raised high. He stood
very still for a long time, then suddenly moved with flashing
speed. The spear went into the water, then was pulled out
again with a long, fat fish flapping on the end of it. He came
back to the bank to put the fish down, and grinned at me.

"We will have enough of *dimral* before the rains cease," he
said. "This night we dine on *pantay*."

He went back out to spear two more *pantay*, then we left
the stream. With the blood from the *fazee* and *dimral* carcass
washed off him, I could see three long gashes near his left
shoulderblade where the *fazee* must have caught him. I quietly searched his mind for the pain he must have felt and did
find it, but it was so well controlled that it barely reached his
consciousness. I soothed it down farther still, then withdrew.

It was nearly dark by the time the fish were ready. The
barbarian had wrapped them in more of the leaf that he had,
then buried them under the still glowing ashes of the fire. I

sat on the veranda of the *camtah*, comfortably clean in body and clothing, working at my hair with the *seetar* brush. The bristles were too short and stiff to be really good, but it was better than nothing, and certainly better than helping the barbarian stack what the *seetar* would carry the next day. My *imad* and *caldin*, and the barbarian's body cloth—called *haddin*—were hung up to dry on pegs on the walls of the veranda in case it rained again.

The *pantay* was delicious, with a delicacy of flavor, given to it by the leaf, that I'd never tasted before. I ate almost all of mine—from the leaf with my fingers—and the barbarian finished his two almost including the bones. He then produced a different-looking waterskin, and took a deep draught.

"Ah, I must remember to thank my friend Dennison for this unmentioned gift," he said, nearly smacking his lips. "I had not thought to taste *drishnak* again until I had returned to my people."

"What is it?" I asked, watching him take another swallow.

"It is a wine made by my people," he answered, then he grinned. "Would you care to taste it?"

"Why not?" I shrugged, taking the skin as he passed it to me. "I could use some wine right about now."

I sniffed at it before drinking, and it somehow had a spicy smell. I sighed a little, annoyed at myself for thinking it would have a bouquet. Considering its source, it would need a lot of apology. I took a swallow of it—and thought my throat was on fire! I could feel it burning all the way down to my stomach, and I gasped in lungfuls of air, trying to douse the flames. The barbarian quickly took the skin from me and pounded on my back.

"Did you swallow wrong?" he asked, his voice filled with a concern he wasn't feeling. Inside he was laughing, and he added, "May I help you in some way?"

"You've already done enough!" I rasped, moving away from his pounding hand. "You did that on purpose so you could laugh at me. I hate you!"

I got to my feet and ran into the darkness to escape his laughter, but the memory of it followed even into the deeper shadow of the *seetarr*. I stood between them near the tree they were tied to, feeling the tears run down my cheeks. The tears were partly from the still burning "wine," but mostly from the barbarian's amusement. I was nothing but an object of ridicule to him, a willful child of no consequence, even less than *wenda*. I leaned against the side of the larger of the two male *seetarr*, and his enormous head reached around to poke at me gently.

"The *seetar* seems to have more sense than I," the barbarian said softly from behind me. "I did not know you would feel the arrow of my laughter, but that has no bearing. I should not have done what I did and I ask your pardon."

I leaned closer to the *seetar* and didn't answer him, and he moved nearer to put his hand on my shoulder.

"Drink this water," he urged, holding a skin where I could see it. "It will help against the burning."

"Why should you care?" I asked bitterly. "What difference would if make to you if I burned up? You could always get another Prime from Murdock McKenzie, and the next one might not be the total loss that I am. It would be a better bargain all the way around."

"You speak again of bargains," he said, pulling me around to face him. It was too dark to see him, but his strength glowed like a mile-high beacon. "I would have you know now that you were given to me by the Murdock McKenzie, not just as a Prime, but as a woman I desired. He is more father to you than you know, *wenda*, and long has he searched for a man for you. He accepted my offer of payment, and now you are truly mine. There will be no others sent in your stead."

My head was swimming, and what he said didn't make any sense. "But—I don't understand. Why would you make an offer for me when you already thought of me as your house-gift from Sandy?"

He chuckled, then rubbed gently at my shoulders with his thumbs. "Although I have traveled between the stars but once, I have traveled many places on this planet of my birth. The custom of house-gift, no matter how well known among my own people, is not followed by other people of this world. Why, then, would I believe that it was followed by the people of another world?"

"But you insisted!" I said in outrage, feeling dizzier and dizzier. "You took me and used me, and insisted that I was your house-gift!"

"You were unbanded," he said, and I could feel his shrug. "On a world of *darayse*, a man insists on what he wills, does as he pleases. None came forward to challenge my claim, but I wished to buy you in a proper manner and so spoke with the Murdock McKenzie."

"Murdock McKenzie can't sell me," I said weakly, trying to stop my head from whirling. "Even if he were my father he couldn't sell me! You don't own me and you know it! You're just trying to—"

I broke off because my knees refused to hold me any longer. The barbarian caught me before I hit the ground, and lifted me in his arms with a soft laugh.

"The *drishnak* is not for *wenda*," he said. "Best you seek your furs now, for we leave with the new sun. There is still far to go before we reach my people."

He carried me back to the *camtah*, and I could feel the vague thoughts of comfort from the *seetarr*. My own thoughts were all confusion as he helped me out of the *imad* and *caldin*. I wanted to argue with him, talk to him, tell him what I felt, but it was as though I'd dropped all of my strings and couldn't gather them together again. He took me in his arms, and it had been so long since he'd last touched me that my body responded immediately. I tried to stop the feelings of desire I was sending to him, but it was beyond my control. His own desire filled me, shrunk me to nothing, the fierceness of it like nothing I'd ever experienced before. He blazed up like a star gone nova, and I was dwarfed and consumed to ashes. I still don't know if I fell asleep that night or passed out.

★ 8 ★

I woke alone again, but this time the light at the leather curtain was the palest of greys. I could hear the stirring-trees sound of heavily falling rain, underlining the annoyance I immediately felt. Didn't that stupid planet every have anything but rain or the threat of it?

I crawled to the leather curtain, intending to get the clean *imad* and *caldin*, but in the dim light of pre-dawn I could see that they were gone from the peg. My rain cape hung there instead, and that annoyed me, too. I went back to the furs, groped until I found the clothing I'd worn the day before, and put it on.

As I went through the leather curtain, the barbarian appeared at the edge of the veranda, stepped onto it, and crouched down. He had two pieces of the meat I'd cooked the day before, and he handed me one of them with a grin.

"After we have eaten, we will pack the *camtah* and go," he said, pushing back the hood of his rain cape. "I would be at this night's camping place as soon as possible so that I may take you quickly to the furs. Never again will a woman without the power have the ability to satisfy me. You are *wenda* without equal."

"Is that so," I muttered, chewing on the meat and staring at him. No men had ever touched me when I was awakened before, and it had been completely my choice. I hadn't really known what I would feel from them, but the polite words that covered hot emotions annoyed me too much to give me an interest in trying. I had a blurred memory of the night before, and I didn't care to feel that small again.

"You and I have a few things to discuss, barbarian," I told him coldly. "I don't like being had. It finally came to me last night that when you agreed with Murdock McKenzie that you would be taking your 'house-gift' home with you, you were bluffing. You were lying to back up his threat."

"The Murdock McKenzie had chosen you to accompany me." He shrugged. "That he did not use a switch to obtain obedience was also his choice. In the face of that, his generosity to you, could I do other than support him?"

"Generosity?" I exploded. "He blackmails me into something I wanted no part of, and you call it generosity? But of course! You would! Well, the game is over. I'm going back to the embassy, and from there I'm going home. Find another fool to do your dirty work for you!"

"I return to my people and my belongings return with me," he answered, refusing to react to my outburst. "I will not find my people at the embassy."

"I can manage on my own," I said, wiping the meat grease on my fingers off on the *caldin*. "It will be my pleasure to tell Murdock McKenzie that you need another victim. As important as he thinks this is, he'll find someone fast enough."

"He has already found someone," the barbarian returned. "And have you forgotten that you were also given to me to band as my own? I paid well for you, *wenda*, and shall not lose my purchase price."

"You might as well forget that nonsense," I snorted. "How long do you think you can fool me with it? You know as well as I do that I'm not for sale and never have been. Even you admitted that your barbaric customs don't apply to my world. I'm a free woman and always have been!"

"But we do not now stand upon your world." He grinned. "We stand upon mine, where the Murdock McKenzie said I might band you. I *have* banded you, and will take you to my people where you shall aid me. Fold the furs, *wenda*, so that I might place them on the *seetar*."

He pulled his hood back on, and went out into the rain again, leaving me to fume. If he thought I would be doing any more of his housekeeping for him, he was crazy. I took the rain cape down from the peg, put it on, then slipped out of the *camtah*.

The barbarian had his back turned, too busy with the pack *seetar* to see me go. I made my way deeper into the woods, fairly sure that I knew the way back to the road. I splashed through the mud beneath the dripping trees, watching for signs of the road, listening for thoughts of predators. I picked up a few fleeting emotions, but they were too far away to worry about.

Reaching the road took longer than I thought it would, but I finally found it. I'd had one close call in the woods when something hungry had picked up my scent, but I'd done the right thing. I'd projected the feeling of being enormous, unconquerable, and very hungry too, and had pretended to turn in the direction of the predator. The thing had felt my projections clearly, and had slunk quickly away.

I walked down the center of the road, wondering what walking there was like when it wasn't raining. The quiet hum of satisfied burrow animals came to me from both sides of the road, keeping me company. I sloshed along in the monotony of the mud, remembering every sloppy step of it to add to my hatred of Murdock McKenzie.

I had almost no warning at all. I picked up stray feelings of boredom and resigned annoyance almost at the same time that I heard the sound of hoofbeats. I looked up in surprise to see three *seetarr* and riders coming down the road toward me, but they were still some distance away. I darted quickly off the road into the trees, hoping I hadn't been seen, but no such luck. The feelings changed to curiosity and interest, and the rhythm of the hoofbeats increased.

I cursed myself for an idiot, and went deeper into the woods. If I'd had the sense to walk at the side of the road, I could have been into the woods before anyone had a chance to see me. Now I had to avoid the riders without getting hopelessly lost.

Suddenly, I felt the curiosity searching in front of me instead of behind. I realized that the riders must have left the road farther up and had swung around to cut me off. I turned back to the road again, sweating under the rain cape.

I was halfway back to the road when the burst of exultation told me I'd been a fool. The man stepped out in front of me, grabbing me easily when I tried to run. He had been on foot, stalking me with the patience and lack of emotion that marked the true hunter, and I'd been wasting my time worrying about the ones who came openly.

"What do you do here alone, *wenda*?" the man asked as I struggled against him. He was almost as big as the barbarian, but I still had to try. "Why do you travel the road without a man, eh?"

"Perhaps she has run away from him to whom she belongs," another voice put in. The other two men had ridden up to us, and were dismounting.

"If she has run away," the third man said with an ugly grin, "we shall not displease her by returning her. She shall find much to occupy her in our company, and shall not run away again."

"She has green eyes." The first one laughed, holding my back up against him with my head up so the others could see my eyes. "I have never had a woman with green eyes."

"It is not her eyes I care to see," the third one said, stepping closer. He opened the rain cape with a single tug, then pulled it off me. They stared at me in silence, their emotions rolling.

"Five-banded," the second man said at last. "Dark-haired, green-eyed, and five-banded. A woman for no ordinary man."

"I, too, would keep her five-banded!" the third man snarled, fear trying to fill his mind. The rain rolled off his rain cape, but it soaked into my clothes and hair. "The one who owns her cannot be the greatest of warriors, else she would not have run away. Do you fear the wrath of one who cannot keep his woman beside him?"

"Perhaps he is but a wealthy merchant," the first said, grabbing at the thought to calm his own fear. "Yes, a fat, wealthy merchant who has the price of such a woman, but not the ability to keep her."

"Aye!" the third laughed, relief flooding him. "She tired of empty furs and went seeking a man. She may now rejoice that she has found three!"

"She is five-banded," the second said quietly. "No merchant would five-band a woman, save were he warrior, too. Let us return her from whence she came."

"No!" the third man said angrily, his blue eyes flashing at the second man. "She has fallen to us, and we shall keep her! My sword is sharp enough to answer any man, merchant or not! Has yours grown dull from lack of use, you may ride on alone! I do not care to ride with *darayse*!"

The second man's jaw set and his hand moved beneath his rain cape, but he controlled the burst of anger he'd felt at the insult.

"I shall not kill you," he told the third man coldly. "I shall leave that to be done by the warrior to whom she belongs. It is his right."

He turned to his *seetar*, mounted quickly, then rode away without looking back. The third man watched him go, then snorted.

"That one is *wenda* himself!" he said in disgust. "Should he find a woman in his furs, he would not know what to do with her. But I, my pretty, do not have that lack. How are you called?"

"That does not concern you," I answered the interest in his eyes. "Would you care to have the price of many women? A price that you yourself may set?"

"What do you say, *wenda*?" he asked, narrowing his eyes. "No woman would be allowed the possession of *dinga*."

"Nor do I have *dinga*," I answered, trying to keep the quiver out of my voice. If I had had any of their money, he would have had it, and me with it. "The *dinga* would be given you if I were taken to the house of the offworlders. It is not distant from here, and the offworlder called Dennison would pay well for me. He has little knowledge of the value of *dinga*, and can easily be convinced to part with much of it."

"It is a thought," the first man said hopefully. "The offworlders are fools, and will pay many times the worth of a woman."

"Perhaps," the third man said, staring down at me thoughtfully. "I would know why the offworlder should wish to buy you, *wenda*. Have you value other than that which may be seen?"

"I have value only to the offworlder," I said carefully, not liking the calculating turn of his thoughts. "The sooner we reach there, the sooner you may have your *dinga*."

"If the *dinga* is there, it shall not stray," he said, putting his hand out to finger a strand of my dripping hair. "I shall see for myself what your worth may be, then we shall speak again of additional value. I will know what I sell before I sell it."

"You cannot . . ." I started, but he pulled me toward him, the heat beginning to build in him. I could feel the first man's desire too, and it made me frantic. They'd both use me before they decided whether or not to take me to the embassy, and they'd spend some time trying to find out why Denny would pay for me. I had no chance of escaping them, but maybe I could distract them.

As the third man slid his hand into the open side of my *imad*, I searched the first man's mind and found the faint jealousy there. It was mostly envy that the other man would have me first, but it was enough. I fanned it carefully and encouraged it a little, and the first man stepped closer to us.

"Hold!" he said sharply. "It was I who captured this woman. Why are you to have her first?"

"It is my right," the third man answered coldly. "Am I not a greater warrior than you?"

I prodded a resentment, and anger flared in the first man. "I am not so poor a warrior that I may be ignored!" he snapped. "Do you think me *darayse*?"

Instead of the anger I expected in return, the third man grew thoughtful. "You are not *darayse*," he said quietly. "We have ridden together under many suns. As it matters to you, do you have the woman first."

The first man was instantly mollified, and I was almost in shock. They weren't going to fight over me—you only fight for something you don't want to share. They had no qualms about sharing me, so there was no basis for argument. I might have had enough strength to force one of them away from me with my empathetic abilities, but I could never have handled two and the necessary running as well; not to mention that I didn't want to give them even a hint as to what I was able to do. The first man pulled me to him with a big grin, taking up where the other had left off, and I struggled ineffectually, trying to think of something else.

Then I caught the flash of fear from the third man, feeling him cover it instantly and stiffen. The first man loosened his hold on me to look over his shoulder where the third man was looking, then released me altogether with a sinking feeling strong within him. I moved to one side where I could see too, and saw an icy mountain of coldly enraged barbarian. Tammad sat stiff on his *seetar*, staring at the other two men.

I moved away farther still, and there wasn't a single word spoken among the three men. Tammad dismounted and they all three drew their swords, the two strangers gripped in despair, but grimly determined to do what they could. First one, then the other of them slipped out of their rain capes, finding themselves appalled to see Tammad merely fold under the right side of his. They needed all the freedom of movement they could get, but he had enough as he was.

The two men separated, going against the slightly bigger barbarian from two sides. Tammad watched them with complete unconcern, waiting patiently for something. When the two men suddenly charged him, his patience changed to satisfaction and the waiting was over.

He moved with the speed that had saved him from the jaws of the *fazee*, and the two men never had a chance. He blocked the sword of the one on his left with his own sword, then cut viciously back toward the one on his right. The man on the right had his sword up for a downward stroke, and the barbarian's blade opened him from side to side. His blood rushed out to join the pouring rain, and the man collapsed to join the trampled mud. He felt no surprise at his death, just a deep, wailing sadness.

The other man had staggered back a step, but by the time he raised his sword again, he stood alone in the battle. He was the one who had been the third man, and his mind cried with a fear that never reached his face.

Tammad moved at him almost casually, bringing his sword down at the man's head with no attempt at deception. The man blocked the blow with his own sword, two-handed, but it still staggered him. Another blow came and another, and each time he had to move back a step. His arms seemed to be having trouble holding the sword up, and finally they could no longer do so. The sword fell from nerveless fingers, and with numbed mind, the man slid to his knees in front of the barbarian. I didn't understand why the core of him screamed and gibbered and shook with a sickness of fear that was worse than the *fazee*'s had been, a sickness that was foam-flecked and rancid blue, until I saw the barbarian raise his sword again, high, high, and bring it crashing down. . . .

I cringed away and quickly turned my back, but couldn't turn away from the voiceless shriek. The man had been so *afraid* of dying, and his sickness soured my soul. To suffer a man's death with him put a big question mark next to the value of the gift I'd thought so much of.

Through the trees I saw the road, and shakily prodded myself into moving toward it. Once I got back to the embassy I'd be all right. I'd bathe, and change into my own clothes, and sleep in a real bed. I was a free woman, and—

"No," the barbarian said, suddenly there to take me by the hair. "We go the other way."

He dragged me over to a small tree, forced my arms around it, then took something from his swordbelt. When he let go of me my wrists stayed together, held by something that hooked the two wrist bands to each other.

"Turn me loose!" I screamed, fighting the chains that held me. "You have no right to do this to me!"

He didn't even bother answering. He moved around behind me, doing something I couldn't see, and there was nothing but calm in his mind—calm and a small knot of anger that made me want to hide. The tree was hard and I was dripping wet, and I couldn't pull loose from the bands that had been forced on me.

When he finished with whatever he had been doing, he came to get me. He separated the wrist bands again and pulled me over to his *seetar*, where the reins of the dead man's *seetar* were already attached to his saddle. He lifted me into the saddle, mounted himself, then headed us toward the road. When we reached it, we collected the second *seetar*, no longer needed by a dead man, and turned up the road.

"I want to go back to the embassy," I moaned, shivering against the chill. I was as wet as if I'd fallen in a river, and the barbarian's rain cape was cold against my back. "This is kidnapping and you know it!"

"A man cannot steal what is his," he told me in that calm, even way of his. After a minute he added, "The *camtah* was left without my permission."

I knew immediately what he meant and tried to slide out of his grip and off the *seetar*, but his arm was a sixth band around my waist. I rocked back and forth futilely, screaming and cursing in every language I knew, but it helped not at all. He was going to beat me again, and there was nothing I could do to stop it.

The pack *seetar* was standing quietly when we reached it. The *camtah* had been rolled and tied onto its back, and there was nothing left of the camp. The barbarian lifted me off his *seetar*, chained me to another tree, then went to the pack *seetar*. When he finally came back to unchain me, the *camtah* was standing again.

He dragged me to the *camtah* without a word, and I was shivering too much to speak. It was difficult to believe that I had ever been dry or warm in my entire life. Once inside the *camtah*, my clothes came off fast, and the barbarian gave me a small cloth to wipe myself with. It didn't go very far, and the water still dripped from the ends of my hair even after I'd wiped it. My furs were on the floor, and I didn't have to be told twice to get into them, but I wasn't just left lying there. The barbarian attached something to the ankle bands that held them together, then he left the *camtah*.

Even with the furs it took a while to stop the violent shivering. The chill was slowly sucked out of my marrow, and by concentrating on the calm, ponderous thoughts of the *seetarr*, I was able to submerge the memory of the deaths of the men. Seeing a man die, no matter how violently, can't compare with feeling him die. The memory would be with me forever, but one day I might be able to cope with it.

My curiosity finally got the better of me, and I moved the furs aside to see what the bands were being held with. If I could remove it, I still had a chance to reach the embassy. My feet were stained with the memory of mud, and the ankle bands, once a bright bronze, were dull with still remaining traces of the mud. The bands themselves were held together with a bronze clip that gleamed between one link of each band. I tried to remove the clip, tried to loosen at least one side of it, but it worked on the same principle that the bands themselves did. I didn't have the strength needed for pressing the thing open.

"Still you do not learn," the barbarian said from the leather curtain. "There is work which must be done before you may return to your people. Before I allow you to return to your people."

He held the dry *imad* and *caldin*, but he also held the switch. I licked my lips from a suddenly dry mouth, then took a breath.

"And how well do you think I'll work if I'm beaten?" I asked weakly. "You'll have to take my word about things that can't be seen by you. If I tell you the wrong things, you'll have no way of knowing that they're wrong, and you won't get what you're after. You need me on your side, not against you."

He sighed heavily, threw the *imad* and *caldin* to the floor, then crouched down to shake his head at me. "*Wenda*, this thought had not occurred to me," he said with considerable patience. "Had I been reluctant to take your council, I would not have accepted you from the Murdock McKenzie. All

have assured me that my cause may be won with your aid.
Should this fail to occur, I will know that true council was
not given me. You will then be rewarded by being unbanded
and given away to any who would have you. Perhaps one
day you may see your people again, but many men will have
passed between the times. If this is what you wish, the decision is yours to make. But for the time you remain my belonging, I will have your obedience."

He forced me to my stomach then, and the switching was
terrible. He held me down with one hand and used the switch
with the other, and the pain made me fill the *camtah* with my
screams. I'd never been treated the way this man, this barbarian, was treating me, and I hated it and hated him. I lost
control and let my pain and desperation flow loose, and the
seetarr bellowed an accompaniment, but the barbarian refused to be touched by it and continued to beat me with calm
in his mind.

Afterward, he sat and oiled his sword until I'd stopped crying, then he had me dress and fold the sleeping furs. He took
the furs and my wet clothes outside while I put on the rain
cape he had retrieved, then I stood by while he folded the
camtah. The roof braces lay flat when he pushed on them,
and the whole thing rolled up into something a *seetar* could
easily carry. The packs had been distributed among the three
spare *seetarr*, and none of them noticed the amount they had
to carry.

In order to resume the journey, the barbarian sat me behind him on his *seetar*, not on the saddle but on the saddle
fur, even though I would have much preferred walking. I sat
astride, the *caldin* being full enough to permit it, and was
forced to hold the barbarian around his broad waist to keep
myself from falling. I cursed myself for a triple-damned fool,
but couldn't stop what touching him did to me in spite of the
pain he had caused, and when the chill came back, I slid my
hands beneath his rain cape to share his warmth.

We rode continuously through the day, eating in the saddle
to make up for the time we'd lost that morning. When we
stopped for the night, I was almost too stiff to stand, let alone
walk. I'd spent the entire, almost endless, day thinking, and
the conclusions I'd come to were inescapable.

I was to be trapped on that terrible planet forever. Something would go wrong with the barbarian's plans, I would be
blamed, and then I would be given away. No one would lis-

ten when I asked to be taken to the embassy, and I would
never see Central or my friends again. Throughout the long
day I'd thought about that, and I was completely resigned to
my fate. I had no chance of escaping the brute who claimed
to own me, and I would never escape the ones who owned
me after him. I would be lost forever.

I wasn't able to eat that night, and even the barbarian's
touch failed to rouse me. I pictured myself at the mercy of
endless brutes, and I cried with deep, hurting sobs. The barbarian was puzzled and held me to him with gentle arms, but
it was no comfort. I cried until I had no more strength left,
and then I slept.

★ 9 ★

The rain still fell the next day, and my world, too, was grey and cold. I found it impossible to look at the barbarian without tears starting in my eyes, so I avoided the sight of him as best I could. I was still able to eat none of the cold meat, so I threw it away when the barbarian turned his back, then folded the sleeping furs without comment when told to do so. The *camtah* was put on another of the *seetarr*, and we began traveling again.

We might have been traveling continuously over the same stretch of road for all that I could tell. The rain fell in thick, steady torrents, the road was an endless stretch of mud, the trees looked the same, the fields looked the same. Sometimes the trees were to the right and the fields were to the left, sometimes the other way around, and sometimes there were no fields at all. Other than that, there was no variation.

We stopped at midday for another meal, but the sight of the meat, white-dotted with its own congealed fat, turned my stomach. I managed to throw it away again, wishing only for a place where the rain would not beat at me, one that did not continually rock from side to side. I could feel the barbarian's eyes on me, feel the puzzlement he felt, but happily he said nothing.

It was late in the day when I almost fell. The dizziness had crept up on me and slowly increased until I clung to the barbarian's rain cape in desperation. My cheek was tight against it, trying to draw every bit of coolness from it, coolness that would drive the dizziness away. The coolness wasn't enough, the dizziness continued to increase, and then my fingers lost

117

their grip. I slid to the left, drawn by the sea of mud beneath, expecting to go down to meet it, but was stopped instead by the giant hand of my captor. He gripped my arm tightly and drew me to the saddle in front of him, frowning as he studied me.

"What ails you, woman?" he muttered, putting his hand to my face. The touch of it was like ice, and I shivered even as it revived me somewhat. He drew his hand away again, leaned me against him, then changed the direction of the *seetar*.

We entered the woods again, found another clearing, and stopped. I didn't know why we'd stopped when there was still light left, but I was too dizzy to care. I sat on the *seetar* while the *camtah* went up, drawing what comfort I could from its grumbling concern.

Once again I was carried to the *camtah*, and once again my clothes were removed. The steadiness of my sleeping furs was a heavenly delight, but they were too warm to have on me. I kicked off the covering one, then held tight to the one beneath me.

"You must remain covered," the barbarian said, waking me from a light doze. He threw the furs over me with one hand, the other holding a small metal bowl from which steam arose. Behind him, through the leather curtain, I saw that it was full night out, and that he had built a small, shielded fire on the edge of the verandah.

"You will eat this and the fever will be gone in hours," he said, folding into his usual crouch. "Why did you not say you were ill?"

"I'm just tired," I mumbled, turning away from him. I wanted to go back to sleep, the only place I could escape to where he couldn't follow.

"This must be eaten first," he said, pulling me back. "Then you may sleep."

I needed help to sit up, and I needed help to drink from the bowl. He'd made a broth from some of the meat, but there was an odd, pleasing taste to it that the meat didn't have. I slowly swallowed it all, then lay down again.

The next time I woke, the barbarian's hand on my face was a good deal warmer. Blurrily, I felt his satisfaction and, through half-closed eyes, saw his smile.

"The fever is gone," he said softly. "The next sun will find you well again."

"I don't want to be well," I mumbled, still feeling the weight of my fate on me. "I want to die and have done with it. Then I'll be free again. Free again."

The sobs came before the tears, and they hurt my chest. But I was too sleepy to cry for long.

The never-ending rain was still there the next morning. I opened my eyes, then decided not to move anymore. If I lay still long enough, it would all be over and done with. I lay there for a few minutes, trying not to notice how hungry I was, and then the barbarian came in.

"Do you now dress," he said, "then we shall eat and be on our way. The day does not grow longer."

"I'm not going with you," I mumbled into the furs. "You said that anyone who didn't prefer death to slavery deserved to be a slave, and you were right. I'm going to stay here and die now, then I won't be a slave any longer."

"So now you feel yourself slave," he said in annoyance. "Very well. It is against the laws of my people to hold slaves, therefore shall I leave you behind me. I will now pack my furs, *camtah*, *imad* and *caldin*. Do you now remove yourself from them."

I stared at his broad, stubborn face for a minute, then set my lips. He was taking everything and leaving me nothing, but I shouldn't have expected anything else. Everything and everyone was *his*.

I got out of the furs without saying another word, then moved past him to the curtain. I didn't like the idea of being outside without clothes on, but I would have died rather than ask him for anything. I moved to the end of the verandah, then remembered something and turned back to him.

"If you're taking everything else," I said coldly, "you can take these chains, too. They *do* belong to you."

"I cannot," he answered, watching me where I'd paused at the end of the veranda. "In honor I may not unband a woman save there be another man there willing to band her himself. The bands you may keep."

"But I don't want them!" I insisted, then forced myself to turn away from him. He'd never listen to a thing I said, and there was no sense wasting my breath. I stepped off the veranda, stood straight, then looked around.

The faint light of dawn put everything in half shadows. As I'd known, the rain still fell, but it fell softly and with more warmth than it had yet had. I was quickly soaked, but it didn't really matter. I went to a tree on the other side of the camp and stood under it.

By the time the barbarian had everything packed, the rain had stopped. He didn't look at me again until he was in his saddle, then he sat for a moment, as if waiting for me to say something. When I didn't, he turned the *seetarr* and rode away.

I waited for something to happen, then I got tired of standing up. I squatted down and waited, but still nothing happened, except that I got hungrier. I looked around again, wondering how long it would take to die. I didn't like just squatting there, wearing not a stitch of clothing, still trapped in those chains. It was embarrassing—and it was boring.

The sun came up, brighter than I had ever seen it. Flying things fluttered around the trees, beasts stretched happily in the woods, and even the mud seemed to settle down quietly. I stood straight and walked out from under the tree, wondering what to do.

The morning wore on and I got thirsty. The waterskins were gone with the barbarian, and the small pools on the ground were too dirty to drink from. I wandered away from the clearing, but didn't go in the direction the barbarian had gone in. With no clothes on, I didn't want to be near the road.

I listened to the feelings of the beings around me, annoyed that they could be so happy when I was so miserable. I hadn't done anything that merited being brought to a strange planet and then abandoned, but I was there just the same, waiting for the one thing that would free me from bondage. Now that I was resigned to dying, how long did it take anyway?

Then I picked up the emotion of a hunting beast, no different from the others in the woods, except that it was closer. I felt its pleasure when it found a scent, and its determination when it began following that scent. I waited a moment to be sure, but there was really no doubt. The scent it had found was mine.

I moved off in the opposite direction, feeling faintly uneasy. How many of the hunting things in the forest would come across me? How many of them would I have to evade? I put together the feelings of being very big, very hungry, and very unbeatable, and projected them at the following animal.

I felt it pause, considering what had just come to it, then it continued on, following my scent.

My heart started pounding and I began moving faster, appalled by what had happened. The beast hadn't believed my projection, or it hadn't cared. It thought of itself as very big and completely unbeatable, and its hunger was greater than mine. It was determined to eat well, and would fight for the opportunity to do so.

I stumbled through the woods, being scratched by branches, fear filling me as it never had before. I projected peace at the beast, contentment, weariness, and even fear, but nothing stopped it. It came inexorably on, patiently seeking the source of the scent.

Suddenly, I stopped dead, feeling the attention of another predator. This one was ahead of me, and it had been attracted by the noise of my passage through the woods. It, too, picked up my scent and came eagerly toward me.

I looked wildly around at the silent and uncaring trees and bushes, not knowing which way to go. They were both so close, and I had no way of defending myself. I grasped the tree I stood near, looking up at the branches that were too far above my head to be reached, then my insides twisted and my eyes were pulled away from the tree. The second predator, the one that had been ahead of me, stepped into sight.

It stood no taller than my waist, but it was lean and muscled all along its five foot length. Its grey and black pelt was wet from the bushes it had passed through, its black eyes gleaming as it opened its fanged muzzle to snarl. I stood petrified, unable to move in any way, and the thing started toward me.

Then a furious roar sounded from the other direction. My head snapped around, knowing that the first predator had arrived, too. It was twice the size of the other, was covered all over with long, silky brown fur, and was absolutely furious that its prey was about to be taken by another beast. The smaller predator hissed and snarled in frustration at the sight of the larger, but it slunk off rather than fight what it knew would be a losing battle.

The big predator turned its head back to me, and I could feel its deep satisfaction and gnawing hunger. It had what it had been after, and it would take it *now*. From twenty feet away, it began to launch itself at me.

My mind found no way to attack it from within, but I

couldn't turn my eyes away. In two bounds it was ten feet closer, and I knew that running would be useless—even if I'd been able to run. Then it left the ground in a savage spring—and twisted in the air, screaming at the shaft in its chest that was ending its life. I watched as it struck the ground, thrashing in the mud in spite of being already dead.

There was a pain in my chest and I gulped in air, not having realized that I'd been holding my breath. Weakly I turned my head and saw the barbarian standing only five feet away with a bow in his hand, and never had he looked so magnificent—or welcome. I wanted to go to him, but instead I squatted down where I was to keep from collapsing in the mud.

"My apologies," he said as he came closer to where I squatted with whirling head in trembling hands. "I am hunting for fresh meat, and did not mean to come between you and the death you seek. I shall continue on my way at once."

He started away again, his thoughts calm, but I was frantic. "No!" I screamed, staggering erect and running after him to throw my arms around him. "Don't leave me again! I'll admit it if you have to hear it, but don't leave me again!"

"What is it that you would admit, *wenda*?" he asked softly, stroking my hair as I shivered against him.

I had to swallow the sour taste in my mouth before I could answer him. "I admit I'm afraid to die," I whispered, closing my eyes. "I'm afraid to die, so I must be a slave. You were right to put chains on me."

"You are a great trial to me," he sighed, continuing to smooth my hair. "It is truly said that the smallest of bands may surround the greatest of difficulties. Know you, *wenda*, that there is much difference between fearing death and not wishing to die. Because you do not wish to die, you do not, *prelta*, become a slave. I, too, do not wish to die, yet I am no slave."

"I don't understand," I moaned in misery, clinging to the pulse beat I could feel in his chest. "I just know that I don't want to be hunted again. That thing was already tasting me, it could feel its teeth sinking into me—"

I broke off at the sickening memory, shuddering beyond my control to stop. I felt again the death of the two men, and I knew that I had almost shared it. The barbarian held me tight against him, and I knew, too, that the shuddering disturbed him.

"I had not realized you would feel this so sharply," he said, almost to himself. "The thing was a mistake. Come, the camp is not far."

He urged me along with him, and I couldn't bring myself to loosen my hold on him. I had come *so close!* If I couldn't submerge the memory, I would never be able to stop shaking again.

When we reached the camp, he made me sit down on the *camtah*'s veranda, dry and warmed now from the sun. I hugged myself, rocking back and forth, trying to gain control of my emotions. I was almost to the point of projecting what I felt, and that couldn't be allowed to happen. The *seetarr* were already snorting and throwing their heads around, and if I let loose, they might stampede.

The barbarian came back with the metal bowl, but it wasn't steaming. He helped me put it to my lips and I swallowed gratefully—until I realized it was that vile *drishnak*. It had had water added to it, but it was still awful, yet he made me drink it all. I coughed and choked until it was down, then he put the bowl aside.

"The *drishnak* will help to calm you," he said, taking my face in his hands to study me. "You are pale yet, but there are no tears. Why do you not cry when there is reason to cry?"

"Don't say I cry for no reason," I muttered, trying to rid my mouth of the *drishnak* taste. "If you were never going to see your home or friends again, you'd cry, too."

"Truly, an excellent reason for tears," he agreed solemnly, but there was some emotion he was holding back on. "I would know how the knowledge of this came to you."

"You told me so yourself," I said, starting to feel warm and a little drowsy. "You're going to give me away to anyone who wants me, and I'll never be able to go home."

"I had thought this was but a possibility," he murmured, his eyes half closed. "Have you decided then to give me no help in my cause?"

"No," I answered vaguely, my eyes meeting his. "But I know something will go wrong, and I'll be blamed. Then you'll give me away because I'm your slave. I want to go home."

"And so you shall," he said softly, letting me lie down right there on the veranda. "Did I not give my word to return you to your embassy? You will give me your aid to the best of your ability, *wenda*, and I shall keep my word. Now you may sleep awhile to restore yourself. Later, we shall continue on."

"Nothing but *wenda* to him," I mumbled, getting very comfortable. "Why can't he see me as more? I'm not crippled any longer. . . ."

I let it trail off because it was useless. I would never be anything but *wenda* to one like him. I wanted it not to matter, but it did matter. It mattered a lot.

I slept for a few hours, and the sun was still bright when I woke. I sat up groggily and stiffly, looking around at the peaceful camp, and then the barbarian noticed me. He brought over a piece of meat and a waterskin, watched silently as I bolted down the meat, then sat himself cross-legged near me.

"Have you restored yourself?" he asked, concern and something else touching his thoughts. I wanted to see what the something else was, but it was too well covered.

"I'm all right," I answered, trying to see through his beautiful blue eyes. "Did you mean what you said before I slept? That you would let me go home?"

"I did." He nodded. "I gave my word. I ask only that you aid me as *you* gave your word to do. Is it agreed?"

His gaze was level and serious, as though the decision were really mine. "What choice do I have?" I asked with a shrug, picking at the outside of the waterskin. "I'm your slave, aren't I?"

"Belonging, not slave," he corrected, and I could feel the flash of impatience that he didn't allow to show. "There is a difference between belonging and slave. The Hamarda, in the desert to the west of my people's lands, hold slaves. These slaves are chained closely and beaten upon whim. Do you not see the difference?"

I fingered the chain around my neck and remembered the last switching. "There's a difference?"

He stared at me, fighting hard to keep his temper, then he took a deep breath and muttered, "There is much to be said to the benefit of tears. Let us see, *wenda*, if we may find a difference. Fetch for me that saddle strap."

I stood up and got the saddle strap he'd pointed to, then brought it back. "Good." He nodded, taking the thing out of my hand. It was heavy leather, thick and stiff, and its edges felt sharp. "Now do you kneel here beside me."

I knelt down, wondering what he was getting at, and was surprised when he took me across his lap and put my arms behind me. When he let go of my arms I tried to get them apart, but the wrist bands were clipped together. He lifted my ankles to him, and in another minute they were clipped tight, too!

"What are you doing?" I asked, squirming on his lap to see if I could get loose. I got nowhere, of course, and his hand stroked my bare bottom.

"I am about to beat you," he announced calmly. "With this strap you so kindly brought. I shall tie you by the throat to a tree, and then I shall beat you. It will, you must know, cut your body terribly, but I may do as I wish with my slave."

"But why?" I asked in anguish. "What have I done?"

"You have done nothing," he answered, his calm completely unchanged. "A slave may be beaten for any reason or no reason. Why do you not run from me?"

"How can I?" I asked miserably. "You've tied me so I can't move."

"But surely this is something you are familiar with?" he pursued in a reasonable tone. "If you are slave and chained, it is never possible for you to run. And you are also always beaten terribly without reason. Is this not so?"

I opened my mouth, then closed it again and bit at the inside of my lip. I knew damned well that he had never tied me up like that before, and that's why I'd been able to run away from him. And I had to admit that the switch, though it hurt awfully, never did more than bruise me a little. I felt the barbarian waiting for something, and I sighed.

"All right," I grudged, staring down at the dirt and grass at the edge of the veranda. "You've made your point. But I still don't like wearing bands or getting switched."

"The bands are necessary and you will grow used to them," he answered with satisfaction. "The switching you may avoid simply by obeying me. I do not give you orders for my pleasure, *wenda*, but for your safety. You do not know the hazards of this world."

He threw the strap away, then reached down to unclip my ankles. I waited for him to do the same for my wrists, but it didn't happen. Instead, his hand stroked me again.

"Now what are you doing?" I asked in exasperation. "I want to get up and get dressed."

"There is no need for haste," he murmured, turning me

over in his lap so I could see his grin. "Know you that I have
seen slave women taken by the Hamarda made to serve their
masters well. I would teach you the way of this, so that
should you someday find yourself true slave, you will know
what is required of you."

At that point I didn't know what to say, but words were
entirely unnecessary, and truthfully I was speechless anyway.
I'd thought I knew something about male-female possibilities,
but those Hamarda were totally unbelievable. The barbarian
swore that the slave women always had their wrists chained
behind them, but he was enjoying himself too much to be
overly concerned with the truth. When I nearly had hysterics
he relented and removed the clip, then comforted me in
a more conventional manner. I wasn't exactly comforted, but
it was a good deal better than hysterics.

Much later, the barbarian had my ankle in his hand and
was trying to tickle the bottom of my foot, when I felt something unexpected. I listened hard to make sure, then leaned
up on my elbows.

"Someone's coming," I told him quietly. "From that way."

He was on his feet and reaching for his *haddin* and swordbelt so fast that I blinked.

"How many?" he asked calmly while dressing himself.
"How far are they?"

"There are two," I answered, "and they're about five
minutes or so away. A man and a woman."

He nodded without taking his eyes from the direction in
which I'd pointed. "I shall greet our visitors. Do you go now
and dress yourself."

I suddenly realized that I was stark naked, and *people* were
coming! I hurried to the pack that held my *imad* and *caldin*,
then went into the *camtah*. By the time I had everything tied
that should be tied and went back out again, the people were
riding into the camp. The girl rode behind the man on his
seetar, a pack *seetar* following along after the first. The man
was grinning broadly, and so was the barbarian.

"*Aldana*, Tammad," the man said in greeting. "This camping place brings an unexpected surprise. I am pleased to see
that you have returned—and in time for the *Ratanan*."

"*Aldana*, Faddan," the barbarian answered. "It was always
my intention to be at the *Ratanan*. This Great Meeting shall
see changes."

"My sword is yours, *denday*," the man said simply, acknowledging the barbarian as his leader. "May we share your camp and join you on the journey home?"

"Of course, Faddan," the barbarian said pleasantly. "Do you step down now and set your *camtah* beside mine. We may use the time of this day to dry from the rains. Have you hunted?"

"Not this day," the man answered, swinging the girl down to the ground and dismounting himself. He was nearly the size of the barbarian, but the girl was more my size. They seemed to grow men larger than average on that world. Both newcomers had blond hair and blue eyes, and the girl stood quietly behind the warrior. She wore *imad* and *caldin*, but in bright patterns rather than solids like mine, and he wore a dark green *haddin*. The girl glanced over at me, and I could see the gleam of a bronze-colored band on her neck.

"I have *peral*," the barbarian told the other man, "also *dimral* against further rains. Your *wenda* may join mine in the preparation of it. I shall build a fire the while you see to your *camtah*."

The other man nodded and led his *seetarr* over to ours. He paused to examine the two *seetarr* that the barbarian had acquired, smiled slightly, then began unpacking.

In no time at all, the fire was blazing and the second *camtah* was up. A large carcass, like the one we'd cooked on the last nonrainy day, was already cut up. The barbarian produced more of the wrapping leaves, and the other man gestured to the girl. She went to him and he stood her in front of him, putting his hands on her shoulders.

"Tammad, I would have you know my *wenda*," Faddan said quietly. "She is called Doran, and I would ask the *denday* to honor me."

"Gladly will I do so," Tammad answered with a grin. "Doran, you are lovelier than your name, and the honor is mine."

The girl smiled sweetly and looked up at Tammad. "The *denday* shall have to earn his honor," she quipped. "I am not minded to agree with Faddan."

The two men laughed and Faddan shook her slightly. "Your agreement is not necessary, *wenda*," he said, trying to sound stern. "This is a matter between *l'lendaa*! Go you now and see to the *dimral*."

"My *wenda* shall aid her," the barbarian said, and all eyes immediately turned in my direction. "She was a gift to me

from her father, whose land lies far beyond the house of the
offworlders. They know nothing there of the banding and
training of *wendaa*, nor are our customs understood by them.
It will require a good deal of teaching, but I shall one day see
her a proper *wenda*."

"A glorious gift," Faddan murmured, examining me with
his eyes, his mind full of approval. "Dark-haired and green-
eyed. And one such as she went unbanded?"

"Unbanded and living as she would," Tammad nodded. "It
is a land of *darayse*, and though many sought her, she accepted none. Her father despaired until my appearance, then
contrived to send her with me upon my departure. Her look
pleased me, else I would not have taken the bother. She is
called Terril."

"An odd name," Faddan mused, "yet one that suits her.
Though she be five-banded, *denday*, she will draw the eyes of
many men."

"This is known to me," Tammad agreed with a shrug. "It
shall make little difference as the *wenda* is now my belonging.
See to the *dimral* with Doran, Terril."

The two men turned away toward Faddan's *camtah* and
the girl came over to me, staring curiously. We put two
pieces of the *dimral* on sticks, and when the meat was in the
fire, her curiosity turned vocal.

"Are *wendaa* truly unbanded in your land?" she asked, and
I could feel her disbelief. "How, then, do men know if they
may have the *wenda* they see?"

"The men ask," I told her, studying the five bands she also
wore. "If the man pleases her, she accepts him. If he does not
please her, she sends him away."

"How many *wendaa* send away *l'lenda*?" She laughed. "You
are no larger than I, perhaps even smaller. Should Faddan
displease me and I attempt to send him away, his laughter
would sound out for all to hear."

"The men of my land are better than *l'lendaa*," I answered,
feeling my tone going stiff. "They need not be forced to
leave. If they are not wanted, they go of their own accord."

"At the bidding of *wenda*?" she snickered. "They must
truly be *darayse*—and more, to care so little for the *wendaa*
of their land. I would not care to live there."

"I do care to live there," I countered. "And I shall return
there soon. Then I will no longer need to wear bands as a
man's belonging."

"The *denday* Tammad is a man among men," she murmured, glancing sideways to where Tammad and Faddan sat talking and laughing. "I have heard much said of him, and many are the *wendaa* who would gladly be his belonging. If you do not please him, why does he allow you to wear the fifth band?"

"I please him well enough," I sniffed, feeling slightly put out. "And he does not *allow* me to wear his bands, but rather forces me to wear them. But he does not please me at all, and soon I shall return home."

"Do not speak foolishly, Terril," she grinned. "If you please the *denday*, you shall remain his belonging. If you do not please him, he shall unband you and find another to care for you, as he has done many times with other *wendaa*. He is not *darayse*, and shall not allow you to be unprotected."

"In my land, I need no one's protection," I said airily. "My standing is such that all look upon me with respect. I shall return home as soon as I wish to."

"And you shall not wish to, save Tammad gives his word," she laughed. "Were you to make the attempt sooner, it would be your wish to remain unseated that day, and perhaps the next as well. The *denday* Tammad will accept naught save obedience from *wendaa*."

"The *denday* Tammad may accept naught in all!" I snapped, feeling my cheeks redden. "I have given *my* word to accompany him for the while, and shall do so despite my own wishes to the contrary. I, too, know something of honor."

I know my head was up as I said that, and she stared at me again in uncertainty. *Wendaa* are supposed to be uninvolved with honor as honor is supposedly a man's province alone. I found that I meant every word I'd said to her, and that it gave me a sense of satisfaction. I *was* honor bound to complete the barbarian's assignment, even if I *had* been tricked into accepting it. I'd been wrong in trying to run away, because acceptance is acceptance. I'd complete the assignment, and return home with no unpaid debts left behind me.

The girl Doran—whose name was that of a pretty blue flower that grew wild—and I finished cooking and wrapping the *dimral* while the men socialized and drank *drishnak*. The fact that they did nothing to help didn't bother Doran in the least, but it annoyed *me* quite a bit. In spite of my own ex-

periences to the contrary, I can't help feeling that catching
the beast is the easy part.

When the *dimral* was all wrapped, it was clothes washing
time again. Another stream—or a different part of the same
stream—helped to take care of that chore, and then Doran
and I were allowed to bathe. I was slightly upset because
Faddan was there in addition to the barbarian, but I was too
desperate to let that stop me. I'd always considered bathing
something to be taken for granted, but on Rimilia it was a
luxury.

The barbarian insisted that Faddan bathe first, so the man
stripped and entered the water while Tammad stood guard.
Faddan let Doran hold onto his shoulders while he swam to
the middle of the stream and back, and she acted as though
she'd just had a brush with death. When he offered to teach
her how to swim and she refused with a firm headshake and
a large shudder, it made a little more sense, but not much.
I'd been swimming since I was a child, and fear of water was
something I could feel in others, but not understand on a personal level.

When Faddan climbed out, Tammad took his turn. After
he'd splashed around a bit to get wet, he came over to me.

"Would you care to visit the center of the stream, too?" he
asked. "I'm a strong swimmer, and there is nothing to fear."

"I believe I would enjoy that," I answered his smile. "The
water holds no fear for me."

"Good." He grinned. "Take hold of my shoulders and do
not let go."

He turned around and ducked low in the water to allow
me to reach him more easily, and I had a nice ride out to the
middle of the stream. The barbarian's muscles rippled under
his skin, his stroke even and sure, but I was a good swimmer,
too. The light stream current was no hazard, so when the barbarian paused to turn around, I let go of him and floated
away on my own.

He turned immediately in the water, searching for me
frantically; I waved to him with a laugh, then dived under. I
didn't go very deep or very far, but when I surfaced again I
didn't need the thunder in his thoughts to bring me his dis-
pleasure. The look on his face was enough to make Sandy's
quadriwagon stop enveloping again, and I didn't understand
it, so I swam closer to him.

"What's the matter?" I asked in a low voice. "I've been swimming for years."

"This should have been told to me sooner," he said coldly, anger and annoyance and an odd tinge of fear filling him. "Do you now return to the bank—*above* water!"

He shoved me in that direction to start me off, then paced me as I swam. I still didn't know what he was so upset about, but he wasn't the only one. Faddan stood on the bank looking and thinking pure grim, and Doran, who stood next to him, wasn't doing much better. When I got to the bank, Faddan reached down and hauled me onto it by one wrist, and the barbarian vaulted out alone a minute later. I stood there dripping and being dripped on by a coldly irate Tammad.

"I do not understand what troubles you," I said to him. "That I am able to swim should not cause such anger."

"That you did not say you are able to swim is reason enough for anger," he answered in a hard voice. "I had thought you close to drowning when you left me! But to behave so foolishly as to swim *beneath* the water! Do you seek to end your life, *wenda?*"

"You cannot swim underwater!" I laughed, finally understanding. "That is what troubles you! There is little to it, *l'lenda*. Would you have me teach you?"

I was feeling pleased that I'd finally found something that that so-superior barbarian couldn't do, but his feelings and reactions confused me.

"Dress yourself!" he ordered, controlling his fury with much difficulty. "We return to the camp."

There was no longer anything to grin at, so I quietly put on the relatively clean *imad* and *caldin* and gathered up the recently washed ones, plus some of the waterskins. Faddan was still glaring at me, and Doran stood behind and to one side of him, shaking her head ruefully at me. The way they all acted, you'd think I'd committed some terrible crime, but I hadn't *done* anything! The barbarian didn't say another word, and we all walked back to the camp in silence.

Once we got there, Doran went to spread her wet *imad* and *caldin* on the roof of Faddan's *camtah*, and I did the same on the roof of Tammad's. I'd barely finished when I was grabbed roughly by the arm and pushed by the barbarian ahead of him into the *camtah*. I was able to turn to look at him when he paused to close the leather curtain, and the gloom wasn't so deep that I couldn't see the switch he was holding. The fury in him hadn't eased off much, and I was suddenly afraid.

"What did I do?" I demanded in a voice I couldn't keep from trembling. "You have to tell me what I did!"

But he didn't tell me. Without a word he held me in place, bared me, and gave me a switching worse than any he had yet given me. I screamed and begged him to tell me what I'd done, but he had no patience for explanations. With the fury was outrage and bitterness, and in my pain I, too, raged and called him barbarian. I was able to keep from projecting, but the barbarian's arm was stronger than my determination to give him no satisfaction. The tears came long before he let me go, and when he was gone, I lay on the floor of the *camtah* near my furs, crying uncontrollably.

A short while later, the curtain was moved aside and Doran came in. She sat next to me and stroked my hair, sympathy and compassion clear in her thoughts. She leaned over me to see what had been done, and a pang of strong, empathetic pain flashed before she sat back with a sigh, smoothing my hair again.

"Truly, Terril, his anger was greater than it seemed," she said softly. "The insult was grave, yet *l'lendaa* do not often take such strong measures with *wendaa*. A lighter switching is sufficient to teach her her place."

"He hates me as I hate him," I choked out, feeling pain deep inside me, too. "I gave him no insult, yet he beat me I hate him!"

"Can you not see the insult you gave?" she asked gently. "I had wondered at your foolish behavior. Know then, Terril, that to taunt a warrior with some lack of ability is insult enough, but to offer him instruction before others is to call him *darayse*. Had you been warrior yourself, it would have meant your life or Tammad's, but the double sound within your name does not make you *l'lenda*. You are still *wenda*, and subject to Tammad's switch."

"I wish I *were l'lenda*!" I answered bitterly, wiping at the wetness on my face with the back of my hand. "It would give me such pleasure to end that—that—*barbarian*! I hate him as I have never hated another!"

"You hate him, you are untutored in our ways, you insult him deeply, yet he keeps you," she mused, curiosity and confusion mingled within her. "I would know the why of it, but the *denday*'s thoughts are not for me to know. Best you rest now till the greater of the pain is past. I shall begin the *peral*, and you may aid me later."

She went out, leaving me alone in the *camtah*, but I couldn't rest. I stretched out on the leather, a fistful of the sleeping furs in my hand, the ache inside and out of me consuming me. I finally knew what had caused the beating, but that didn't make me hate him any less. I hadn't insulted him on purpose, but that had made no difference to him. He beat me as if I were less than a *seetar*, and he kept me only for the help he needed. Not a woman but a *thing*, to be endured until it was used and then discarded with relief. The tears flowed easily down my cheeks again to my outstretched arms and I lay still, wishing that the predator's hunt had been successful. The feel of its teeth in my flesh could not have been as severe a pain as what I felt inside me then.

When Doran called me, I went outside the *camtah*. The sun was low in the sky, and the two warriors were with the *seetarr*, checking hooves and mouths, running their hands over high, broad backs. Neither one of them turned as Doran gestured me over.

"The *pearl* must be turned constantly," she directed, nodding at the relatively small animal that was skinned and spitted over the fire. It had been seasoned with bits of the wrapping leaf, and had already been cooking awhile.

I took over at the crank of the spit, squatted down, and turned the thing as I stared into the fire. Doran went inside Faddan's *camtah*, but I was grateful for what she'd already done. I was sure she wouldn't have called me at all if she hadn't had to.

As I turned the animal, I tried to pretend to myself that I was unawakened, that I didn't know the feelings of the warriors near the *seetarr*. They were both aware of me as I crouched near the fire, but pretending didn't help. I still felt Faddan's faint sympathy and curiosity; I also felt the hard knot of tangle in the barbarian, not the least trace of tenderness or regret in him. A stone he was, and he cared nothing for me.

When Doran pronounced the animal done, Faddan lifted it off the spit, placed it on a leaf, and cut it up into quarters. There was more in my quarter than I could possibly eat, but I accepted it silently and carried it away from the fire that the other three sat themselves near. It was dark enough to find a good shadow, and I crouched in it, waiting for the meat to cool.

The conversation between the men slowly came to include Doran, and there was laughter shared among them. I crouched in my shadow and ate as I watched them eat, realizing there was more than physical distance separating me from them. They belonged together on their world, but I was an intruder who didn't fit in, an outsider, for all that I knew their language. Before very long, I put the meat aside and simply watched them.

The conversation continued for a short while after they'd finished eating, then the barbarian stood up. Doran stood too, but with an odd sort of hesitation. Faddan stayed seated, but he smiled and nodded at her with deep satisfaction, so she turned, still hesitantly, to the barbarian. He reached his hand out and stroked her cheek gently, then took her arm and drew her into his *camtah*. Faddan made himself more comfortable by the fire.

I closed my eyes, but eyes are easily closed, and even open they wouldn't have seen what there was to be felt inside the *camtah*. Doran teased lightly for a short while, but only to hide the tinge of fear she felt. Her mind quivered slightly when she was first touched, but she soon settled down to pleasurable acceptance. The fear disappeared completely and didn't return, because he was *gentle* with her, gentle and tender! Tenderness for her, beatings and no regret for me. I lay down on the dark ground and curled up tight, feeling his satisfaction grow higher.

"It is late, Terril," Faddan's voice came suddenly from above me. "Come, you are to share my *camtah* this night."

I curled up tighter, wishing him away from me, but he was *l'lenda*. He picked me up with no effort, carried me to his *camtah*, and put me down on furs. The smell of the *camtah* was different, and the furs were *hers*, but she didn't need them. She had *my* furs, and she had—I wanted to cry, but it hurt too much.

"The *denday* honors me this night," Faddan said, feeling very pleased, deliberately ignoring my tight-clenched eyes and fists. "As it is Doran's time, it is my hope that Tammad will give her his child so that I may raise it among those of my own that Doran shall give me. It is high honor to raise the child of a *denday*."

I didn't answer him, and couldn't keep myself from probing at the other *camtah*, searching for the least indication of dissatisfaction. I reached to his mind and hers, but there was nothing but shared pleasure there, nothing but the happiness of two people together. I put my fingers in the band around my neck and pulled at it, not caring how the chain dug into my neck and fingers.

"It is our way, Terril," Faddan said gently, forcing my fingers away from the band. "It does not mean that Tammad no longer considers you his belonging. He has told me that he shall not unband you."

I opened my eyes to the shadows to find that his swordbelt and *haddin* were gone, and I suddenly realized that he was untying my *imad* and *caldin*! I tried to get away from him, tried to get out of the *camtah*—but he was *l'lenda*. His strength kept me where he wanted me, the *imad* and *caldin* were removed, then he lay down to take me in his arms.

"The *denday* does not wish you to be alone this night," he murmured, holding me up against the warmth of his body. "He does me further honor by asking that I see to you. I shall ease your hurt as best I may."

He used me then as *l'lendaa* do, and his gentleness was bitter to me. I didn't want to be used, but more than that I didn't want *his* gentleness! I struggled only a short time, then lay quietly and let him do as he wished. I wasn't a slave to be chained and beaten, oh no. I was no less than a belonging—to be given to any man approved of by him to whom I belonged. I lay quietly in the cloaking darkness, seeing the difference clearly.

★ 10 ★

I was awake before everyone the next morning. I dressed quickly and quietly, leaving Faddan asleep in his furs, then went out into the pre-dawn stillness. The dark mass of *seetarr* were aware of me and I could feel their hunger, so I gathered up the leftovers of the last night's meal and divided it among them. I gave a little extra to the barbarian's mount, and the gigantic male rested his face on my shoulder as he chewed, thinking soothing thoughts at me. I stroked his neck awhile, letting him feel my gratitude, then turned back to the camp.

"How long have you been awake?" the barbarian asked softly as I stopped short to keep from running into him. His deep calm was back, and I hadn't even felt it through the turmoil in my own mind.

"Not long," I answered, dropping my eyes and starting to step around him. His hand touched my arm, and I was stopped. "No, I won't run again," I said, answering the question I knew was in his mind. "I gave my word and I'll keep it."

"The switching was too harsh," he said, still touching my arm. "I would offer my apologies."

I nodded without saying anything, feeling the way my throat burned, making it hard to swallow. There was no sense of apology or regret anywhere in him. His hand went down, and I continued on back to the camp.

The first rays of the sun were just beginning to put color back into everything when Doran appeared, looking radiantly happy. She hugged me in an effort to express the joy of her feelings, and I patted her arm in understanding. A minute later Faddan emerged from his *camtah* and she ran to him, throwing herself into his arms. He laughed softly and hugged her, and she nestled close to him.

"How passed the night, Faddan?" the barbarian asked conversationally as he handed out pieces of *dimral* to all of us. "My *wenda* treated you well?"

"Aye, *denday*," Faddan answered, and I could feel his eyes on me where I stood, slightly off to one side. "I did not lack in the absence of Doran."

"Good," the barbarian said. "And what thought you of the special gift she brings to the furs?"

"Special gift?" Faddan echoed in confusion. "My apologies, Tammad, but I saw no special gift."

There was a giant surge in the barbarian, but he had control of it again before I could analyze it and he said, "Perhaps I am mistaken, Faddan. Her ways are still strange to me. Let us eat and seek the road once more."

We all ate in silence, then Doran and I gathered up the things to be packed by the men. With the *camtahh* rolled and tied in place we were ready, and Faddan put Doran behind his saddle before he mounted. The barbarian turned in his own saddle and put his arm out to me, but I knew where I belonged, where it was best for me to be.

"The day is clear," I said, looking at the ground. "I am to walk in your track."

He backed the *seetar* slightly, then leaned down to grasp my arm and swing me up to the saddle fur behind him.

"You are to do as you are bidden," he answered evenly, but I could feel the anger toward me again. "You shall not walk when you are told to ride."

His mind was made up, and there was nothing I could do about it. We moved off toward the road, Faddan and his *seetarr* going first. Doran held tightly to him, pressing herself as close as possible, indescribable contentment in her at the contact. I put my fingers in the barbarian's swordbelt, and held on that way.

At sundown we made camp again, and I helped Doran with the animal Faddan had shot late in the day. She skinned the thing herself because I didn't know how to, and I realized that skinning was supposed to be a woman's job. There were a lot of things I didn't know how to do, and the barbarian had had to do them all. No matter how I tried to deny it, I *was* helpless in the barbarian's frame of reference, helpless

and worthless. It was enough to make any able person want
to avoid me completely, and it was no wonder that the barbarian looked at me as he did.

When the meal was done, Faddan and Doran went happily
to their *camtah*. There had been vegetables of some sort with
the meat, and Doran had found them. I had merely washed
them at her direction, then watched her wrap and place them
beneath the fire. The men had been full of praise for both of
us, but the accomplishment hadn't been mine, so the praise
hadn't touched me.

I had wandered down to the *seetarr* again, and was assuring Tammad's large male that I was fine, when I felt the barbarian near me. His usual calm had been interrupted by a
flash of annoyance, and that had brought him to my attention. I sighed a little, wondering briefly what I had done this
time, then turned to face him.

"It is time to be in one's *camtah*, not among the shadows,"
he said, looking down at me with no trace of the annoyance
reaching his face. "Do you now come with me."

I followed him without comment to the *camtah*, and then
inside. He turned away to remove his swordbelt and *haddin*,
and when he turned back, he saw that I was already out of
the *imad* and *caldin*. He hesitated briefly, strong control over
his emotions, then he sat next to me on my furs.

"Read for me this man Faddan," he said softly. "Tell me
what you see of him."

So I was to be tested. Well, the notion wasn't unreasonable,
and I'd been close enough to Fadan long enough to have
formed a few conclusions. I composed myself for serious
work, and closed my eyes.

"Faddan is a strong man," I reported, rechecking my data,
"strong in his loyalties and strong in his beliefs. He is not as
quick-tempered as some, and will use his anger rather than
let it use him. He believes in you and is loyal to you, but
does not fear you. His fears are well known to him and accepted by him, and are therefore manageable to him. He
weighs both sides of a question before making up his mind,
and would make a good leader, but needs someone to look
up to."

I opened my eyes, and could see his face pointed toward
me, his attention sharp on every word I'd said.

"It is true," he mused. "You know the man as I do, yet I

have known him since we were boys together. Truly, your gift shall be of great value to me."

He took me in his arms then, but I felt no satisfaction over the value I had to him. It was a value any Prime would have had, not a personal value. I made no effort to stop my desire from reaching him, and his satisfaction was so close to that of Faddan's with Doran that I couldn't tell them apart. Of course, he was only receiving my projections and building on them, but for the time I could tell myself that his feelings were his own. I knew then that I could never mean anything to him other than as a Prime, but at least I could pretend. I was his belonging, but he would never belong to me.

★ 11 ★

We traveled another two days and Doran taught me what she could, but I had little aptitude for being a woman on Rimilia. The first night I tried putting the vegetables to cook on my own, and managed to burn my hand well in the process. It was all I could do to keep from projecting the intense pain, and the *seetarr*, especially the barbarian's mount, bellowed frantically until the rider had smothered my hand in a salve that deadened it. I had been so shocked at the burn that I hadn't even had the sense to dampen the pain myself, and when the barbarian had finished with the salve I ran from him, shame making me want to hide. I used my own intense emotions as a block between me and the barbarian, unwilling to face the disgust I knew he would be feeling. I was still a burden to him, Prime or no. I stayed with the *seetarr*, taking comfort from them, resigned to the fact that many things were beyond me, but the barbarian's increased annoyance and frustration when he came for me, still cut deep.

We reached cultivated fields early on the last day, and by late afternoon we entered a surprisingly large town that was on the bank of a river. Murdock McKenzie's report had mentioned that there were many such towns, inhabited by the most advanced group on the planet, Tammad's people. We rode downhill into the town, the road becoming a broad central street. There were a lot of people moving around busily, making the place alive with the activity of their doings. Most of the men were dressed as warriors, but some few of them wore long, loose, wide-sleeved robes over their *haddinn*, and of these, most wore no swordbelt. The women, all in *imad* and *caldin*, were banded to a greater or lesser degree, but all were banded. I was almost shocked to see how many of them had small children with them.

We rode slowly down the street, and every man we passed greeted Tammad by name. The barbarian returned the greetings, also by name, and many of the women stopped to stare at him, longing clear in their faces and thoughts. When they saw me behind him they frowned, but they weren't overly upset. Obviously I wasn't the first to be banded by him, although my dark hair might be something new. Almost without exception, every man, woman and child's hair was some shade of blond.

The buildings we passed were of various sizes, but all were one-story affairs and each stood close to the next, some of them separated by a cloth-covered stall with items for sale on the counters. The items were examined by people near the stalls, but only men did the buying. If a woman was alone, all she could do was look.

We pulled up in front of a wide building that had extra wide and high doors, with a large sign on it that had a picture of a *seetar*. Doran and I were swung to the ground, and the men dismounted.

"Remain here," the barbarian said as he and Faddan tied their *seetarr* to tall posts that seemed to be provided for the purpose. "We will not be long."

He and Faddan disappeared inside the building, and I glanced at Doran. She stood calmly and patiently, waiting until the men would finish their business and return. I sighed a little, then tried to match her.

In a very few minutes, standing in the hot dirt of the street became uncomfortable. I shifted from foot to foot, wishing the barbarian had given me those buskins Denny had mentioned. Mud might be messy, but at least it didn't burn. I looked around to help me forget about my feet, and found that almost every man passing by had his attention on me. I was stared at frankly and openly, and their grins said the same thing that their minds did. I expected to be annoyed but I wasn't, and I didn't understand it.

There was a small, narrow patch of shadow on the ground to my left, thrown by a tying post, so I moved over to it. It wasn't large enough to shade anything, but it felt good on the bottoms of my feet. Men and women went by on the street, and little children played in the dust.

I felt the rage suddenly then, and it was almost unbelievable that everyone else hadn't felt it, too. It was so strong it
pounded at me, but people continued to pass by unconcerned.
I turned quickly in the direction it came from, seeing the
seetar standing to the right of the building that the barbarian
had gone into. It stood in an alleyway that probably led to
the back of the building, staring out at the crowd of people,
its rage increasing.

Abruptly it trotted out of the alleyway into full view, increasing its pace, bellowing its intention to trample and
destroy. It wore no bridle or halter, and when the passersby
saw it they moved fast to get out of its path. Everyone ran—
except some of the children who were paralyzed with fear. A
number of the warriors turned back and ran toward the children, but from the speed the *seetar* had picked up it was easy
to see they'd never make it.

I blocked out the horrified screams and desperate shouts
and drew calm about myself, moving at a run toward the
seetar at the same time. I knew that the great mass of emotions was too much for the *seetar*, that it was more sensitive
than normal to the people around it. It didn't understand
what it was feeling, and the result was intense rage. If it
wasn't stopped, it would kill everyone it could reach.

I projected calm at the *seetar*, and its giant head snapped
around to me. Changing course without slowing down, it
came directly toward me. I stopped running and waited, urging it to come and share my peace. I put my hand out, sym-
pathizing with its pain and offering understanding, and I felt
its rage ease, allowing its loneliness and confusion to show
through. I comforted the confusion, soothed the loneliness,
and the giant beast stopped in front of me, nudging me
gently with its nose. I stroked the nose, assuring the beast
whatever help it was in my power to give.

"Never have I seen such a thing!" a man said from the
awed and silent crowds. There was a murmur of agreement
from the others, but mostly they were too numb even to
think. I took the opportunity to help the beast raise a small
and feeble barrier in its mind, and the barrier calmed it even
more.

"What has happened?" another voice demanded, a voice
that was all too familiar. I turned to see the barbarian and
Faddan coming out of the building, accompanied by a third

man. Faddan hurried over to a pale and shaking Doran, but the barbarian and the other man came over to me.

"*Denday*, I do not believe what I have seen with my own eyes!" a man said, coming out of the crowd. He was the same man who had spoken before, and he stared at me with the disbelief he spoke of. "The *seetar* was mad, yet she stopped it with naught save the sweep of her arm!"

"I know this *seetar*," the man who had come out of the building with the barbarian said shakily. "It was left with me for resale, yet I could find none to control it. A mad beast, locked away from all it would destroy, and here it stands! How came it here?"

"From there," I said, pointing toward the alleyway. "It stood there seemingly lost, and I but called it to me."

"Called it to her!" the man from the crowd snorted. "It would have trampled all in its path, and nearly trampled *her*. The why of its stopping is beyond me!"

"She has great facility with *seetar*," the barbarian said evenly, but his mind boiled with a monstrous anger—aimed again at me. I knew I'd somehow failed him yet again, and I looked down at the dirt in defeat. "I shall send the *seetarr* to you when they are unburdened, Jezzar," he continued to the man who had come out of the building with him. "Do you see to their sale. Come, *wenda*."

I started to follow him back to his mount, but discovered that I, too, was being followed. The *seetar* kept directly behind me, and I stopped in confusion.

"I shall take the *seetar*," the man from the building said in a kindly way. He produced a leather rope from behind him and started to put it around the *seetar*'s neck, but the *seetar*'s eyes blazed and it rumbled warningly. He stepped back immediately, as did everyone else, but the beast calmed again when I put my hand on its neck. It lowered its head to my shoulder, and leaned there comfortably.

"The beast wishes to band her as its own," the man from the crowd laughed. "Tammad, you must needs do battle for your *wenda*."

The barbarian folded his arms across his chest and grinned with true amusement. "I have often done battle," he said, "but never with a *seetar*. And what need would it have for my *wenda*? It is *wenda* itself."

The crowd roared laughter at this, and it was true. The *seetar* was a female. I had to calm her again because of the

laughter, but it was becoming increasingly easier to do. The
barbarian came closer and studied the *seetar* carefully, then
turned to the man Jezzar.

"I would buy her from you, Jezzar," he said. "As the only
alternative seems to be to sell my *wenda* to you, I shall have
to offer a good price."

"I would prefer the alternative, *denday*." Jezzar grinned,
looking at me appreciatively. "The *wenda* is one I, too, would
keep five-banded. Yet I cannot take your price for the *seetar*.
It would have done great damage had it not been stopped,
and in gratitude I would gift it to you. It will do well as
breeding stock."

"My thanks, Jezzar," the barbarian said warmly. "You
shall have the first of its offspring. Come you *now, wenda*,
and bring my *seetar*."

He turned back to his mount again and I followed, feeling
the old annoyance all over again. I let him lift me to the
saddle behind him, the female *seetar* still sticking close to me,
and we continued up the street through the parting crowd.

After we had gone a short way I muttered, "She's mine."

"Did you speak?" the barbarian asked mildly, turning
slightly in the saddle.

"I said the *seetar* is mine," I repeated in a louder voice.
"She did not come to you for comfort."

"Ah, I see," he murmured. "You called to the *seetar*, but
not aloud. And she needed naught save comfort?"

"She needed understanding, too," I said, "but comfort most
of all. I comforted her and she's mine."

"But *wenda* cannot own property here," he said in a
smooth, easy way. "You are my belonging, and what was
yours is now mine. How, then, may the *seetar* be yours?"

"She is *mine*!" I insisted stubbornly. "Take her if you can!"

"Now you give my own words back to me." He laughed.
"You are able to call to her and I cannot. The *seetar* is
yours."

He faced forward, and I sat there behind him trying to figure him out. I'd expected a fight from him over the *seetar*,
but he'd given up any claim to her just like that. It could
have been that he thought he would own her anyway when I
left, but I didn't think that was it. It was almost as if he
didn't need to prove his superiority in so small a thing, almost as if he were rewarding me for proving my point with

his own arguments. He was feeling pleased, and I didn't understand why.

Faddan and Doran turned off at a building, raising their hands in farewell, but we kept going until we came to a much larger building than any of the others, even though it was still single-story. It stood to the left of the road, was faced with some sort of stone, and had a double-doored entrance at the top of two steps. The doors were made of wood, but were metal braced, and a higher, *seetar*-sized door was all the way to the right. We made our way to the *seetar* door, and it opened for us. An older man stood there, grinning up at Tammad.

"It is good you are returned home, *denday*," he said. "All is as you left it."

"I would expect no less, Bollan," the barbarian answered. "I shall unburden the *seetarr*, and would have your Gilor await me in the hall."

"It shall be done, Tammad." The man nodded, then stepped back out of the way. We rode past him, my *seetar* a bit nervous, and entered a covered alleyway that led to the rear of the building. There was a heavily fenced in, partially roofed corral about twenty feet from the back of the building, and that's where we went. When we were all inside the corral, the man called Bollan closed the corral gate behind us.

"Do you now see to *your seetar*," the barbarian said, setting me down on the ground. "I shall be occupied with the others, and there is fodder aplenty."

"I don't mind taking care of her," I said, watching him dismount. "As long as you remember that she *is* mine."

He snorted briefly in amusement, then turned to the four *seetarr* he had to tend to. I looked around and found a nice piece of carcass for my girl, then encouraged her to eat it. She didn't need much encouragement as she was very hungry, but she wasn't used to being fed without an aura of fear about her. I stroked her side as she chewed, aware of her deepening happiness.

Suddenly I was nudged very gently from behind, and turned to see Tammad's saddle *seetar*, less his saddle and bridle. He snorted very softly at me, and let it be known that he was hungry. I shook my head in mock annoyance, then chose another piece of carcass for *him* to eat. I went back to my girl then, but the big male picked up the meat in his teeth and carried it over to us before he began eating. I laughed softly, and stroked him, too.

"My *seetar* cares for you," the barbarian said from where he stood watching my group. He had all of the packs and halters off the animals, and they were searching for food. "I had not understood this, but you knew of it."

It was more a statement than a question, but I nodded anyway. "I knew. His thoughts are very lovely and calm—and comforting."

"So you sought comfort from him—and not escape from me," he said with a small smile. "I had thought it the latter. Come to the house with me, *wenda*."

I assured my girl that I would not be far away, then walked over to him. He looked down at me in a strange way, his emotions confusing me for a minute, but then their meaning was obvious. His pleasure came from being home again, his relief due to the fact that I was still relatively in one piece. If I had managed to do something serious to myself, it would have been inconvenient to his cause. He stroked my hair briefly, then led the way to the house.

The back door opened into a moderate-sized entrance hall, which had four doorways. A handsome older woman stood quietly in the hall, smiling warmly when she saw the barbarian.

"I am much relieved that you have returned, Tammad," she said. "I feared that this journey would swallow you forever."

"There are still many journeys to make, Gilor." The barbarian grinned. "I am not yet to be swallowed. I would have you know my *wenda* Terril, and ask that you see to her hand. It was burned on our journey here."

"Gladly will I do so," Gilor answered, looking me over. "Bollan has already had me put furs for her near yours. Do you wish food?"

"See to her hand first, then we both shall eat," he directed. "And do *not* allow her to aid in the cooking of it! She must heal before she faces further peril."

He strode out through one of the doorways and Gilor watched him go, then turned to me with a grin.

"Such a sour expression!" She laughed. "The *denday*'s *wenda* does not care for his humor?"

"It was not humor," I told her dismally. "I burned my hand attempting to cook for him. I shall not make the attempt again."

"You must do more than make the attempt," she said firmly, wagging a finger at me. "Think you the *denday* shall keep his bands on one who cannot tend to his needs? One may spend only so much time in the furs."

"I am banded for reasons other than cooking or furs," I told her, staring at the floor without seeing it. "Your *denday* cares nothing for me, and shall soon return me to my own land. Then shall he search for one who knows the way of his needs. That one is not I."

"I would see the burn," she said after a moment, holding her hand out. Although reserved, she was a friendly person, but would not allow her curiosity to ask further questions. I gave her my left hand, and she unwrapped the dirty bandage from it.

"It has begun to heal," she said, studying the large, round, shiny-red sear on the back of my hand. "It is fortunate that salve was applied to it. Come, I shall add more salve and a clean bandage."

I followed her through one of the doorways other than the one the barbarian had taken, finding a short hall that led to a large kitchen. There were four young girls moving about in there, but they stopped to stare at me when we walked in. Gilor was wearing four bands, but the younger blondes had only one each, and that on their left ankles. Not only was there little friendliness in them, but two of them were down-right hostile—inside. Overtly, they smiled.

"Do you return to your work," Gilor said to them. "Is the *denday* to turn away guests at his door so that you may stand about and gape? Terril shall not disappear, and you may know her when the men are seen to. Quickly, now!"

The girls grinned and turned back to what they'd been do-ing, but they still had their attention on me. I was being sized up, but with different feelings from the ones the men had shown. Gilor found a pot of salve and a clean rag and took care of my hand, then went to a large kettle that hung on a hearth and scooped out two metal platesful of what looked like stew. An oversized goblet was filled from a pitcher, two smaller shallow-bowled, long-handled versions of the kettle-scoop were put near the plates, then she turned back to me.

"Do you carry your own plate," she directed. "I shall take Tammad's."

"I would take the *denday*'s *trejna* to him," one of the girls interrupted, coming over to stand in Gilor's way. She was tall and big-busted, with a very pretty face.

"It matters not." Gilor shrugged, looking around her. "There are other things requiring my attention. Terril, go you with Rapan. She will show you to Tammad."

The girl Rapan smirked and picked up the plate, scoop, and goblet, then gestured with her head for me to follow. I took the other plate and scoop and went along, but not happily. Rapan was one of the two who had felt hostility at my appearance, and that hadn't changed. She still felt hostile, but she was also determined about something. I followed her, wondering what she was going to do.

We went back to the entrance hall, then through the doorway that the barbarian had taken. The doorway was hung with a piece of material, and the material parted to show a large room that was wood-paneled and decorated with weapons. It had long, wide windows, but the windows were barred and could be shuttered. Tall torches hung as yet unlit from sconces on the walls, and what seemed like hundreds of pillows were scattered all over the floor on top of a furlike carpet. The barbarian stood looking out of one of the windows, but he turned when we entered.

"*Trejna* at last!" he said, grinning at what Rapan was carrying. "I shall not miss the taste of *dimral* after so long a time with little else. Give it here, Rapan."

"Aye, Tammad," the girl said with a coy smile aimed at the barbarian. "I, myself, prepared it for you, hoping it would please you. You have been so long away, we thought you had forsaken us." She handed him the plate, but held the goblet to the side and back away from him as he reached for it, rubbing herself on him as he moved closer. "My father will be here to greet you this night, Tammad. He would not be displeased were you to speak with him of me."

"And so I shall, Rapan," he answered, leaning over just a little farther to take the goblet from her. "His switch has too long been kept from its proper use, and he shall know of it."

"But—you would not!" she protested, feeling a deep upset and frustration. "Tammad, I long to be yours! I would please you more than she whom you have this time banded. I beg you to ask my father for me."

The barbarian had crouched to set his plate and goblet on a small, very low table, but he stood straight again to place his hands on the girl's shoulders.

"Rapan, it is not seemly that you speak so," he told her gently. "Your father sent you to me so that you might be seen by my warriors more easily than in his house. He hoped for a good match for you, and had found one even as I prepared to leave on my journey. You shall be banded this night, *wenda*, but not as mine."

"I shall not!" she screamed, twisting away from his hands. "I shall go with no other!"

She raced out of the room, anger and hurt filling her so completely that she had forgotten all about me. I sighed for her, then turned to see the barbarian watching me.

"Do you sit beside me as we eat," he said, folding himself onto a large pillow. "There shall be many warriors here this night, and I wish your presence as well. Tell me, *wenda*, are you able to know truth from falsehood too in a man?"

"Sometimes," I answered, sitting on a pillow near his. I wasn't used to the angle, and almost tumbled off it onto the floor. His control was masterly—not a trace of the vast amusement he felt reached his face. "But there's no need to try being diplomatic," I added. "Your laughter is something I can always feel."

"I but remembered my experience with your *chairr*." He grinned, leaning over to the small table to scoop up some of the stew. "Each man does best with his own belongings about him. This night you are to read my warriors, *wenda*. I suspect a follower of my enemies is among them, but each has been with me too long to be lightly accused. I would be pleased to learn that I am mistaken, yet are you to seek earnestly."

"I'll do what I can." I shrugged. "If the man feels no guilt over betraying you, or if there's someone who dislikes you personally but would never betray you, there could be some confusion. Keep the point in mind."

"I shall." He nodded. "The final decision is ever mine to make. Why do you not eat?"

I looked down at the plate of stew in my hand, then used the small scoop to try some of it. It was spicy and very tasty, so I began eating. After a minute or two, I looked up again.

"That girl Rapan is in love with you," I told him quietly. "You still see nothing wrong in giving her away to someone else?"

"The girl is very young," he answered, giving most of his attention to his food. "Yet even that has no bearing. She is not mine to give, *wenda*, but her father's, and he, too, knows that what she feels for me is not as deep as what she may one day feel for another. He has made a wise choice for her, and awaited only my return to give her to the warrior who desires her. In this manner, she will not think herself stolen from me in my absence."

We went back to eating in silence, but I was still disturbed. The giant barbarian was as calm as ever—wasn't there a woman anywhere he cared about?

He kept his eyes on me until both our plates were empty, causing me to grow increasingly uncomfortable under that light-blue stare. I knew he was waiting to say something else, but I had a feeling it had nothing to do with the men he wanted me to read. After the last bite was down, I found I was right.

"*Wenda*, there is yet another matter to speak of," he said, and his mind and tone had hardened. "The last switching you received was, as I have said, too harsh. But for that, you would now ache mightily. Never again shall I see you risk yourself as was done this day, else you shall feel my wrath in your deepest parts. Are my words clear to you?"

"But I was in no danger," I protested, feeling the blazing edges of the wrath he'd mentioned. "That *seetar* wouldn't have. . . ."

"That *seetar* had to step but once to put an end to you!" he interrupted in that cold fury he was so good at projecting. "Best you remember what I have said, as I shall not warn you again! Return these plates now to Gilor, and say that she is to find clean *imad* and *caldin* for you. I shall send for you when I require your presence."

He handed me his plate and scoop, but kept the goblet. I took the things without another word, then went looking for Gilor, finding her easily just outside the curtain in the small entrance hall. She laughed softly and led the way back to the kitchen to get rid of the plates, then again to the hall and through yet another doorway and hall to a large room with sleeping furs in the middle of it. It had pillows scattered around the floor, a tall, barred window and little else, but I was sure the room was the barbarian's. Gilor closed the room's door, then turned to me.

"I shall fetch the *imad* and *caldin* in a moment," she said with a twinkle in her eye. "First, I wished to ask if you still believe the *denday* does not care for you. I had thought you to be wrong, and now I am sure of it."

"And I am sure I am not wrong," I answered, curious as to her interest. "Nothing has occurred to make me believe otherwise."

"Heard you not his words?" she demanded in outrage, her fists on her hips. "He does not wish you to risk yourself. Are those the words of a man who cares nothing for his *wenda*?"

"Those are the words of a man who cares only for his Prime," I answered bitterly. "Were I to die now, he would be inconvenienced, therefore he threatens to beat me to make me obey him. Yet I, too, care nothing for him or his beatings. I shall do as I please."

"So you care nothing for him, eh?" she mused, staring at me through narrowed eyes. "I know not the ways of such in your land, Terril, yet do I know the look of a woman who longs for a man. Your need seems deeper than Rapan's yet strangely, for you wear his bands, more hopeless. This I do not understand."

"There is little to understand, Gilor." I shrugged, feeling that understanding was important to her. "He does not see me as a woman, though he uses me as one. And gives me to other *l'lendaa* as one. I am not accustomed to obeying men, nor am I accustomed to being handed about among them. I shall not allow it any longer."

"Terril, these are *l'lendaa* you speak of, not *darayse*," she warned. "Have a care as to how you anger them. Tammad will not hesitate to teach you your place."

"He has already taught me my place," I answered, beginning to feel the anger that had been building so long, "Beside him when he has need of me, beneath him when he desires me, behind him when he tires of me. I shall now find my own place."

"Which will be where?" she asked, a bit nervously. "There are no others."

"Then I shall create a place," I said, starting to think about it. "It cannot be impossible for one of determination. I shall consider it."

I sank down onto the furs, then stretched out comfortably. There had to be a way out of the rut of *wenda*, and if I didn't look for it, I deserved whatever I got. I couldn't very well complain about how *he* treated me if I let him get away with it without a murmur.

Gilor stood where she was for another minute, then turned silently and went out. I tossed some ideas around until she came back with the clean clothing, then asked about a drink of water. The barbarian had gotten a drink with *his* meal, but I hadn't. The request resulted in a pitcher and goblet being brought in, so I decided to see how far things could go.

"Gilor, I would also like a bath," I announced. "Is there a place for bathing here?"

"We bathe in the river," she answered, "but the sun is nearly gone. Best you wait for the new sun."

"I have little care for waiting," I insisted. "Surely something may be done?"

"I know not what." She shrugged. "There has been no provision made for such things. Do you now change to the new *imad* and *caldin*, so that. . . ."

"I shall not," I interrupted with determination. "I shall not wear clean clothing if I may not bathe."

"The word was not mine." She shrugged again. "The *denday* will not be pleased."

"I care little for his pleasure." I shrugged too. "You may tell him if you wish."

"I shall," she said, giving me a calculating stare. "If you wish his attention in such a manner, so be it. I would not care for attention of that sort."

She turned and went out, and I leaned back in the furs. I wasn't very eager for the sort of attention Gilor was talking about, but it had to be risked if things were going to change. The barbarian might never see me as a woman, but I'd force him to see me as something other than a tool.

It didn't take very long before the door opened again, but this time it was my nemesis himself, filling the doorway as he came through it. My insides twinged when I saw the switch he carried, but I tried not to let it ruffle my calm.

As he came toward me I said, "What made you change your plans?"

He broke stride and frowned. "My plans have not changed," he said. "They are as they were."

"Not if you use *that* on me, they're not," I countered, nodding toward the switch. "I can't control myself well enough after a beating."

He thought about it in annoyance for a minute, but as far as he knew, I was telling the truth. I'd been too far off-bal-

ance to use pain control when I should have, but I was beginning to pull myself together again.

"There is perhaps enough time for a light switching," he
mused, studying me as I lay in the furs. I wanted to be so
many things to him, wanted so much to have everything I
couldn't have. Beat the Prime and use her in the furs, force
her to do her job and then return her with indecent haste. He
couldn't see me in his world, but at least he would know I
was there.

"Could be," I agreed evenly. "I know by now that I can't
stop you, but it might not be the best of ideas. I won't go
back on my word to help you, but there are other things I
can do to make my presence even more unpleasant than it
has been. I've been conditioned against doing most of those
things, but I think I can break through it now. Would you
like me to try?"

"What things do you speak of?" he asked curiously, and it
was interesting to see that his curiosity was genuine. He really
did want to know more about my "power."

"Well, I can project to men just as I do to animals," I said
slowly. "You've felt nothing but general or accidental projections, and those not even at full strength. Try this."

I put together a clear picture of my emotions during the
last switching, the pain, the shame, the frustration of not
being able to stop it, and imposed the picture on his mind.
There was a great deal of resistance in my own mind during
the process, but I worked in spite of it. His face flushed red
when he had the picture, and his free hand went back behind
him as he literally felt everything I had felt.

"Pain is an emotion too, you see," I explained as I felt him
clamp down to ease what he was experiencing. "As an emotion, I can project it any time I wish, and in future I shall,
but not only to you. If I'm given pain, everyone within my
radius will feel it. I'll leave it to you to make the explanations."

"I now understand your point," he said in a choked voice.
"Truly, *wenda*, you have learned the lesson well. Right lies in
the ability to do, and you have proven your right. What is it
you wish?"

"Merely a bath," I answered. "Then I'll be glad to change
my clothes."

"You shall have it," he said coldly, then turned and walked
out. As soon as the door closed, I gave in to the exhaustion

that had been trying to claim me and lay without moving. Projecting a specific picture to humans is extremely draining, and my top range was about twenty-five feet, but that didn't matter. The only thing that mattered was that the barbarian believed me, and he did. My place was beginning to change.

It took a while to restore myself, but by the time I did, my bath was ready. Water had been heated in the kitchen, and a large wooden tub had been brought in, but I had no intention of being too choosy. I bathed in the kitchen with a good deal of contentment, barely noticing the giggles of the three girls. What I did notice was that Rapan was no longer with them.

By the time I was dressed in clean clothes and had my hair brushed, it was full night outside and the torches had been lit. Drying around the five bands had been extremely annoying, and my success with the switching episode tempted me to see what could be done about those chains. I'd have to give it some thought, but the next day would be soon enough.

I was just coming in from checking on my *seetar*, when I met Gilor in the entrance hall. She smiled briefly and said, "Tammad would have you join him in the meeting hall. You may take a plate to him at the same time."

I almost protested the idea of serving him, but then realized I might need an excuse to be where he was. I followed her to the kitchen to collect a big platter of meat chunks, then went back through the curtain to the large room, which was now torchlit and no longer empty. At least forty men lay about on the pillows, each holding a goblet, some few helping themselves from the platters the three young girls were passing around. The strong, blond *l'lendaa* laughed and spoke with each other, and in the midst of them sat a relaxed Tammad.

I made my way among the men on the floor, trying to be casual but having a hard time of it. The men I passed followed me with their eyes, their appreciation vocal as well as emotional, more than a few of them snatching at the hem of my *caldin*. It came to me then to wonder what would become of me if the barbarian were somehow killed. Those men were nearly the same size as their *denday*, and it struck me hard that the only thing that kept their hands off me was the fact I wore bands. Unbanded, I could have been taken by any or all of them, and the nearest peacemen would be too far away to do any good. I hurried a little, and got to the barbarian as soon as I could.

Tammad looked up as I reached him with the platter, and he gestured toward the low table near him.

"Do you set it there, *wenda*," he directed with a faint grin. I looked in his eyes, and suddenly *knew* that he'd guessed my thoughts about his men. I put the plate down, feeling that I'd lost more ground than I'd gained, and he pulled me to the floor near him. "You must have a care how you deal with me," he murmured in my ear. "Should I be unable to defend my right to you, you would pass to another who has not given his word to return you to your people. Your power would then be of little aid to you, as possession of an offworlder *wenda* would be jealously fought for. Think on it."

He leaned away from me to greet some newcomers, and I did think about it. Needless to say, I didn't like the trend of the thoughts.

In another minute, two men walked in together and came directly over to the barbarian. One of them was a good deal younger than the other, but they were both trim fighting men in their prime. They crouched down near us and grinned.

"*Aldana*, Tammad," the older man said. "It is good that you have returned. Kennan here has been most impatient."

"Aye, *denday*." The one called Kennan grinned. "Though had I known you traveled to band a *wenda* such as this one, I might have traveled with you."

The older man laughed along with Tammad and clapped Kennan on the back. "Truly said, Kennan," he chuckled. "The *wenda* is indeed worth a man's traveling for. Faddan, too, speaks highly of her in the furs. Are there others of her sort in the land which you visited?"

"Many." The barbarian grinned, enjoying the blush on my cheeks. "She and her sisters are unused to the ways of *l'lendaa* and have much to learn, yet should she do well, the others will not prove difficult to take. They live among *darayse* and welcome the appearance of a man."

"So *you* say!" I snapped, finding it impossible not to remember how the women had clustered around him at Jan's party. "My sisters care nothing for great hulking brutes, and would welcome you with the lack of their presence did they but know your purpose!"

The three men laughed at that and the older man said, "She has a sharp tongue, *denday*, and does not seem to enjoy her place as your belonging. Was she taken during battle?"

"No battle, Loddar," the barbarian said, taking a strand of

my hair to toy with. "She was gifted to me by her father, he knowing full well that the *darayse* of his land would not challenge my taking of her. Though broken in body, her father is true *l'lenda*."

"I do not see Rapan," Kennan commented, looking around the room. "She has not taken ill?"

"Rapan remains near her furs," Tammad answered, glancing at the older man. "She insists she will belong to no man, and refuses to join us here."

"Ah, *wendaa*," Loddar sighed, shaking his head. "And she is but the first of my daughters. I wish you joy in the banding of her, Kennan. You may find little joy thereafter."

"Kennan shall not be father to her, Loddar." The barbarian laughed. "Therein lies a great difference."

"True," Loddar grinned, "and a difference all men may appreciate. I shall fetch her, Kennan."

He stood straight again and left the room, and Kennan watched him go with a grin. "I see I shall have little peace for a time," he said to Tammad. "My *wenda*, too, does not come willingly."

"It keeps a man from becoming set in his ways," the barbarian commented, his eyes on me. "Spirited *wendaa* make the struggle more interesting."

"The men of *my* land have more pride than to force themselves where they are not wanted," I put in casually, examining my nails. "Do *l'lendaa* know nothing of pride."

Both men stiffened slightly, then the barbarian shook his head. "Fortunate is this one that she was born *wenda*," he said to Kennan, then tugged at my hair. "Know, would-be warrior, that it is ever a part of *wenda* to challenge the man who would take her. To submit meekly would make her slave, and *l'lendaa* do not care to possess slaves. A man's true match, however, may be taught to accept him in time, and thereafter give herself to him willingly. It would be foolish to expect such acceptance on first meeting."

"I have heard that your *wenda* is called Terril." Kennan chuckled. "Has she also been taught the use of a sword?"

"She must first be taught the lifting of one," the barbarian answered dryly. "Now comes Loddar with your *wenda*."

We all turned to see Loddar coming back through the curtain with a struggling bundle of girl over his brawny shoulder. The other men in the room roared laughter and pointed, and the three other girls stared in reluctant fascination. Loddar brought Rapan over to us, and set her on her feet in front of him, turning her to face Kennan.

"Know, daughter, that this warrior has purchased the right to band you," he said with his hands on her shoulders. "He is called Kennan, and shall take you this night."

"He shall not!" Rapan said stubbornly. "If I may not have the man of my heart, I shall have none at all!"

"The matter is one for *l'lendaa* to decide," Loddar answered her. "*L'lendaa* have decided. You may now band her, Kennan."

Kennan grinned and pulled a small chain from his sword-belt, catching Rapan as she tried to slip away from Loddar's hands. Loddar made no attempt to stop her, nor did he touch her again, but Kennan didn't need his help. He forced the struggling girl to the floor, put his band around her right ankle, then removed the band from her left ankle with one surge of his well developed muscles. He handed the open band to Loddar, then pulled Rapan to her feet.

"Now are you my belonging, Rapan," he said, stroking her long, blond hair. "You shall not regret it."

"I shall give you no pleasure," Rapan said through her teeth. "You will not possess me long!"

"He will possess you as long as he wishes to," Tammad put in from beside me. "Do not forget he is *l'lenda*. Do you use my house as yours, Kennan."

"My thanks, *denday*." Kennan grinned. "I shall do so now."

Kennan took Rapan by the wrist, then headed toward the curtained exit. Rapan was pulled along, but she turned to give Tammad a desperate, pleading look before the curtain closed her from sight. She was feeling miserable and frightened, not nearly as defiant as she'd pretended to be.

Loddar sighed, sat himself down near Tammad, and helped himself to one of a number of goblets that stood on a nearby low table.

"Kennan shall be a good man for her," he said to Tammad, "yet her pleasure may be slow in coming. She pines for you, *denday*, and she is as yet unbroached. Too, Kennan has waited overlong to possess her, and patience comes with greater age than he has yet achieved."

"The matter will be seen to between them," Tammad said quietly. "Should she be his true *wenda*, it shall require the effort of none save them to prove." The two men sat in silence for a minute, then the barbarian tugged harder at my hair. "Come you closer to me, *wenda*," he directed. "I am weary from our travels, and the new sun shall show much work as yet undone."

He pulled me to his chest and folded his arms around me, but I knew it was just camouflage. He had pinched me on the word, "work," reminding me what I was there for. I put Rapan out of my thoughts, closed my eyes, and went to work.

It's sometimes difficult for empaths not to be accidently caught up by and submerged in the sea of emotions always surrounding them, and purposeful submersion is a relief and a release both at the same time. To me, it had always felt like taking a deep breath after ages of being forced to breathe in small, unsatisfying gasps, and I let myself slide into the sea current with a good deal of pleasure. The general sense of emotions swirled and blended and I bathed in it freely, sometimes floating, sometimes swimming against the current. There were so many men there, all feeling relaxed and happy. I touched each lightly, just in passing, moved on to the next, then abruptly stumbled over a well-hidden rock and didn't need to float any longer. Most of the men who saw the barbarian holding me felt amused over it, some with wry, lighthearted envy, but the last man I'd come to felt no lightheartedness. He was forcing complete unconcern, but underneath was a well-controlled mass of jealousy and hate. There was no loyalty there, I knew, and never would be.

I checked the others in the room, finding a man who was scornful of the barbarian, but there was no active hate involved. The rest were unremarkable, lacking criticism of any sort. I withdrew from the sea and opened my eyes again, then decided on a way to announce that the job was done.

"There is very little air in here," I said, sliding quickly out of the barbarian's grasp. "I shall return to my quarters."

I started to get to my feet, but the sash of my *caldin* was pulled hard, throwing me back onto the barbarian's chest.

"You have not been given my permission to leave," he said in a mild tone, faint annoyance tinging his thoughts. "Do you now ask for such permission."

I studied his broad, handsome face for a minute, then said, "The air elsewhere is preferable to that which is here, O *denday*. May I go in search of it?"

A choking sound came from Loddar which was quickly muffled by his hand and turned-away head. The barbarian threw him an annoyed glance, then turned his attention back to me.

"Indeed you may, *wenda*," he answered evenly. "And I shall aid you in your search."

He got to his feet in one fluid motion, pulling me up with him, then headed out of the room, hauling me along behind him by the sash. I had a good chance to look around before the curtains closed behind me, and had no difficulty spotting the two men I'd found earlier. I was pulled all the way back to the barbarian's room, and the door was slammed closed behind us.

"Who's the man sitting directly under that overgrown axe?" I asked before my—"owner" could open his mouth. All of the emotions rolling and building in him stopped abruptly and he frowned down at me.

"That is Caffar," he answered. "Why do you ask?"

"Because he doesn't care for you," I said. "Such deep, strong hatred and jealousy isn't an everyday thing. If I had to bet on someone, it would be him, with the extreme left-hand man in the group of five over on the other side of the room as possible second choice. He thinks he's better than you are, but who knows? He may be right."

Tammad stood for a few moments deep in thought, then finally remembered I was there and nodded at me.

"You have done well," he said quietly. "I had not known it could be accomplished so quickly." He started toward the door, but stopped short of it and turned back to me. "Should you again speak to me as you did this night, *wenda*, you shall feel the switch no matter what the consequences. You have my word."

He continued on out and closed the door behind him, leaving me disgusted and depressed. I hadn't wanted to dig at him, either in front of his people or alone there in the room, but there was something about him that made me want to reach him and jostle him around. I wanted to shake him out of that rigid control and know what he was feeling deep inside him, but all I'd succeeded in doing was to set myself up for another switching. Which would bring me even more trouble when he discovered that I'd been lying about projecting.

I got slowly out of my clothes then into the furs, tired from the long, eventful day. I looked around in the dim torchlight, seeing things that were alien to my way of life, also seeing the empty furs next to mine. Those furs were longer and wider than mine, quite a bit longer and wider. It was foolish of me to want to sleep there instead, as it was obvious I would never fit. I turned my back on them and tried to sleep.

The presence of someone else brought me partway out of a deep, sound sleep. The someone moved around briefly then came closer, and the furs were tucked a little more tightly about me.

"*Wenda sed* Prime," a deep, soft voice murmured tonelessly. "*Ti l'lenda queren?*"

The voice said nothing more, and deep sleep came again.

★ 12 ★

When I woke in the morning, I dressed and went to the kitchen for something to eat. Gilor and the three girls were there, and I had the impression they'd been up for hours. Gilor looked at my hand but didn't change the bandage, and then gave me a large bowl of something thick.

"I do not believe I care for the appearance of this," I said, studying the coarse-grained contents of the bowl. "Is there no meat at hand?"

"The meat is for *l'lendaa*," she said with slight annoyance. "*Wendaa* make do with such as you have. Eat quickly, Terril, as there are many things which must be done this day. The *denday*'s house does not exist of its own."

She turned away to do something else and I watched her for a minute, then looked back at the bowl of thick meal. It wasn't very appetizing, and I'd grown used to having meat for breakfast. Leaving the bowl on the nearest board, I waited until everyone's attention was definitely elsewhere, helped myself to a chunk of meat, then left the kitchen.

The meat wasn't *dimral*, and it was very tasty. I ate it with enjoyment, then went back to the kitchen to refill the water pitcher. Gilor, having noticed the still-full bowl, watched me curiously, but she didn't comment. I had my drink, replaced the pitcher in the barbarian's room, then went outside.

My *seetar* was happy to see me, and I was happy to feel her contentment. She chewed at her own breakfast as I stood near her, and once again I was pushed at gently from behind. The barbarian's mount had come to greet me, but this time he wasn't hungry. He rumbled at me softly, pleased with the calmer tenor of my mind, then turned his attention to my girl. She felt his attention and was puzzled by it, and he was amused.

I stayed with the *seetarr*, brushing first my girl, then the barbarian's male, until they both shone a glossy black. When I finally stepped back to wipe away the sweat and admire my work, the two *seetarr*, understanding that I was through, proceeded to lower themselves to the ground and roll around contentedly. I don't know whether or not they heard my groan, but their comforting thoughts reached me at the same time as the barbarian's laughter.

He stood just outside the corral fence, and it was fairly obvious that he'd been there for some time. His calm thoughts never brought him to my attention when I wasn't seeing him, and I didn't care for it. I resolved to be on the alert for him in the future.

"That is ever the way with *seetarr*." He grinned, letting himself into the corral. "They must be well tied if the brushing is not to be undone."

"From now on they can stay unbrushed," I said sourly, watching the two ingrates grunt and roll around with the deepest of enjoyment. "Who am I to interfere with their contentment?"

"Learning will come to you with experience," he said, looking me over with a critical eye. "You, too, appear to have rolled in the dust. You may bathe in the river when you join the others for the washing of clothing. My warriors will be there to guard you."

"Your warriors can guard whatever they like," I answered, brushing my hair back out of my eyes. "I'll be bathing in my tub in the kitchen."

"The tub has been removed," he said, folding his arms. "You shall bathe in the river or not bathe at all. Here, *I* am *denday*. Do you wish to take my position, you must face me with sword in hand. Is this your wish, O would-be warrior?"

"Why is my bathing in the kitchen a challenge to your position?" I asked in annoyance. "I didn't say *you* had to bathe me!"

"I should not have allowed the tub to begin with," he answered, his tone still even. "Your obedience is not so remarkable as to merit reward. I was taken by the surprise of your power, but shall not allow such to occur again. Do as you will, *wenda*, but know that disobedience shall bring you punishment—as with other *wendaa*. You may bathe in the river, but may not swim. Come you now to the house."

He headed back toward the house and I threw the *seetar* brush away and followed, silently cursing his stubbornness. He was determined to keep me as nothing but *wenda*, and if I tried to disagree he'd reach for the nearest switch. I'd tried to bluff my way out of the corner, but he'd called my bluff and now I had to walk more warily than before. If he ever found out that he'd backed down on nothing but an empty threat—

Gilor was waiting in the entrance hall, and she smiled pleasantly when she saw me, then spoke to the barbarian. "May I now have the use of her, Tammad? There is much to do with Rapan otherwise engaged."

"You may have her, Gilor," he answered with a faint grin, looking me over with a good deal more amusement than he was showing. "Teach her what there is of kitchen work, so that it shall no longer be a mystery to her."

He strode on out through the curtains, and Gilor laughed softly. "You have now found a new place, Terril, yet shall it soon become familiar to you. Come, I shall explain your duties."

She led the way to the kitchen while I seethed quietly. She and the barbarian both were having a grand time at my expense, but it might be possible to disappoint them. The mysteries of a kitchen were ones I had no intentions of reading.

Gilor had me wash off some of the *seetar* smell, then gave me a large bowl filled with some sort of pod vegetable. She showed me how to open the pod to reach the vegetable inside, providing another bowl to hold the shelled results. When she'd watched me do it once and was satisfied, she started to turn away, then changed her mind.

"Terril," she said hesitantly, "during the last sun you spoke of being a—a Prime. I would know the meaning of such."

"It is merely my position in my own land," I answered, inspecting the pod vegetable unenthusiastically. "A position of high respect—and no menial labor."

"I know of such." She nodded, the hesitation immediately gone. "In a manner of speaking, a *wenda denday*. The Revanas to the south are ruled by *wendaa*, and sacrifice all captured *l'lendaa* to them. Yet now are you the belonging of Tammad. Best you forget that which is past, and learn ways of your new land. It is in my mind that the *denday* shall not unband you."

Not until I've done his job for him, I added silently as she walked away. And a job that would not be long in coming. There was no telling how long I would spend at Tammad's house, but it couldn't be too long. The *Ratanan* was soon due to convene.

I spent the next hour or so getting on Gilor's nerves. When she came back to check on the pod vegetables, she found that I'd damaged most of them and had mixed in a fair amount of shell with the vegetable. Her annoyance was of a pleasing intensity, and it didn't take much of a touch to make her pull the whole thing away from me. She tried me on stirring a thick soup next, and was appalled at the amount of soup I managed to slosh onto the floor. After she'd inspected the metal plates and bowls I'd supposedly scrubbed with sand, she gave up altogether.

"I shall inform Tammad that should he wish to have sustenance for his guests, he must find other use for you," she said with her fists on her hips. "It is beyond my comprehension how *wenda* may grow to your size and still have learned nothing. Here, take to him this *trejna* and be gone!"

I took the bowl of stew she thrust at me and escaped, pausing near the curtain to the meeting room only long enough to remove all traces of my grin. Wholehearted cooperation can often get you out of unpleasant situations a good deal faster than stubborn balking.

I pushed the curtain aside to see about a dozen men sitting in a loose semicircle near the barbarian. The men were wearing those robes I'd noticed earlier, and most of them held piles of cured animal skins and pieces of charcoal. One of the men to the barbarian's right was speaking to him.

". . . and should the raids continue, *denday*, I shall have nothing for the people of our city," he said firmly. "How may my caravans arrive intact when the savages are allowed to ride unmolested?"

"I shall have a number of my warriors accompany your next caravan, Voldar," the barbarian answered. "And should there be the need, we shall ride out in full strength at the conclusion of the *Ratanan*. We cannot survive without the caravans."

"It is good you have returned, *denday*," another of them said. "As merchants, we must have the support of warriors if we are to see our city live and grow, but not many of the *l'lendaa* are able to speak with us without insult, uninten-

tional as it may be. To be merchant does not make a man
darayse."

"You yourself are proof of that, Naggas." The barbarian
grinned. "Though a merchant these many years, you still remain true *l'lenda*. It is good for a man to show others that
new ways may be learned with ease."

"Less with ease than with hard work." Naggas laughed.
"Though there is much to commend the life of *l'lenda*, still
do I find the many demands of a merchant's life more fascinating. And you, Tammad, have done exceedingly well as
denday of our city, far better than the *denday* who was."

"The man knew little of a city's needs." The barbarian
shrugged. "We are fortunate that he knew equally little of the
use of a sword. Bring the *trejna* here, *wenda*. I would taste it
before the mold sets in."

The other men chuckled, and I realized I'd just been standing there listening. As I carried the bowl toward him, I tried
to control the light blush on my cheeks, but couldn't seem to
do it. I always did *something* wrong in front of him.

"A *wenda* worth the banding," the man Naggas commented in approval as he stared at me. "Should you tire of this
one as you did the others, Tammad, I would buy her from
you."

"Best you bear in mind what you have learned as a merchant, Naggas." The barbarian grinned. "The most attractive
bolt of cloth may be useless for practical purposes. This one
shall take much teaching yet before she is worth the banding—if ever she is worth it."

"You misbegotten son of strangers," I choked as the merchants laughed. As if I were there because I'd asked to be! I
took the bowl of *trejna* and threw it at him with all my
strength, then turned and ran from the room.

I slammed the sleep room door behind me and went to the
window, totally unable to control the misery I felt. "Useless"
he'd called me, and it wouldn't have hurt nearly so much if it
hadn't been true. On Central, I was respected as a Prime; on
Rimilia, I was useless. I put my hand on one of the window
bars, and the gleaming, bronze-colored wrist band caught my
eye. I looked around, saw an empty dagger sheath on the
floor in the corner, went and got it quickly, then forced it under the band. If I pushed hard enough, the band would open,
and I didn't care how much it hurt as long as the bands were
off!

"No," the barbarian said, suddenly right behind me. "The bands shall stay as they are."

He twisted the dagger sheath out of my hand, making me furious. "What for?" I demanded harshly. "I'm obviously not fit to wear them. Go and find a kitchen queen to band and leave me alone! And I don't care if you beat me for throwing things at you. If I ever get another chance, I'll do it again!"

"You shall not be beaten," he said gently, holding me against him in spite of my struggles. "Do you not know, warrior, that it is fitting for a man to speak well of another man's *wenda*, but not of his own? It was not my intention to give you insult, yet I had forgotten how deep ran your pride. I ask your pardon."

"Just leave me alone," I repeated in a whisper, not even struggling any longer. "Take your bands and your furs, and forget about me until it's time for me to do my job. I'll sit in a back room somewhere and not bother anybody."

"You shall remain in my bands as well as my furs," he said softly, stroking my hair. "All know of your presence, yet even had they not known, I would not allow you to do such a thing. It would not be fitting."

He picked me up then and carried me to his furs, and it was impossible not to respond to him. He echoed my projection more strongly than ever, showing that my projection was stronger than it had been, which wasn't surprising. He finally left me there in the furs, and when he was gone I had the usual trouble moving.

The upset reached me before I was physically aware of anyone's presence. I turned my head to see Rapan in the doorway, and she stared at me, shaking her head.

"I do not understand," she said in confusion. "Had he just visited me, I would be wrapped in bliss, yet you seem less happy even than I. Does it mean nothing to you that you wear his bands?"

"Wearing his bands means more than you know," I answered bitterly. "Were it possible, I would gift them all to you, then *you* might have the pain of his touch."

"There is none more gentle than Tammad!" she said indignantly, holding her head angrily high. "His every word and gesture, the wisdom of his ways—none may compare! Though Kennan's touch was pain to begin with, even *he* has gentleness within him. Am I to believe the *denday* is less than Kennan?"

"You may believe as you wish," I said tiredly. "A man need not be concerned with being gentle with one whom he cares nothing for. He keeps me in his bands and furs as a monument to the fitting. For all else, I am useless."

She started again, unable to understand or answer me, then said, "Gilor bade me fetch you to a meal. Afterward, we go to the river to wash clothing and bathe. You are to come now."

You are to come now. There was always something to do or somewhere to go on *that* world. I got to my feet, straightened the *imad* and *caldin*, then followed her to the kitchen. Gilor looked at me and frowned, then gestured toward a bowl of *trejna* without saying anything. I took the bowl, ate what I could of the *trejna*, then left the rest and picked up my pile of dirty clothing. Beneath the two sets of *imad* and *caldin* was a familiar looking brown *haddin*, which made me wonder how strong the river current was.

When everyone was finished eating, we took our bundles of wash to the front door, where a half-dozen *l'lendaa* were waiting to escort us. A small dirt road to the right of the main road led to the river, and Rapan and the other girls walked ahead, the girls whispering question after question, Rapan answering each casually and with a shrug. The *l'lendaa* followed along a short distance behind Gilor and me, and Gilor chuckled.

"The others ask Rapan of Kennan," she said softly to me. "They, too, look forward to first banding, and have great curiosity. Is it not so with all *wendaa?*"

"It is not so in my land." I shrugged. "My friends and I chose our first men casually, knowing there was little difference between them. It mattered not which we chose first."

"And now you yourself have been chosen, and it matters a great deal," she murmured. "Tammad is *l'lenda*, and shall do with you as he pleases. It is this which disturbs you, is it not?"

"I care nothing for what pleases your *denday*," I said, kicking a small stone down the road ahead of me. "He deems me useless, and I would be free of his bands and gone from the sight of him."

"He does not deem you useless in all ways," she commented, looking at me from the sides of her eyes. "I have rarely seen him in such high spirits as when he left you earlier, yet you do not share his high spirits. Is it possible to give a man such pleasure and yet be untouched yourself?"

"I am touched," I answered heavily. "I am touched with pain as always. Why must he take me so hard, Gilor? Though he cares nothing for me, is it beyond him to see what he does to me? He sees the pain of others, so why does he not see mine?"

"Do you show pain in his sight?" she asked gently, shifting the things she carried to her left arm so she could put the right one around my shoulders. Her compassion was strong, and I wanted to cling to it the way the *tenna* had clung to me. "From the little I have seen, Terril, you show him nothing of your pain. A man often loses himself in the enjoyment of his *wenda*—the deeper his enjoyment, the deeper is he lost. Yet Tammad is a man who would guard himself did he but know of your difficulty. Why do you not speak to him of it?"

"And be deemed more useless still?" I asked. "I would sooner have the pain than ease it in such a manner. I have shown him weakness too many times to wish to add to it."

"There is no shame in showing weakness." She smiled softly. "It is one of the ways *wendaa* are more fortunate than *l'lendaa*. It is for *l'lendaa* to be strong come what may; we need not be troubled by so foolish a thing. To be free to show weakness brings a strength of its own."

"Strength," I echoed, staring at the small clouds of dust our feet kicked up. "Once I, too, had strength. Now it is gone, taken from me by the one who has taken *me*. Soon I shall be returned to my own land. Will my strength be returned also?"

"A woman gives her strength to the man she favors." Gilor smiled more broadly, squeezing me. "In such a way may she then share his strength. Tammad shall not unband you as quickly as you believe, Terril. I have seen him many times with *wendaa* he has banded, yet never has he seemed so satisfied. He shall keep you long, I think, and perhaps allow you to bear his child. It is a great honor to bear the child of a *denday*."

"Bear his what?" I asked in shock, staring at her wide-eyed. "I shall do nothing of the sort!"

"The choice is his." She laughed contentedly. "Should he wish you to have his child, you shall have it within you in spite of your protests. Have you never borne a man's child?"

"Never!" I answered with a shudder. I knew the man was a barbarian, but to do something like that! Happily, I was well protected, and would remain protected until I was safely back on Central.

We heard the sound of *seetar* hooves, and turned to see twenty *l'lendaa* riding up the main road toward the far end of the town. After thinking about them for a minute, I decided that they were road guards like the ones we'd passed on the way into town. There hadn't been a sign of them showing, but I'd hardly been able to miss the alert attention of so many minds. The town looked to be wide-open and undefended, but that wasn't the case.

We reached the river after another few minutes of walking, and there wasn't anyone else in sight. Gilor mentioned with a grin that they usually went earlier, but the *denday* could not be denied his enjoyment. The guarding *l'lendaa* laughed at that and looked at me, and the young girls giggled. All, that is, but Rapan. She just took her clothes and began washing them.

When all the clothes were washed—with soft, lumpy soap that Gilor had brought along—it was time to bathe. Three of the *l'lendaa* had their backs to us, eyes moving constantly in all directions, hands resting lightly on weapons, but the other three stood with folded arms and lazy grins, staring straight at us. The *wendaa* didn't seem to notice the stares; they just stripped happily before slipping into the water. I did the same but more quickly, wondering if there really was danger around. *Wenda* guard detail could always be a reward for good behavior.

I used some of the harsh, lumpy soap in my hair, then relaxed a bit and just soaked. I was disturbed slightly by what Gilor had said about the barbarian's satisfaction, but finally decided that she was wrong. He was pleased with me in the furs and in my job capacity, but he wouldn't dare try keeping me after the *Ratanan*. I wasn't just any stray girl, I was a Prime! He couldn't decide to keep me in his bands and in his house forever. Bracing myself against the river current, I made myself believe that.

The *l'lendaa* didn't let us bathe long as the river was higher than normal due to all the rain that had fallen. The current wasn't impossibly strong, but the other women didn't know how to swim and the men were nervous. I climbed out with reluctance and dressed quickly, sneering at myself for not swimming in spite of the barbarian's orders. Myself sneered back with a very vivid picture of the switch that would have

been used on me, and asked dryly how well I would have
been able to control the pain *during* the switching. I said
nothing to that, but added the question to the rest of my wor-
ries.

When we got back to the house, we went around to the
rear and spread the wet clothes over tightly stretched pieces
of netting, then weighted the corners of the clothes down
with rocks. I thought we'd be going back into the house then,
but only Rapan went in. The rest of us followed Gilor
around the house to the main road, and from there into the
town.

There were just as many people about as had been the last
time, and we made our way slowly through the crowds.
There were many women there, some alone, some with men,
but the majority of them had small children either in their
arms or by one hand, and some had both. I found myself
curious about the older children, but seeing one of the men
with a boy about seven and a girl about eight reminded me
of another of their customs. The women looked after the children until they were about five, then the men took over their
training, boy and girl alike. The women bore children for
their men, but the children belonged solely to the men. If a
woman was sold after having a man's child, the child did not
go with her.

"See you there," Gilor said softly to me, nodding toward a
woman who wore two usual bands and also a leather headband. The woman was well advanced in pregnancy, but
moved her swollen body easily. "That *wenda* swore to us all
that never would she bear a man's child; she now carries his
third, just as reluctantly as the first two. The *l'lenda* to whom
she belongs cares more for the getting of his children than for
her humor. Should he find a more willing and attractive
woman, he will sell her, yet until he does, she acts as she is
bidden. The choice ever beongs to *l'lendaa*."

"There are some choices even beyond *l'lendaa*," I answered
with a good deal of satisfaction. "Why does she wear the
band about her hair?"

"The headband is to show that she is with child," Gilor explained. "There are *l'lendaa* who would buy a woman with
child sooner than one who is not. It is proof that the woman
is not barren."

"Your ways are exceedingly strange to me," I admitted.
"On our journey here, your *denday* and I were joined by one

of the *l'lendaa* and his *wenda*. The *l'lenda* asked the *denday* to honor him by using his *wenda*. I was told that the *l'lenda* hoped to see his woman with child by the *denday*, but he was given no more than the single opportunity. Should she indeed find herself with child, how are they to know if the child is truly that of the *denday*, or merely of the *l'lenda* himself?"

"Tammad rarely needs further opportunity." Gilor laughed. "Yet it matters not. The child shall be considered as belonging to the *l'lenda*, and shall be watched carefully for signs of greatness. Should the signs become apparent, the child may claim kinship to the *denday* and thereby further himself. The *l'lenda* shall have the honor of raising the child, and thereby gain greater stature. In such a thing, there is satisfaction for all."

"Strange," I repeated, shaking my head. "There is much to think upon here. Where do we go now, Gilor?"

"We go to replenish the stores of the *denday*," she answered. "Other *l'lendaa* may hunt and trap for the *dinga* to buy that which they wish to have, or they may sell the use of their swords to the city in return for the *dinga*. Tammad is too burdened with the problems of all, and therefore must have his needs supplied without *dinga*. The merchants give willingly, glad that he is there to aid them. We go first for the vegetables our own gardens do not produce."

We made our way into a building that had shelves and boxes filled with vegetables of all sorts. Gilor picked and chose what she wanted then led the way out again. I'd never seen a building filled with food like that, and it was an odd sight. My own house's chef had the food delivered to it already cooked and placed in stasis. The chef had only to remove the stasis field and deliver the dish. I'd once, as a child, seen raw food, but in nothing like the quantity that that building had held.

We made the rounds of all the food buildings, passing now and then at the stalls that held cloth and jewelry. There was finer cloth than that which our *imadd* and *caldinn* were made of, and the women stared at it lovingly. I had the feeling that the cloth was ours for the asking, but Gilor didn't ask. She just sighed a little, then went on to the next building.

We got back to the barbarian's house loaded down with packages, but I was wearier than carrying them around accounted for. I'd had to spend a good deal of energy defending myself from the people of the town, and I wasn't used to

it. Men and women alike seemed to know who I was, and the
feelings of desire and envy and curiosity had almost been
staggering. I'd noticed that very, very few of the women were
even four-banded, let alone five, and that seemed to add
something to the emotional overtones. I felt pale with my efforts, and the relative peace of the house was very welcome.

Meat and vegetables were put up quickly to cook, and Gilor set me to putting clean goblets on trays. I did it automatically, encouraging my inner self to relax and regather
strength, and by the time the food was ready I'd almost come
back to normal. Rapan came in, saying that Tammad and
Kennan were ready to eat, and that she and I were to join
them. Two platters were given to each of us, one of the girls
coming along to carry the goblets. The men were alone in the
meeting room and were naturally served first, then Rapan
and I were able to sit and eat.

Kennan and the barbarian were in a good mood, joking
with each other as they ate. They each listed all sorts of defi-
ciencies in their respective *wendaa*, but with big grins and
broad winks. Rapan blushed and looked down at her food,
but I stared at the men and weighed my plate in my hand.
The barbarian got the message and laughingly changed the
subject.

When all the food was eaten, the two men drank briefly
from their goblets, then stood up, inspecting Rapan and me
lazily. Rapan got quickly to her feet too, but I stood more
slowly, wondering what the men were up to. Kennan felt a
strong sense of expectation, and the barbarian was controlling
himself firmly.

"Kennan and I have spoken," the barbarian announced
with his usual calm. "I have been asked to honor my guest,
and have agreed to do so. In return, I have gifted to my guest
the use of my own *wenda*, whom he shall use as his until the
return of his. Rapan, you are to come with me."

Rapan was delirious in her excitement, but the announce-
ment affected me differently. He always seemed to be taking
one woman or another with him, palming me off on the man
who was *wenda*less. I said, "The *denday* may take all of the
city to his furs, but I grow weary of *l'lendaa* without end.
Find another to console Kennan. I have no interest in him."

I started to turn away, but Kennan grabbed my arm in his
oversized hand. "The *denday* has spoken, Terril." He grinned.

"You are mine until Rapan is returned to me. Come you now and show the proper respect."

"Respect for whom?" I snorted. "There are none about worthy of respect!" I waited until the flash of anger loosened his grip the least little bit, then pulled away and ran out of the room. I could feel him right behind me, but I wasn't running aimlessly. I went straight out the back door, across the twenty feet, and into the corral.

My *seetar* was on her way to me even before I'd shut the corral gate. She knew that something was upsetting me, and she was concerned and angry. I met her a short distance away from the gate, leaning against her huge side as she nuzzled my shoulder comfortingly. I'd sleep with the *seetarr* if I had to, but I would not go with Kennan. Just because that barbarian periodically tired of *me* didn't mean that I wanted to go searching for new talent, too. And Gilor had been so certain about his satisfaction. A lot *she* knew.

The corral gate opened again almost immediately, showing Kennan standing there. He was as big as all *l'endaa* and his annoyance was completely in proportion to his size, but I had an ally of my own and my ally made Kennan look small. He started toward me without hesitation, but a snort and deep rumble from my *seetar* made him falter, then stop altogether.

"Come you here, *wenda*!" he ordered sternly. "You must emerge from there at some time, so this action avails you naught! The *denday* has gifted you to me for the present, and with me you shall be!"

"The *denday* may fill your furs himself," I called in answer. "I shall not! Think you to deal with this *wenda* I stand beside as easily as you deal with Rapan? You may make the attempt if you wish, Kennan, but I shall not leave here!"

Kennan put angry fists on his hips, but I was answered from another quarter. "You *shall* leave here, *wenda*," the barbarian said as he came into the corral behind Kennan. Rapan stayed at the fence and watched us all wide-eyed.

The barbarian started toward me, ignoring the warning rumble of my *seetar*, slapping his hand sharply against his thigh. Suddenly his saddle mount appeared next to him, and the big male let his nose be rubbed with a good deal of satisfaction, then joined his rider in advancing toward me.

It all happened so quickly, I barely had time to see it, let alone anticipate it. I stood to my *seetar*'s left, and the barbarian walked to his *seetar*'s right. When the two males were

three feet away, my *seetar* charged the man with a squeal of
rage, but the male *seetar* moved unbelievably fast to block
her. The man darted around the two *seetarr*, grabbed me before I could even blink, threw me up on his shoulder, then
raced out of the corral. His male was having a hard time
stopping my female without hurting her, and when Kennan
slammed the gate closed behind us, the male *seetar* simply
got out of the way. My female came crashing into the fence,
but the heavy, reinforced wood held her weight, and she was
helpless to keep the barbarian from carrying me back into the
house.

I was taken to his sleeping room, and wasn't put back on
my feet until the door was closed firmly behind us. The barbarian stood and studied me, so I folded my arms and stared
back at him.

"Again you disobey me," he said with a curious lack of anger. "Kennan shall have you for as long as I have Rapan."

"The *Ratanan* will be long since forgotten before *she* gives
you up," I snorted. "I didn't come here to settle down with
Kennan."

"I am aware that you came only to serve me, *wenda*." He
grinned, enjoying the double or triple meaning. "Yet there
are other services to be performed, and you shall obey me in
all things. Return to Kennan and ask his pardon."

"I won't do it," I said with a headshake. "Why do you always have to include me in your bed-hopping? If you want
me out of the way, just say so. I wouldn't dream of interfering in your—affairs of honor."

"The matter with Rapan is more important than it seems,"
he said softly, coming over to run his hand over my back
beneath the *imad*. I shivered slightly and moved away, but he
just grinned a little. "Sooner would I have *you* in my furs,
l'lenda-wenda, yet I must wait until Rapan is seen to. I cannot give her child, but must do all possible to give her
freedom from the attraction she still feels for me, if not for
her sake, then for Kennan's. Go you now to Kennan in
obedience to my word."

"I refuse," I answered, steeling myself for the beating I
knew was coming. I would not go willingly to *any l'lenda*.

The barbarian shook his head with a sigh, then took my
wrist and towed me out of the room. Kennan and Rapan
stood a short way down the hall, and we stopped in front of
them.

"My *wenda* is now yours," he said to Kennan, pulling me closer to the big *l'lenda*. "You have my permission to punish her lightly for the insult she gave you. It is more fitting than punishment at my hand."

"The insult shall be totally wiped away." Kennan grinned, getting a good grip on my arm. "Come, Terril, and we shall discuss the giving of insult—and its consequences. Rapan, go you with Tammad."

Kennan dragged me back up the hall past the barbarian's room, and I turned once to see the barbarian standing there watching us, seemingly totally oblivious to Rapan who gazed up at him lovingly. Once again, someone else had gentleness to look forward to, while all I had in store was punishment. I looked away from the man who had put me in chains, and didn't look back again.

Kennan's sleeping room was no different from the barbarian's. He threw me down on his sleeping furs, then crouched to tell me what would have happened to me had I been male and spoken as I had. He didn't leave out the least gory detail, and when he was through, he stood again to remove his *haddin*.

"Rejoice that you be *wenda*, Terril," he summed up, throwing the *haddin* from him. "You may not lose your life through insult, yet still shall you regret your words. The *darayse* of your land do not dwell in ours."

He caught me as I tried for the door, then proceeded to make me regret what I'd said. My *imad* and *caldin* were quickly removed, and he used me as *l'lendaa* do, but he also used me in the most embarrassing and humiliating of ways. I was helpless to stop him, my tears of frustration and shame simply giving him greater pleasure. He felt himself morally right, and there was nothing that would change his mind.

I lay in misery next to him as he rested, asking myself what he would do next, when the door to the room flew open and Rapan ran in. She threw herself into his arms sobbing wildly, and his surprise was genuine.

"Rapan, what ails you?" he asked, holding her tight to comfort her. "What has happened?"

"Take me away from here!" she begged, trying to get even closer to him. "I had thought him gentle, but Terril spoke truly! He—he—caused me such pain, Kennan! Please take me away!"

"As quickly as I am clad," he assured her with a gentle

hug, then disengaged himself from her viselike grip. He dressed fast, added his swordbelt, then helped her to her feet and out of the room. His emotions were tender concern, great happiness, and deep gratitude. He had also completely forgotten about me.

I tried to soothe down my own emotions, but often that's too much like a medic trying to fix a wound on his own back. I could calm myself in times of crisis, but ordinary emotional upheaval was too much to work through. My own emotions blocked my control, and made the effort a waste of time.

"So Terril spoke truly," a quiet voice said from behind me. "And why did Terril not say to me that which she said to others?"

"Would it have made a difference?" I asked tonelessly, not even turning to look at him. "What do you care about what happens to me as long as I'm here and healthy enough to attend the *Ratanan*? I'm a useless female, wearing your bands only because you have no other choice. *Ahresta wenda*."

"You are not *ahresta*!" he said angrily. "If you were truly unwanted and kept only out of pity, five bands would not be necessary. I have already been asked many times if I have tired of you as yet! Such does not occur with *ahresta wenda*!"

"That's only because they don't know," I said, lowering my cheek to the furs. "Maybe if you give me away often enough, they'll begin to believe you."

"It was my duty as host to gift you to Kennan," he said harshly, moving toward me. "Also you must learn to soften your words with *l'lenda* lest they take insult! Too long have you been used to the men of your world who—"

He had unexpectedly crouched down to turn me to face him, and my gasp cut his sentence short. I'd been unprepared for the sudden movement, and the pain had gotten away from me. I controlled it quickly, but not before he had seen.

"What has been done to you?" he demanded with a frown, looking me over carefully. "Kennan was told he might punish you lightly. Did he mistake my meaning?"

"He understood," I told him stiffly. "What he did wouldn't have hurt so much if it hadn't been for—"

"My use of you earlier," he finished heavily when I didn't. "It is now completely clear to me why you seek comfort and protection from *seetarr*. You have no *l'lenda* you may turn to. Lie still until the pain has passed."

He stretched out next to me and took me gently in his arms, stroking my hair soothingly. When I felt him trying to project safety and peace at me I could have cried—particularly because that's exactly what I did feel just then. He held me as if I meant something to him, and in spite of the pain I understood Rapan's comment about bliss. I was almost lost between his giant arms and mighty chest; but I never wanted to be found again.

The pain eventually eased as most pain does, and I told him so because I felt he had something else he was waiting to do. It was cold when he took his arms away, and I dressed quickly as he stood there, then followed him out into the hall. He hesitated near the door to his sleeping room, but made up his mind fast and threw the door open.

"Go you now to your furs," he directed. "I would have had you with me at the meeting this night, but it is not necessary. It is more important that you rest."

For the *Ratanan*, I thought, and straightened up a little. "I'm all right," I told him. "What did you want done at the meeting?"

"Will you never learn to obey my word?" he asked with fists on hips. "You were told to seek your furs, and you had best do so lest *I* seek my switch! Go you *now*!"

His thoughts were as hard as his tone of voice, so I went into the room without further comment. He stood and waited again until I was between the furs, then he came and tucked them closer before going out and closing the door behind him.

I lay very still after the door had closed, because his action with the furs had triggered a half memory. I remembered someone tucking me in before, and I was sure it had been he. He'd said something that other time, and it took a few minutes before I had the words back, then I was shocked.

"*Wenda sed* Prime," he'd said. "*Ti l'lenda queren?*" "A woman who is called *Prime*. How may a warrior contend with such?"

I couldn't believe it, but it had to be true! There had been such a strong feeling of longing to go with the words that I was surprised I could have forgotten it. He wanted me, but felt that I was beyond him, out of his reach. And thinking that *he* was too good for *me*, I'd taunted him and called him—barbarian. His patience with me, his protection of me, the times he'd apologized—never once had I apologized to him, yet *I* had called *him* barbarian!

I searched for his calm control, wanting to go to him, but found his familiar pattern among many others. I lay back in the furs, remembering the meeting and cursing it soundly. Why did he have to be among so many men just at *that* time? It wasn't fair, but very few things are fair. I'd just have to wait until he got back.

The furs were very soft and comfortable. I waited for him to come back until my eyes closed of their own accord.

 ★ 13 ★

When I woke in the morning, I stretched lazily then groaned when I realized that Tammad was gone again. I had a faint memory of his holding me as we both slept, but he hadn't awakened me and he hadn't touched me otherwise. I dressed quickly, determined to find him, but his pattern was nowhere in the house, so I went to the kitchen instead to find Gilor.

"Where has Tammad gone?" I asked as soon as I saw her. She was patiently stirring a big kettle of something and didn't answer immediately.

"The *denday* has gone about his business," she finally said. "He has instructed me that you are to rest this day, eat well, and be given no work. For one who cares nothing for you, he is indeed generous."

"Have *you* never been in error?" I asked defensively. "He keeps close to himself and does not allow his feelings to reach me, but now the truth is known to me. Gilor, what may I do for him?"

"You may obey him." She laughed, looking over at me with happiness in her eyes. "You are to eat, rest, and do no work."

"But I wish to *do* something for him!" I protested. "Is there no plate to carry, no *haddin* to be washed, no—"

I broke off and closed my eyes, feeling the meager list of useless, menial chores echo and ache inside of me. There was nothing I *could* do for him that other women couldn't do ten times better. I was still useless, and couldn't imagine why he would want me.

"Do not let sadness touch you," Gilor said gently and compassionately, coming over to put her arm around me. "That he cares for you is the telling point. All else may be easily seen to and learned by one who is willing. Are you now willing?"

I looked at her, understanding that my "cooperative" assistance of the day before hadn't fooled her, then nodded my head. I might be left with no unburned skin on my hands, but I'd do my damnedest to learn.

"Good," she said and patted my shoulder. "I shall be pleased to teach you that which you must know the moment Tammad gives his permission. This day you must eat and rest, therefore shall you take a bowl and begin to do so."

She dippered out a bowlful of thick whatever and handed it to me, and I could see there was no sense in arguing with her. She was not about to disobey Tammad, and her mind was firm. I took the bowl glumly, used the small scoop—and felt my eyebrows rise at the taste. It was coarse and gritty, but it had a light, sweet flavor unlike anything I'd ever eaten. I emptied the bowl quickly, but had it taken firmly out of my hands when I tried to clean it. Gilor was annoyed, and I was banished from the kitchen.

I wandered around for a while, bored by total inactivity, then went outside. My *seetar* waited anxiously at the corral gate, and I hastened to assure her that I was all right. She half-sensed my still twisting emotions and snorted dubiously, but calmed down enough to lie in the sunny grass where I could sit too and lean against her. I relaxed in the sun with partially closed eyes, trying to arrange my thinking into something resembling lucidity. When Tammad's male came over hesitantly, I stroked the nose he put in my lap without really seeing it.

I spent the rest of the day with the *seetarr*, and there wasn't a sign of Tammad. I tried to go with the other women when they left for the river, but one of the *l'lendaa* marched me firmly back into the house. The *denday* had left word that I wasn't to go to the river, and there was no arguing them out of it. I managed to avoid insulting anyone, but I was left with such a sour mood that I took some meat to nibble on and went back to the *seetarr*. For the rest of the afternoon I wondered why everyone else found it so easy obeying the *denday*, while I always had such difficulty. Maybe it was a matter of point of view.

At sundown I went back to the house, knowing in advance that Tammad hadn't yet returned. Gilor wrinkled her nose when I got within sniffing distance, and immediately sent for the large wooden tub. I didn't want a bath just then, but I got one anyway, as well as a lecture on what a man dislikes in a woman. As the strong smell of *seetar* was high on the list of dislikes, Gilor was not about to let me hurt my own cause.

After I was dry, brushed, and into clean clothes, I was allowed to eat. I crouched near one of the sputtering kitchen torches, eating mechanically and staring out into the night. It was quiet and peaceful outside, warm and comfortable inside, and not much different from Central. Oh, there were a lot of broad differences, but specific items like sky and trees and food and shelter were all the same. It was not difficult thinking myself home.

When the meal was finished, Gilor came by to take the plate and tell me it was time to sleep. I flatly refused to budge from the spot until Tammad got back, and she just shrugged and walked away. Five minutes later Bollan took her place, and there was no refusing with him. He might have been older than most of the other men I'd seen, but he was still straight and tall, and he was still *l'lenda*. He escorted me to Tammad's sleeping room, waited with folded arms until I'd undressed, then quietly shut the door.

I lay in the furs, determined to stay awake this time until Tammad came back, and I wasn't sleepy enough to lose control. I waited half the night, but he never did show up.

"Time to awaken, small warrior," a voice murmured in my ear. I knew immediately who it was, and couldn't help smiling.

"About time you got back," I mumbled, putting my arms around his neck. "What took so long?"

"The preparations were many." He chuckled, putting his hands somewhere other than near my neck. "All is now complete, and we must be on our way. The *Ratanan* comes whether we attend or no."

"The *Ratanan*?" I said, trying to sit up straight. "Are we leaving today?"

"If ever you arise," he said, moving back to look at me. "Was my word obeyed during the last sun?"

"For the most part," I hedged. "I didn't know we were leaving today. You could have told me."

"There was no need for you to be told," he answered, watching as I got into the *imad* and *caldin*. "Had you obeyed my word, you would have been properly prepared. Come you now for something to eat. We leave as soon as we are done."

He straightened from his crouch and led the way to the kitchen, where a sleepy-looking Gilor was waiting with a bowl of thick whatever for me and a chunk of spiced meat for him. I ate the whatever without comment, but much of its flavor disappeared in the face of the meat. The good part about the upcoming trip was that I, too, would soon have meat for breakfast. Thick whatever is not enough to face the day on.

We went out the front of the house to find a double line of fifty *l'lendaa* already mounted and waiting for us in the just-dawn chirping. There were a good number of pack-*seetarr* on leather leads, and quite a few of the *l'lendaa* had women mounted behind them. Tammad's big male was saddled and ready, and Tammad walked up to him.

"A moment," I said quietly, putting my hand on his arm. "I do not see my *seetar* here."

"Nor shall you," he answered, checking the saddle straps. "That one is too easily enraged to be taken along." He turned, lifted me by the waist, and set me down on the saddle fur. "Your place is there, and there you shall stay."

He was up into the saddle before I could even begin to argue, and then we were off down the road. I was so annoyed I just held onto his swordbelt with my fingers as the rest of the party moved off with us, but after a few minutes I put my arms around his waist and leaned against him. His pleasure was so apparent that it made me glad my *seetar* wasn't there.

We stopped for lunch by the side of the road, and the *dimral* was passed around. *Dimral* isn't as good as the spiced meat Gilor makes, but it stands up to spoilage better, and is almost always used when traveling. Some of the *l'lendaa* came over to eat with Tammad, and there was a lot of good-natured joking around. When the food had been finished and everyone started back to his own *seetar*, one of the men paused near Tammad.

"My *wenda* feels certain that the night shall produce the desired results, *denday*," he grinned, slapping Tammad on the shoulder. "Again I must thank you for honoring me."

Tammad grinned back and turned to lift me to the saddle fur, not missing the narrow-eyed look I gave him. His grin broadened as he climbed into the saddle, but when I muttered, "Preparations, huh?" he laughed out loud. He continued to laugh when I resolutely put my fingers back in his swordbelt, and stubbornly refused to stop until I held him around the waist again.

I'd expected us to camp in the woods that night, but sundown came close and there was no sign of our stopping. Just at dark the column paused, and one of the *l'lendaa* rode up to us to hand Tammad a bundle of material. Tammad took it and turned off into the woods, leaving the rest of the column on the road.

"You shall wear this *imad* and *caldin*," he said, handing me the bundle when we were out of sight of the column. "The *Ratanan* ground is not far ahead of us, and I wish you to have the status of *rella wenda*. Thus shall you be able to enter the *dendarsa camtah* with me."

I nodded and let him slide me to the ground, then started changing clothes. The *imad* and *caldin* were brand new, of a soft, rich-feeling material, and I knew the colors would be bright and compelling. *Rella wendaa* were not for breeding but for showing off, and only some of the most prominent leaders had them. If being a *rella wenda* would gain me entrance to the *denday*'s tent, then I would be a *rella wenda*. It was better than sneaking up on the outside of the *dendarsa camtah*.

I found a pair of buskins in the center of the bundle, and put those on, too. It seemed so long since the last time I'd worn shoes of any sort that the buskins felt strange to my feet. I rolled up the old *imad* and *caldin*, and handed them up to Tammad.

"Before we continue on, I have one question," I said as he swung me up behind him. "You have a habit of telling me nothing I don't need to know on the spot, so let me be as general as possible. Is there *anything* that I'll need to know once we reach the *Ratanan* grounds? Having surprises sprung on me doesn't make for good working conditions."

"There is nothing that comes to mind," he said, thinking about it carefully. "Should you find something you do not understand, ask me and I shall explain. I do not wish you to be at a disadvantage."

"Fair enough," I agreed, and we headed back toward the column. When we reached it, we all continued up the road, and in less than an hour came to the *Ratanan* ground.

The area was to the left of the road in a broad, clear field that stretched for miles. Hundreds of *camtahh* were pitched in the field in groups, and in the midst of each large group was an oversized *camtah,* more a pavilion than anything else. It was too dark to count the exact number of pavilions, but there should have been twenty-four, one for each of the other twenty-four towns represented. Tammad and his people made the twenty-fifth, but the *Ratanan* would have begun on time even if some of the twenty-five hadn't been there.

The separate groups were dotted with campfires, which made it easier to see where we were going. We made our way between two of the groups, the *l'lendaa* of each group coming out to greet Tammad as we passed, then reached a wide, empty space. Most of our *l'lendaa* began choosing places to dismount, but five of them, all without *wendaa*, stayed near Tammad as he changed direction slightly for a pavilion that was even larger than the others, and also stood alone. There were *l'lendaa* standing near it, and we stopped among them.

"*Aldana,* Tammad, *aldana!*" many of them called with broad grins, then came closer as I was swung to the ground. "You are a welcome sight, as is your *wenda.* There are few about to equal her."

"Aye, Hannas." Tammad laughed as he dismounted. "She is comely to a small degree. Is Rommar as yet in attendance?"

"He sits within," the one called Hannas answered with his own laugh. "Besides him, one may also see his *rella wenda.* Garrad will be pleased at your arrival."

All the *l'lendaa* within hearing laughed aloud at that, which made me curious. There was some amusement they were sharing, and I wondered what it could be.

Tammad removed his swordbelt, handed it, along with the extra dagger, to one of his *l'lendaa,* then went toward the pavilion entrance. I followed behind, feeling the itch of what I usually called a hunch. It was more a matter of receiving definite signals, and worked a good deal more accurately when I was awakened. I had the feeling that my presence there had been well planned for, and would not arouse undue curiosity where it shouldn't be aroused. It would be interesting to see if I was right.

Tammad pushed the entrance hanging aside, and the light from the interior spilled out into the night. He opened it only wide enough to let himself step through, then stood there for a moment, to let his eyes adjust, I thought. There were greetings called to him from within the pavilion, and I stopped just behind him, feeling the patterns of many men, but not able to see them. Then he stepped suddenly aside and I was framed in the opening, almost two dozen pairs of eyes staring directly at me.

There was complete silence for a very brief time, then normal conversation began again and one of the men rose and came toward us, a big grin on his face as he looked at me.

"Tammad, I expected you before this," he said, pausing near us to study me. "Though I believe I see the reason for your delay. *Sarella wenda.*"

I smiled pleasantly at the man who had called me an unusually beautiful woman, and Tammad grinned back at him. "She is adequate, Garrad," he said fondly. "How has the time passed for you?"

"All too quickly," the man called Garrad answered with a rueful smile. "There are many more things requiring a *denday*'s time than he has the time to give them. As you well know. Come and seat yourself, and share the *drishnak.*"

He turned and led the way back toward his place among the cushions, not far from the silken back wall of the pavilion. A group of men sat there, grins on their faces and welcome in their minds, but Tammad stopped in the middle of the fur-covered floor to grin at a man on the far right. The man stared back without expression, but furious hate was strong within him. A really beautiful woman sat near him, long silky blond hair falling past her waist, a definite green tinge to her lovely blue eyes.

"*Aldana*, Rommar," Tammad said in a casual drawl. "I see you are again accompanied by your *rella wenda*. She is even more tempting than I had remembered, and you are generous to share the sight of her."

"No more generous than you, Tammad," Rommar answered, almost in a growl. "A *wenda* such as yours is rare indeed, and I would know how you came by her."

"She took a fancy to my furs and followed me." Tammad grinned broadly. "Was I to see her walking the roads unprotected? I shall keep her for the time, and perhaps she may one day suit me."

Rommar outwardly controlled himself at that, but the banter made his mind seethe even more furiously. It was obvious now that I was supposed to be a counter to the other man's *rella wenda*, and I was forced to admire Tammad's thought processes. He must have had that eventuality in mind as far back as our first metting on Central, accepting me as the help he needed, knowing how easily I would fit in. *Sadayin l'lenda*, brainy indeed.

Rommar leaned back slightly, pulling his *wenda* to him. The girl looked at him with an adoring but cowed gaze, then curled up tightly against his chest.

"So you fail to suit him, eh, *wenda*?" Rommar said to me. "My Nalar would not dare to fail to suit me. She is just as I wish her to be."

"That is easily seen, *l'lenda*," I answered with an easy nod. "Perhaps it is more difficult suiting one such as Tammad."

Every man in the pavilion roared with laughter, but Rommar didn't see any humor in the comment. He scowled at me, strong anger filling his mind, but Tammad's pleasure came to me even more strongly. He reached out and stroked my hair, then led the way to where Garrad was awaiting.

"A rare *wenda* indeed." Garrad grinned as Tammad lowered himself to the cushions. "She has almost the sound of *l'lenda* to her. I, too, would know how you came by her."

"She was gifted to me by her father," Tammad answered, pulling me down, not next to him, but into his lap. "He found her pride too great for so slight a form, and asked only that she be taught moderation and obedience. Do you now heed my words, Terril. I am flattered by your exalted opinion of me, yet did you come too close to insult with Rommar. Have you need of another lesson in the consequences of insult?"

"I spoke very carefully so as not to give insult," I told him, and grinned up into his half-amused eyes. "Had I intended insult, I should have added that Tammad does not use fear to see himself suited. No true *l'lenda* would."

Tammad wearily rubbed his eyes with one hand while the other *l'lendaa* around us guffawed. Garrad was vastly amused, and he clapped Tammad on the shoulder.

"She is well named, my friend," he said with a huge grin. "I have no doubt but that your sword has often needed honing since the acquisition of her. Have you yet worn out a switch?"

"Not through lack of effort," Tammad answered dryly, giving me a stern look. "Should Terril wish me to again make the attempt, she need but speak in such a fashion once more.

The laws of the *Ratanan* forbid the use of weapons, yet say nothing of the use of a switch."

"Does Tammad truly seek to make me fear the switch?" I asked innocently, running a finger over his chest. "I had not thought he had need of such."

"All men have need of aid with *wendaa*." Tammad grinned. "And should you continue to do as you now do, you may be sure that I shall take you in this very place, in spite of the amusement of my brothers. This, too, would be fitting punishment for your pride."

I snatched my finger away from his chest as the men laughed again, wondering if he was really telling the truth. That he was easily aroused by me I already knew, but would he really—right there in front of everybody—I took a shaky breath and decided not to try to find out.

Tammad was given *drishnak* by an ordinary serving *wenda*, and the evening wore on. When large platters of meat chunks were passed among the *l'lenda*, I tried to take a chunk and got my hand slapped. Tammad chose one for me instead, but I didn't make a fuss about it—I was too hungry, and too busy studying the men in the pavilion.

All the men in Garrad's group had their attention on Tammad so they were easy to read, as was the group around Rommar, who were constantly taking turns glancing our way, but the uncommitted *dendayy* who ranged themselves with neither side were another matter entirely. They were trying hard for neutrality, but most of them tended to lean more toward Rommar, and that wasn't good. It hadn't been hard to see that Rommar was leader of the opposition.

I stayed in Tammad's lap, facing away from everyone else and holding him around with my eyes closed, but I wasn't trying to snuggle or hide. I was preparing reports on the uncommitted *dendayy*, pinpointing what I could of them so as to make identification easier, too. It wouldn't have helped much to try to describe the large, blond *l'lendaa*, and I didn't know their names.

I finished what I could of the preliminary reports, coming back to awareness of my surroundings to find that Tammad and his friends had had more of the *drishnak* than the meat chunks. Their minds were as blurry as their laughter, and when one looked at me it was with a good deal more heat than previously.

I made the mistake of trying to get out of Tammad's lap,

and was pulled back firmly and smacked hard on the bottom for not having first asked permission. Tammad's emotional control was still good, but it was a lot sloppier than it had been because of the *drishnak*. I had no trouble telling that he was on the verge of being thoroughly angry with me again, so I stayed where I was to avoid more unpleasantness. I couldn't count on his judgment in the sort of condition he had gotten himself into.

Before very much longer, every *l'lenda* in the pavilion was limp. One or two of them still had the strength to hold onto a goblet, but I doubt if they knew what they were holding onto. The girl Nalar was nearly crushed beneath Rommar's arm, but she was making no attempt to get away from him, and I could understand that. My own owner had opted for holding me down on his lap in an obvious and potentially painful way. If I tried to move before he was completely out cold, I would definitely and embarrassingly regret it.

I had just about decided to try prying the fistful of my *caldin* out of Tammad's hand, when the *l'lendaa* who had been left outside began filing into the pavilion. They were chuckling and talking quietly to each other, but separated once they were inside to go to their various *dendayy*. One of Tammad's men got me loose with a single pull, then he and two others lifted Tammad and began carrying him out. I found out why the standard retinue was five in number when one of the far gone *dendayy* tried to resist being carried out. I turned my back on the battle and followed Tammad's body.

The *l'lendaa* carried Tammad past the *camtahh* that had been set up, to a smaller pavilion that was obviously his. They took him inside while I paused to take a deep breath of the fresh night air, a moment later discovering a *l'lenda* at my elbow. I looked up to see a grinning Faddan studying me.

"You do not seem to care for Tammad's state," he told me with a chuckle. "Had you hoped to have him conscious and aware of you?"

"I had hoped for a long conversation with him," I answered blandly, staring him straight in the eye. "Now it must wait for the new sun."

"Aye." Faddan laughed, deeply amused. "All—conversation—must wait for the new sun. I bid you a pleasant sleep, Terril."

He walked away, still chuckling, and I stood outside the pavilion, seeing the campfires range into the distance. I was tired from the day-long trip, drained from studying the men in the pavilion, and the night wasn't as peaceful as most people consider it. Emotions are more intense at night, and though a lot of people slept, those who were still awake made up for the sleepers. I stood slumped in the night, wondering where *I* was supposed to sleep.

"The *denday* calls for his *wenda*," one of the men announced as the three who had carried Tammad into the pavilion filed out again. "Still does he sleep, yet still must his word be obeyed. Do you now go to him, *wenda*."

I felt annoyance even as I stepped into the pavilion. Their *denday* was dead drunk, but I was still expected to obey him. There was a small torch burning feebly in one corner of the pavilion, and I could see Tammad stretched out on his furs. His *haddin* had been removed, and it lay to the left of the furs near his swordbelt. Tammad himself moved restlessly on his furs, his mind empty but for a small yet definite annoyance. He tossed a bit and mumbled, reaching around as if searching for something.

I removed the *imad* and *caldin*, folded them carefully, then slid into my furs, which were, unsurprisingly, right next to Tammad's. He continued to toss around, his annoyance growing, until his arm happened to fall across me. Immediately I was pulled to him, held tight in a grip that was unbreakable. The annoyance in his mind began fading at once, letting him lapse into a deep, restorative sleep. I rubbed my cheek against the chest I was pinned to, and had no difficulty at all in finding sleep of my own.

★ 14 ★

My head throbbed in painful rhythm to my heartbeat, and I had to force my eyes open. It took a minute to realize that the pain wasn't my own, but that of the mighty warrior who sat groggily next to me. Tammad was definitely awake, and when he saw me watching him, he made a valiant effort to control what he was feeling.

"Did you sleep well?" he asked, reaching out to smooth my hair. "There is much for you to do this day."

"I can see that," I answered, holding back a superior grin. "Isn't there anything you can do for that headache?"

"I must wait for it to abandon me," he sighed, stretching out in the furs again. "It is the price one pays for the foolishness of too much *drishnak*."

"As long as you admit it's foolishness, maybe I can help," I said, moving close to stroke his forehead. "Relax your control and let me try."

His muscles eased up somewhat, the action making him wince inwardly at the uncontrolled pain he felt in his head. I surrounded the pain as best I could and soothed it, urging it down to a level he could handle. His surprise didn't keep him from immediately exercising control over what was left of the headache, and his hands kept me from moving away again.

"Truly are you *wenda* without equal," he murmured, enjoying the feel of me against him. "I am again as I was, for you have taken the pain from me." He paused to frown in thought, then demanded, "You have not taken the pain as your own?"

190

"No," I laughed gently. "With you around, I don't need anyone else's pain. Do you still plan on beating me?"

"Should the need arise." He nodded without hesitation. "All men must know that there is ever one greater than they somewhere in the world. I would not have you insult the one who is greater than I, and end his belonging to be punished for insolence. Sooner shall the punishment come from my hand, to be given in full measure, yet not without concern. It is my duty."

"Your duty need not be so carefully seen to, O *denday*," I answered ruefully. How do you argue with someone who's going to beat you because he cares for you? "I'll be too busy doing my job to get into very much trouble."

"Such is my sincere hope," he answered, a faint grin appearing on his face. "You may begin when we have had our meal."

"I've already begun," I said, enjoying his reaction to this second surprise. "Last night, while you were building the foundations of a headache, I was doing what I was brought here to do."

"Then I am the laggard." He grinned more widely, slowly moving his hands on me. "What have you learned?"

That was a question I had no trouble answering. "I've learned that my *aman* is nonexistent when you do that." I groaned, holding tightly to him, then added, "There are no other *l'lendaa* about *now*."

"There soon shall be." He laughed, prying me away from him and forcing me flat. "Therefore must you tell me now that which you have learned. We may not have further opportunity."

I groaned again as he held me still, then took a deep breath. "We'd better make the opportunity," I disagreed. "I've read the men, but I don't know them and can't tell them apart until I see them individually. We'll have to walk around and visit."

"Such is no hardship," he mused, already planning it. "The *Ratanan* allows for much mixing and visiting. Do you now dress yourself, and we shall eat."

He stood to do his own dressing, and after a minute I followed suit. The man was highly frustrating and extremely unfair. He had the *Ratanan* on his mind, and couldn't be lured away from his purpose. I remembered the real we had experienced together, and felt a strong urge to rape *him*—if only just that once. If he hadn't been so big. . . .

Breakfast was waiting in the form of spiced meat chunks, courtesy of the women who had been brought along. My shiny new clothes proclaimed that I was to have nothing to do with the preparing of food, and I can't honestly say I was disappointed. My mind kept centering on the reports I'd put together, and cooking under those circumstances would have cost me a good deal more skin. My hand was no longer covered or salved, and seemed to be healing. I didn't want to press my luck.

After we'd both had some water, we began our visiting tour. Faddan, Kennan, and Loddar came along with us, but I wasn't half as surprised at seeing them as seeing the one called Caffar—the one who hated Tammad. He was among the rest of our fifty, and I didn't understand why.

The tour began with a quick call on Garrad, who was on his feet but just barely. Tammad smiled gently, wished him a speedy recovery, then moved on. Garrad stared after him, a new respect beginning to form. Once the headache was gone, the respect would grow.

We spent a good deal of time with ordinary *l'lendaa*, both out of courtesy and out of necessity. It was impossible to ignore someone without giving insult, and the *dendayy* needed time to come out of the fog. After a couple of hours, though, they all seemed to be whole again, and I was impressed. Tammad's headache was gone completely, with no trace left that it had ever been there.

There were cleared spaces in front of the *dendayy* pavilions, and I soon found out their purpose. Matches between individuals and groups of *l'lendaa* began, and the spirit of competition was high. They all started with weaponless wrestling matches, and I still don't understand how they could consider something like that fun. When one or the other hit the ground he hit *hard*, and there was no question about the pain he felt.

As we approached a group, I recognized the *denday* as one I had drawn a few conclusions about. I plucked at Tammad's swordbelt, gesturing him close when he turned.

"This one needs to be bested at something," I whispered low. "Does that help you?"

He nodded slowly, considering what I'd said, then continued on toward the pavilion. The *denday* stood with his men, watching as two of the *l'endaa* sweated and grunted, seemingly not noticing us. We stood silently too, waiting until one of the men had caused the other to concede, then Tammad turned to the other *denday*.

"*Aldana,* Miggan," he said pleasantly. "Your men seem as fit as ever."

"And ever shall they be," Miggan answered neutrally. "I believe in nothing else. How fares your city, Tammad?"

"Well," Tammad answered. "Our caravans are beset by the savages, yet still we prosper. Have you also been attacked?"

"Aye," Miggan said, and spat disgustedly to one side. "We shall soon have the savages in our *camtahh,* should we continue to fight them singly. We must band together and force them to return from whence they came."

"I, too, believe so." Tammad nodded. "This *Ratanan* must see it done." He glanced toward the cleared space, where another two men struggled, and grinned. "There is fine sport to be had for those who wish to take it, yet it is unfitting for a *denday* to sport with his *l'endaa*. A pity, for I feel the need for such sport."

"Often, I, too, feel such need," Miggan said in the same casual tone while his attention focused on Tammad. "As we are both *dendayy,* let us see to our mutual need."

"An excellent thought," Tammad answered, as though the idea had never occurred to him. "After this match, we shall take our turn."

Miggan nodded, and they both turned back to watch the wrestling. I ignored the wrestling and watched the two *dendayy,* hoping that I'd guessed right. Miggan had been difficult to read until his control had slipped with the intake of *drishnak,* then his superior intolerance had been easy to feel. He had sat alone in the pavilion through his own choice, but not through feelings of unfriendliness. Often a man has difficulty socializing with people he considers his inferiors.

The match ended with a final crash, allowing Tammad and Miggan to step forward before anyone else could do so. They removed their swordbelts to the yells of encouragement from the *l'endaa,* then began measuring each other with their eyes. Neither man felt any doubt, and I wished I could say the same.

They started circling warily, arms out and away from their bodies, bodies bent slightly down and forward. They were both in magnificent condition, strong, healthy brutes bred for battle. Tammad was somewhat the taller, but Miggan made up for the negligible difference with slightly more weight. Their blue eyes were locked on each other, their blond hair stirring not at all in the gentle breeze.

Then suddenly Miggan moved. The mighty Tammad was raised high in the air to be slammed down hard on the ground, but he rolled and was up again immediately, to return to circling with a grin. The pain of landing was not allowed to enter his conscious mind, and seconds later it was Miggan's turn to be raised and dropped, but Miggan, too, quickly regained his feet. His control was not as good as Tammad's, and the pain was felt, but it was totally ignored.

A larger and larger crowd was gathering, and I was only able to keep my place because Tammad's three *l'lendaa* saw to it that no one stood in front of us; and it was a good thing they did—behind the giant *l'lendaa*, I would have missed it all.

The crowd cheered and laughed each time one of the *dendayy* was thrown or locked in a hold, and they cheered and laughed often. Tammad and Miggan were well matched and both knew what they were about, but Tammad's greater control and agility slowly pulled him ahead. Finally, Miggan was taken by the neck and tripped, but when he tried to get to his feet again, he found a knee in his back and his arm twisted in a vise. He tried futilely to escape the hold, then gave in to his overpowering weariness.

"I yield," he gasped out, almost shocked at the words that came from him. Tammad released him immediately, and they both stood, breathing hard, to face one another. Miggan stared briefly then said, "Never had I expected to say those words, Tammad. You are *safeety l'lenda*."

"I, too, have rarely faced such an opponent." Tammad smiled, ignoring the fact that he had been called a superior warrior. "You do me honor by sharing my sport, Miggan. Perhaps we may fight side by side against the savages."

"I would find much pleasure in such an undertaking," Miggan said, nodding slowly. "Aye, much pleasure. Will you share *drishnak* with me, Tammad?"

"Gladly." Tammad grinned as he reclaimed his swordbelt. He put his extra dagger behind him again, and Miggan eyed the dagger in the sheath.

"A lovely weapon, that," he said, nodding at the dagger. "May I see it?"

"Certainly," Tammad answered, handing over the dagger. "It was a house-gift from a close friend, chosen carefully from among many others. I prize it highly."

"So should I," Miggan said, handing the dagger back reluctantly. He collected his own swordbelt, then led the way to his pavilion. Tammad followed, but not before gesturing to me. I went along, and once inside saw that the pavilion was divided in half by a drapery, no sleeping furs being in view. I realized why when a woman came out from behind the drapery. She was five-banded and smiling pleasantly, and her eyes lingered briefly on my *imad* and *caldin*.

"Ah, Padir." Miggan smiled. "Do you fetch the *drishnak* for the *denday* Tammad and me. We drink to victory and defeat."

Padir nodded and left the pavilion, and Miggan's glanced slyly at me.

"My *wenda* is called Terril," Tammad supplied, noticing the other man's slight frown. "Does her presence disturb you?"

"No," Miggan answered, studying me carefully. "She is truly *sarella wenda*, yet do I feel that to merely show a woman demeans her. I intend no insult, Tammad. I merely speak my mind."

"No insult is taken, Miggan," Tammad answered easily. "I feel as you do, though there is no dishonor in also showing a woman who is to be used. My *wenda* is *rella wenda* only for the *Ratanan*."

Miggan thought about that for a minute, then began to laugh heartily. "I see that Rommar has been bested even more than he knows," he guffawed. "His *rella wenda* has been outdone by a *wenda* who is intended to bear children! She shall give you daughters to steal your sleep, Tammad. I know whereof I speak."

"Aye, sons are much the easier to raise." Tammad laughed, eyeing me in a very proprietary fashion, which made me feel extremely uncomfortable. I knew he couldn't give me children, but he sounded so *sure*. . . .

"Here is the *drishnak*," Miggan announced as Padir came back in with a skin. He was feeling very brotherly toward Tammad, and that's what we'd been trying for. As soon as I confirmed that, I ignored the two drinkers for my own thoughts.

Since there was a lot of territory to cover, we didn't spend

too much time with Miggan. I heard nothing of Tammad's
excuse for leaving, but it must have been a good one; when
he tugged gently on my hair to get my attention, Miggan was
still feeling brotherly. Miggan grinned fondly at me, too,
which annoyed me, but he never noticed the annoyance. He
just walked us to the pavilion entrance and lifted a hand in
farewell.

The next *denday* we came to didn't have to be fought with
or drunk with. I told Tammad to ask any question and
thereafter just listen, and when we walked away the *denday*
was feeling as brotherly as Miggan had felt. The man was
bigger than Tammad and tended to speak a good deal more
slowly than he used a sword, and most *l'lendaa* had no patience for listening to him. When Tammad listened, not only
with patience but with interest, the gigantic *denday* was
pleased out of all proportion to the effort. He didn't fail to
compliment me, but I was glad to be away from him. He
remembered me from the night before, and still felt what he
had felt then—which was definitely not brotherly.

We went back to our own pavilion for the midday meal,
and Tammad insisted that we eat inside. It was cooler and
darker out of the bright sun, and once my eyes had adjusted
to the difference, I saw that the sleeping furs had been moved
to the back of the pavilion, and pillows had been scattered
near the front. The drapery that had bisected Miggan's pavilion was available in ours, too, but our drapery was drawn to
one side, leaving the pavilion whole. Tammad sat himself on
one of the pillows, then gestured me down near him.

"I do not understand the way of your power," he said
when I was seated. "You read those men easily and well, yet
their thoughts should not have been open to you. Are you
able to explain this to me?"

"Maybe so, but I don't think you'll like the explanation," I
answered, leaning back a little to study him. "The advice I
gave you was pure guesswork—educated guesswork, true, but
still only guesswork. Do you still feel that sure about me?"

"I would be a fool to doubt you now." He grinned, taking
a mouthful from his bowl of stew. "In what manner do you
'guess'?"

"When I read a man, I see only his emotions," I explained,
after taking a deep breath. "Then I have to interpret the emotions, and that's where the guesswork comes in. Miggan's
feeling of standoffish superiority might have stemmed from a

deeply buried inferiority complex just as easily as from never having been beaten. I had no way of knowing which it was, and therefore had to guess. Just as I guessed that that gonadal gargantua was frustrated through lack of vocal expression. His frustration could have come from general disbelief on the part of others, too—or any one of another half dozen reasons. Do you understand what I mean?"

"Perhaps in part," he answered slowly, chewing over what I'd said as carefully as he chewed the stew. "Were you taught this—interpretation?"

"For many years," I nodded. "I thought I was infallible until the first time I made a mistake. Then I had to admit I was only human."

He ate quietly for a while, then he looked at me as he never had before. "This power of Prime," he mused. "Is it something to be handed from father to son—and mother to daughter?"

"It—doesn't often happen," I said weakly, putting my bowl of stew aside untasted. I didn't want him to know that my gift was a dominant trait and showed up in every generation after the first. He *couldn't* give me children! He *couldn't!*

"Once would be enough," he commented, going back to his stew with a satisfied feeling. I sat and fretted until he noticed that I wasn't eating, then I stuffed down what I could. It was a relief to get back to visiting *dendayy.*

The hours went by and we made conquest after conquest. I'd been lucky enough to guess right in every case, and Tammad followed my directions without a murmur, although he always added a personal touch that never failed to make a good situation better. He and I made a very effective team, and each time we left a pavilion his hug or caress was warmer. The only thing that kept me going was the thought that he'd given his word to let me go back to the embassy.

There's very little excuse I can make. That we'd walked all over the camp to the very outskirts of the *camtahh* was true. That it was nearly sundown and I was tired both mentally and physically is also true. That still doesn't excuse the fact that I almost missed them. If I had, few of us might be alive today.

We stood just within the last line of *camtahh*, talking to our latest convert. He was a man who disliked everything, but who perversely felt guilt about his dislikes. Tammad had discussed nothing but the dislikes of the majority of the *den-*

dayy, making the man feel less alone. The man still disliked him, but if he ever supported anyone, it would be Tammad.

I let my mind and eyes wander over the remainder of field just past the *camtahh*. The sun was setting in that direction, which made one want to look away, but it was so empty and peaceful that it drew me. I closed my eyes and let my mind wander alone—and then I felt it. I snapped back and double checked, but there was no mistake. That empty, lifeless field held dozens of human mind patterns, patiently waiting to be allowed to explode, which was going to happen soon.

My eyes flew open, and I knew I had very little time. Desperately I groaned and doubled over, holding myself with one arm and clutching for Tammad with the other. He broke off in the middle of a sentence and turned to me immediately, his emotional control rippling.

"What ails you?" he asked, reaching for me with anxious hands. As he bent down, I put my arm around his neck, pulling his ear close to my lips.

"I'm all right, but there are men hidden in the field beyond," I whispered raggedly. "I think they're going to attack."

Only his eyes moved, and he looked at the field through attentive slits. With no perceptible hesitation he picked me up, then turned back to the *denday*.

"My *wenda* has taken ill," he announced in normal tones. "I must return her to my *camtah*." Then his voice dropped and he whispered, "Savages in the field beyond. Alert your *l'lendaa*."

The other man barely blinked before answering, "I shall accompany you," then added low, "This is our attack signal."

He pursed his lips and whistled a calm tune, and it was barely in time. Just as the *l'lendaa* in the area started over at a run, the savages attacked. They were on their feet and racing in, screaming their challenge and swinging their swords, almost before it was possible to accept the fact of their presence. They went from invisible to visible in the blink of an eye, and were very hard to see in any event with the setting sun at their backs. The *l'lendaa* shouted their defiance and ran to close with them.

Tammad put me down fast near a *camtah*, growled, "Remain here unless they approach," then turned away to join the battle, drawing his sword as he ran. I stood near the side of the *camtah* and watched what was going on, never having seen anything like it in my life.

The savages crowed with delight as they fought, the delight unfading even when they fell with mortal wounds. They had their entire bodies and faces dyed a deep orange, thick white lines painted here and there over the orange. The *l'lendaa* within earshot had come, but the camp was spread out too far for others to notice the battle.

Swords rang and thudded, men cursed and laughed, savages went down happily, *l'lendaa* died reluctantly. It was a bedlam beyond description, and I found the savages' emotions worse than any I'd yet come across, because they made no sense. Their reactions were almost insane, and I felt repelled by them as well as fascinated. The professional side of me probed deep for explanation, and found the possibility of one: an odd numbness at the back of their minds suggesting the likelihood of drugs.

Many of the savages were down sooner than it takes to tell about it, as they made no attempt to defend themselves, relying only on all-out attack. The tactic would have been a good one with anyone else, but *l'lendaa* were too sure of themselves in battle. They parried the attacks and followed with attacks of their own, and the savages went happily to what they were looking forward to. Some few of the *l'lendaa* died also, but most were just wounded here or there, some worse than others.

The battle was nearly done when I saw what Tammad had gotten himself into. He had been fighting two of the savages, and had been doing better than all right when Faddan, who had been fighting near him, slipped in his own blood and went down. Before the savages could end Faddan, Tammad sprang to his defense, standing over him and fighting not two but four, while the other man tried to stop the flow of blood from his thigh quickly enough to help. Another two of the savages yipped their glee and joined the others, sure that six of them could down the lone *l'lenda*.

Tammad's sword was metallic lightning, flickering here and there without stop, flashing at the savages and keeping them at a distance. There was grim battle joy in him all the while, a release from tensions and conventions that civilized men never experience. But it was a deadly purification, one that could end him as quickly as it could end his opponents.

When I saw the last two savages join the other four, my insides knotted. No matter how good Tammad was, the odds were against his survival. I couldn't just stand there and watch it happen, I had to *do* something, but I was too far away. I left the side of the *camtah*, trying not to be noticed by *any* of the combatants, and moved closer.

By the time I was twenty feet away, I was nearly frantic. One of the savages was down with his head split open, but Tammad was bleeding from too many places, and Faddan was dizzy from loss of blood, unable to get to his feet again. The savages were going to launch themselves at Tammad, intending to sacrifice as many as necessary so that one, at least, would reach the mighty *l'lenda* with a fatal thrust.

I crouched down where I was, forcing calm and gathering every bit of strength I had. I closed my eyes for concentration and dredged up the feelings I'd experienced that day in the rain, of the man who had died with such a great fear of death choking him. The experience was nauseating to feel again, but I ignored my own reactions, intensified the horror and fear, and then projected it at the five savages. Dividing the projection was the hardest thing I'd ever done, but I *had* to do it.

The savages felt the projection below whatever they'd used to numb themselves, and the impact on them was terrible. They wailed in the deepest despair, feeling the horror of death as they'd never allowed themselves to feel it before. Through it all, I felt the presence of another savage not far from me, but there was nothing I could do about it. My strength was draining fast, but I had to hold the projection as long as possible.

In no more than a matter of minutes, my strength was gone and I slumped to the ground, completely played out. No one but a Prime would have been able to hold a projection even that long, but the thought was hardly comforting. I didn't know if I'd held it long enough, and I didn't know what had happened to the savage who had been near me.

I forced my eyes open to see Tammad still engaged with the last two savages, just as an arm circled my waist and pulled me from the ground. The savage laughed insanely as he began carrying me away, and I was even more helpless than ever. The savages were of a size with the *l'lendaa*, and I couldn't have managed another projection literally to save my life. I was being carried toward the empty field, and once we got past the last *camtahh* in line, there would be no one to stop us.

I was trying to find the strength to struggle even slightly when the savage stopped suddenly, laughed a maniacal laugh, then dropped me in a heap. I lifted my head to see that Tammad stood in our way, his eyes hard, his bloody sword raised high. The savage yipped out a challenge and charged, concerned as usual with nothing but attack. Tammad took the smashing blade on his own broad weapon, then quickly swung his sword down. The savage's arm flew severed from his shoulder, and a moment later, his head rolled after his arm. My own head was too heavy to hold up any longer, so I let it fall until it reached my wrist.

"How are you hurt?" Tammad demanded, turning me quickly so that I rested against his arm. "What was done to you?"

"I'm not hurt, just tired," I answered weakly. "Projection is hard work."

"So it *was* you who touched the savages," he said, staring down at me. "From their faces I do not wish to know what was done, but I *will* know why you came out from safety."

"I couldn't reach them from where I was," I explained reasonably. "I had to get closer to be within range, so they would—" I broke off short, realizing what I'd said only from the look on his face. I was too tired to think clearly, and should have kept my big mouth shut.

"Within range," he repeated flatly, a sharper anger adding itself to the controlled rage he already felt. "So you lie as well as disobey. The life of a woman among the savages is not a pleasant one. You risked being cut down, and nearly found yourself taken—all through lack of obedience to my word. It shall not go unnoticed."

He stood then, looking around to see that the battle was over. Women appeared to tend the wounded, and by really trying, I got to my knees. Tammad noticed my struggle, bent, and lifted me in his arms.

"We return now to our *camtah*," he said, but his mind was not as calm as his tone. "You shall eat and rest and restore yourself. When you are as you were, your disobedience shall be punished."

"You can't mean that!" I protested as he carried me along in the gloom. "I was only trying to keep you from getting killed! Would you have been happier getting killed?"

"I am *l'lenda*," he answered stiffly, "and have faced death many times. It is fitting that I should do so." He paused, looked at me in an odd way, then added, "Sooner would I see this *l'lenda* dead than you."

"But you can't beat me!" I wailed.

Damned barbarian. He did.

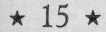

★ 15 ★

I lay in my furs behind the closed drapery, bored and unhappy, but unable to do anything about it. I'd been ordered in no uncertain terms to stir not an inch, and I had no doubts about what would happen if I disobeyed again.

When we'd gotten back to the pavilion the night before, I'd pulled myself together enough to get some water, clean rags, and salve for Tammad's souvenirs from the savages. He hadn't been hurt badly, I was relieved to see, but there's no such thing as being hurt well, I got the wounds washed and medicated, then went after something for us to eat. After the meal and a strong pull on a *drishnak* skin, Tammad went off to see how Faddan was doing, and I had time to rest and think.

I had no trouble resting, but my thinking was anything but clear. I had risked myself, a Prime of the Centran Amalgamation, for the sake of an essentially worthless man from backward Rimilia. Something like that would have been laughed at and condemned by everyone I knew; it would have been considered insanity. Once, I would have considered it insanity too, but that wasn't possible any longer. The man had risked himself more than once for me, and if the situation recurred, I would do the same again.

But was that the only reason? Was I just repaying a debt that I owed, cancelling an obligation? I tried to tell myself that it was so, and failed miserably. I would not have risked myself for just anyone no matter how many times they had saved me, but I hadn't even thought about myself when I saw Tammad in danger of death. He was more than a worthless

man from a backward planet, but just how much more I was
afraid to think about. He cared for me, and I cared for him,
but how far did that care go?

I brooded until he got back, then had no further opportunity for brooding. He lectured me in a cold voice, telling
me exactly how many ways I'd disobeyed him, and didn't allow any interruptions. After the lecture came the switching,
and a royal switching it was. I felt the wrath he had once
spoken of, and a good deal more, and by the time he was
through I heartily regretted everything I'd been guilty of. I
was sent to my furs to contemplate my sins, and Tammad
went off to the *dendarsa camtah* alone. Instead of contem-
plating, I fell asleep.

The next morning, right after eating, it was my turn to lecture. Tammad had limited his *drishnak* intake the night before, and was eager to continue converting *dendayy*, but I
wouldn't be going along with him. He made me describe the
mannerisms of the men involved and add my guesswork, then
gave me my orders about staying put. Considering how irritated he still was with me, I didn't even try to argue. I stayed
put, but I didn't particularly like it.

I heard him get back at midday, but he stayed in the front
part of the pavilion and I could feel that he was deep in
thought. I left the furs and went to the drapery, peering
around the side of it to see him stretched out on the cushions.

"May I come out now?" I asked when I felt that he was
aware of my presence. When he didn't answer I added a
small, "Please?"

"Have you thought upon the reasons for your punishment?" he asked, moving his eyes to me. When I grimaced
and nodded he smiled. "Dress yourself then and join me. Our
meal will soon be brought."

I went back and dressed in record time, then came out
from behind the drapery just as one of the women brought in
two bowls of stew. She hid her amusement well enough, but I
felt myself blushing anyway. The way I'd yelled the night before, the entire camp must have known about my beating.

When the woman was gone, Tammad gestured me over to
him. "You have done very well so far," he said with warmth
as he handed me a bowl. "There was a mistake in your esti-
mation of one man, yet was I able to turn it to my advantage. When the discussions begin with the new sun, you
must read the others again and weigh the manner in which

they receive my words. I shall broach the most important subject last."

I nodded again and sat carefully, then studied him. "What exactly is it that you want for your people?" I asked after a minute. "I know you have some specific purpose in mind, and I'm curious about it."

"My purpose is clear." He shrugged, eating some of his stew. "I would have my people survive and prosper. Is this so different from the wants of others?"

"No," I answered, "but you yourself are different from others. I think you want to be *denday* of *dendayy*."

"How may a man hide from one who sees as deeply as you?" He laughed. "Such is indeed my intent, yet the time is not right for the thing. All things come in their proper time."

"So I've heard," I murmured. "At least no one can say you have no ambition. What would you do as *denday* of *dendayy*?"

"I would see that my people survived and prospered," he answered neutrally. "Do you now eat quickly so that you may see the competitions between cities. They began earlier, and much honor shall be won by the city which triumphs most. I shall have no need of you here."

"Then you're not going," I said, knowing it as a fact. "You have something more important to do, and it doesn't concern me." I looked down at my bowl then added, "I'll leave as soon as I'm through."

"Do not feel *ahresta*!" he said sharply, reaching over to take my face in his hand. "I would have you beside me always, yet there are matters I must see to alone. It would not be fitting to have *wendaa* present."

"*Wenda!*" I snapped, pulling back away from his hand. "When you come right down to it, I'm still nothing but *wenda*! Handle your matters alone and be damned!"

I got to my feet and stalked out, trying to bury my hurt beneath layers of fury. The question of *wenda* had nothing to do with why he wanted me out of the way and I knew it. He was going to discuss things he didn't want me knowing about, that's why I'd been offered time off to see the fair. He didn't trust me enough to let me in on his secrets, and that really hurt.

I'd left my bowl of stew almost uneaten, but I wasn't hungry at all. I wandered around from camp area to camp area, stopping occasionally to watch the goings-on. There were wrestling matches, knife throwing matches, swordfights, riding contests, and archery contests. The *l'lendaa* enjoyed them all, either participating or watching, their women in the crowds along with them.

I saw one pavilion that had been opened completely, and every man in it had a woman in tow. Other, unaccompanied men ringed the pavilion and examined the women with interest. As I watched, one man entered the pavilion and approached another who was holding a woman's arm. They spoke briefly, *dinga* was exchanged, and the man who had been alone left with the woman. I noticed that she was one-banded, and realized that she had just become the belonging of the man who had paid for her. She hadn't felt terribly upset by the exchange, in fact she was rather excited, and I couldn't help shaking my head. Was I the only one who was disturbed by such things? Did the women really prefer such a life, or were they just used to it? I didn't know, and probably never would.

The contests went on for the rest of the afternoon, but at sundown the crowds began breaking up. I continued to wander, reluctant to go back to the pavilion. I hadn't paid attention to where I was going, but paying attention wasn't necessary. I could find my way back by following the patterns of our people, so I just wandered wherever the whim took me.

The campfires were beginning to show more sharply against the darkening sky. I moved behind a line of *camtahh*, still full of my own thoughts, and a group of figures moved out of the shadows to surround me. I looked up in surprise to see Rommar directly in my path, six other *l'lendaa* completing the circle around me.

"*Aldana, wenda,*" Rommar said with an expressionless face, staring down at me. "You wander far from the *camtah* of Tammad."

"I mistook my direction," I answered, matching his evenness of tone. "I should return at once, for the hour is late."

I tried to step around him, but he moved just enough to block me again. His emotions were calm, but I could feel a sort of excitement in the minds of the others. It didn't take much ability to suspect that I had trouble.

"Tammad shall not seek for you as yet," Rommar informed me. "He speaks with his followers of matters of great import. The number of his followers has increased beyond my expectations, and this disturbs me. There is little I may do to alter the situation, yet must it be altered. Perhaps Tammad will be good enough to act for me."

I didn't even see the slap coming, but my head rang with it, my cheek turning to burning needles. I cried out at the pain, trying to protect myself, but the second slap touched my other cheek with fire, and he wasn't even exerting himself. The circle closed in tight, someone stuffed a cloth in my mouth, and it didn't take very long, but I had to use pain control even before Rommar's fist reached my stomach. I lay curled up on the ground, nauseously dizzy and bleeding from one corner of my mouth, and there was still no anger in him. He had hurt me unemotionally and for a purpose, but I had nothing to do with that purpose.

The men were satisfied with what had been done, and I lay still for a few minutes after they were gone, then got rid of the gag and got painfully to my feet. My *imad* was ripped, my *caldin* was dirty, and I was expected to do something. I had a fairly good idea about what that something was, but I had no intentions of doing it. I got my bearings with a bit of difficulty, then started back to my own area.

Even with pain control, it was harder going than I'd expected it to be. My stomach kept wanting to cramp up, and that made walking difficult. I kept to the shadows as much as possible, breathing heavily from the exertion, but about halfway there Loddar found me. He saw me before I was aware of him, and he hurried over.

"Terril, what has happened?" he demanded, lifting my face gently to see the bruises more clearly. A screaming anger filled him, and he lifted me from the ground. "Tammad was wise to feel concern over your absence," he growled. "There will be blood spilled over this!"

He hurried back to the pavilion, moving carefully so as not to hurt me further. There weren't many people about, for which I was grateful, and not having to walk let me work at restoring myself a little. By the time we got there, I was prepared to do what had to be done.

Tammad looked up as we entered, his annoyance disappearing immediately as he jumped to his feet. A deep ache filled him as he took me from Loddar, and he briefly and gently held me to him before setting me down on the cushions.

"How badly are you hurt?" he asked in a choked voice, his

finger carefully daubing at the blood on my mouth. "I shall have his life for this, I swear it!"

"He wishes you to make the attempt," I got out, not able to soothe his ache. I needed everything I had to keep from groaning and showing what a really good job Rommar had done.

"His wish shall be answered," he said grimly, rising to his feet again. His rage was a monumental thing, harsher than anything I'd care to face. "Loddar, stay you with Terril and see to her. I shall return shortly."

"Aye, you shall indeed return shortly," I said in disgust to his broad back. "Bereft of all you have worked for, but filled with a boy's satisfaction. Your honor shall be intact."

He whirled back to me, his face twisted with anger. "Am I to congratulate him on his treatment of my *wenda*?" he demanded in a roar. "Am I to become *darayse* and overlook his crime?"

"Are you to hop to his bidding as a child obeys its father?" I countered. "This was done for no purpose other than to force you to break the laws of the *Ratanan*! Your voice cannot be heard by the others from the distance of your own city, and I would wager a goodly amount that he now sits surrounded by innocents who would condemn only you for baring a blade. He would be left here, and you would be gone! Is this what you wish?"

He stared at me, his mind in turmoil, and Loddar stepped closer. "*Denday*, she has the right of it," he said slowly. "I, too, would have faced the man with thirsty blade, yet she sees more clearly in spite of her pain. *Sadayin wenda*, as well as *sarella*. Her thoughts and actions do credit to her name, and I salute her courage."

"My small warrior," Tammad said, smiling slightly in spite of the ache that had reclaimed him, "is he to give you pain and suffer nothing himself in return, *l'lenda wenda*? I would indeed be *darayse* were I to allow such to happen."

"His pain shall come at the defeat of his schemes," I said, starting to feel dizzy again. "Should you bitterly discuss the happening with others, burning to know the identity of one who would do such a thing, no thoughts of *darayse* would arise. Also, should he admit the deed out of desperation, there would be few to stand with him. He may yet give you the opportunity you seek."

"I am not to know who did this?" he asked in surprise. "How may I not know?"

"Through great fear of *l'lendaa*, I shall speak no name," I answered weakly. "You may then suspect, but you may not know."

"Fear of *l'lendaa!*" Loddar guffawed, sticking his thumbs in his swordbelt. "Never have I seen *wenda* with so little fear of *l'lendaa*. Rommar shall indeed regret his actions."

"I will not be satisfied until he is beyond regret," Tammad said softly, sitting down next to me to stroke my hair. "Loddar, do you bring water, and have a broth prepared for my small warrior. I feel her pain is deeper than she would have us know."

Loddar nodded and left, and I closed my eyes, drawing strength from the hand that touched my hair. In a short while my face was washed carefully, and a short while after that the broth was brought. Again it had the strange but pleasing taste to it, and it went down easily into the void in me. I was then carried to my furs, undressed, and allowed to sleep.

It was still very dark when I awoke, and I moved carefully, testing for pain. Between my own efforts and the medicated broth there was none, but Tammad's mind was instantly alert, centered on me with worry and fear. It was almost a shock to realize that he did feel fear, but the fear wasn't personal, it was for me. His Prime's work was nearly done, but he wasn't afraid for his Prime. He was afraid for *me*.

"Are you in difficulty?" he asked softly, moving closer on his furs. His hand took mine and held it, swallowing it almost completely.

"The pain is gone," I answered, glad that he couldn't see the bruises on my face. The dark gave me a courage I never thought I'd need, and I added in a small voice, "Tammad, may I share your furs?"

"Terrillian *hama*," he breathed, drawing me to him as a great joy filled him. "Never before have you spoken my name, nor asked to come to me. I had almost given up hope."

"Tammad *hamak*," I murmured, thrilled with calling and being called beloved. "I had not had the courage nor sense to speak before this. More fool I."

"Foolish perhaps, but never a fool." He chuckled, holding me tight. "All will be well now."

It wasn't well, it was indescribably wonderful. I gave myself happily, and he accepted my gift gently, tenderly, yet still with passion. His desire was great, but he satisfied it with duration rather than intensity, allowing me to share my strongest feelings in order to increase his satisfaction. The night surrounded wishes fulfilled, and never had life meant more to me.

★ 16 ★

The morning was beautiful, and even my almost constant yawning didn't spoil it. Tammad laughed at the yawns, and I grinned along with him even as I blushed. The night had been too good to regret the loss of sleep.

I followed Tammad to the *dendarsa camtah*, which had been opened all around so that the gathered *l'lendaa* could hear the discussions within, and I was very glad there was no mirror available. I was dressed in a fresh *imad* and *caldin*, but I could gauge the bruises on my face by the fury and pain Tammad felt every time he looked at me. I had the company of a full dozen *l'lendaa*, and they would stay with me until Tammad was free again.

The morning was spent discussing the problem of the savages, and victory was very sweet. Rommar was unalterably opposed to a united effort against them and spoke convincingly for his position, but Tammad's arguments were even more convincing. The *dendayy* supported Tammad, and I was glad I hadn't scratched the itch to project a bit of general agreement and belief. Tammad's victory was completely his own, and Rommar soured further with defeat.

The *dendayy* took the midday meal together, so I took the opportunity to go for a bath. Tammad gave reluctant permission for me to visit the stream on the far side of the camp, and his *l'lendaa* were just as jumpy as he was. They didn't know who had attacked me the night before, but they hadn't needed Tammad's orders to keep a close eye on me. Every time they looked my way, their lips tightened and their minds seethed.

211

The stream was a very welcome sight, and I stripped quickly and stepped into the water. It was cool and refreshing, doing a lot to ease my tiredness. I washed quickly, then stood up to my shoulders soaking, a small smile of memory on my lips due to the night before.

I was brought back to reality by a brief cramp, then was shocked to see dark red swirling in the clear water below me. It was obvious that I was bleeding, and my first thought was that I'd been injured by Rommar's attack on my stomach. I fretted over the idea for a minute or two, and then another possibility presented itself. It was nonsensical and impossible, but my body might have been telling me that I was pregnant!

Shakily, I told myself that that was ridiculous. I'd had my six month anti-pregnancy treatment, and it had never been known to fail. I had lots of time until the next treatment was due, as the last treatment had been taken care of just before I'd left for Dremmler's sector. I cast my mind back, trying to pinpoint the exact date of treatment, then closed my eyes. I'd been treated almost two months before I'd left on my last assignment.

But it still couldn't be! I was supposed to have warning when my protection wore off. Strong cramps that couldn't be missed were the warning, and I hadn't had those. I hadn't felt anything like—my argument stopped and another part of me laughed at my blindness. I'd had the cramps, all right, but I'd thought it was Rommar's doing. My body had warned me, but I'd missed the warning. Now it was taking great pleasure in telling me that it was pregnant, that it had finally gotten around the restrictions I'd imposed on it. Abrupt lack of protection like that made a woman immediately vulnerable, and the bleeding was a confirmation of impregnation that also couldn't be missed.

I stayed where I was for the ten or fifteen minutes it took for the bleeding to stop, and happily the *l'lendaa* saw nothing of it. I was numb for a while, but then I examined my emotions and found only part of the shock I'd expected. I didn't want to be pregnant, but it wasn't the terrible thing I'd pictured, and I felt no different. Then I asked myself honestly if I could have gone home even if I hadn't been pregnant, and I honestly had to answer no. Tammad was the man I wanted, but he was an earthbound deep-spacer on Central. He belonged with his own people, and I would have to stay wherever he was.

I climbed out of the water and dressed, wrapped in a calm that didn't have to be forced. I hadn't thought about what would happen after the *Ratanan*, but now I had to think about it. My *hamak* would take me back to his city, and then I would tell him my news. He had enough on his mind at present, and didn't need to be distracted.

I got back to the *dendarsa camtah* shortly after the discussions had begun again, and I could feel Tammad's relief all the way from the back of the crowd. I looked through a gap in the bodies and smiled at him, and his answering grin warmed every part of me. Various unimportant city matters were discussed through the afternoon, but I paid close attention so that my report on the *dendayy* would be as complete as possible.

That night after the evening meal, I gave Tammad my report. We discussed possible reactions to various arguments for the establishment of the Centran complex, and I was told which of the *dendayy* should be read again and more completely. I filed the instructions away for the next day, then joyed in the touch of my *hamak*. He was fiercely pleased with me, and my admiration for his abilities couldn't have been greater. He was a *denday* without equal, a *l'lenda* without fear, a man without doubt. I loved him.

The next two days were unremarkable. I listened to the discussions, read the men, made countless suggestions, and discovered more about Rommar. He, too, was a man with a purpose, but his purpose was to keep Rimilia isolated, and separated within her isolation. He feared and hated the idea of unity, but I couldn't discover why. I tried hard enough, in order to counter the man better, but I had no luck.

The night of the fourth day, Tammad came back to our pavilion in high spirits. I looked at him questioningly, and he grinned.

"I have just outlined the arguments I plan to use in the next discussions," he said lightly. "As the subject to be discussed is the Centran Complex, Caffar was most interested."

"Caffar?" I blurted. "But isn't he the one who—"

"Who is in the employ of Rommar?" He chuckled. "Indeed he is. Soon Rommar too shall hear of my plans."

"You gave him counterfeit arguments!" I pounced, finally seeing the point. "When tomorrow comes, he'll be totally unprepared!"

"Such is to be hoped." He nodded, pulling me to him so he

could run his hands over me. "Upon sword or dagger, it shall soon be decided. No other could have given me the aid you have supplied. You are truly *l'lenda wenda*, my Terrillian *hama*. Should victory come, it shall be yours as well."

"I could ask for no more than to share it with you," I said, meaning every word of it. We had worked together, and no matter what happened, we'd both know we'd done our best.

The next day was bright and sunny, but it felt as if there should be lightning flashes. The tension was high among the spectators of the talks, and even the *dendayy* were showing signs of unrest. Everyone knew what was next on the agenda, and they knew, too, that any decision made could change their lives forever. Excitement flickered all around, but absolute silence descended once the *dendayy* were in their places. Tammad didn't move from his cushion, but his voice rang out clearly.

"It is time that we speak of a matter of import," he said to the others. "The last *Ratanan* saw a decision that must now be changed, else our world may be lost to us. I would speak in favor of what is called the Centran complex."

"And I would speak against it!" Rommar put in loudly. "The *denday* Tammad would have us believe that the offworlders mean us no harm, that our lands shall not be taken from us, that our ways shall not be interfered with. This is but the dream of an aged *wenda*, who fears the night and so reassures herself with fantasy. These offworlders, these *mondarayse*, seek to take what is ours with words. I, for one, mean to greet them with sword in hand, and thereafter watch them scurry back to their flying houses, never to return again!"

Ragged yells of agreement broke out here and there among the spectators, but the rest kept silent. Once the noise had died down, Tammad leaned back and inspected Rommar.

"The *denday* Rommar is fearless indeed," he drawled. "To face the weapons of the offworlders, which may destroy a man completely from as far away as those farther trees, with naught save sword in hand, is something I, myself, would not care to do. The offworlders may scurry indeed—directly to their weapons."

Rommar was slightly off-balance, but he didn't let it show. Instead, he sneered at Tammad. "And if these weapons should be used? I am *l'lenda*, and unafraid to die! Not all here be *darayse*!"

"True," Tammad agreed quickly before anyone else could react to the words. "Yet not all here be *l'lenda* either. What is to happen to our lands, and children, and *wendaa* once we have died uselessly? Dying is effortless, and may be achieved by the lowest of creatures. To live, to survive and prosper, requires *l'lendaa!*"

This time the cheers were for Tammad, and that infuriated Rommar. "And *how* are we to live?" he demanded. "As scraping servants to the *mondarayse*? They shall steal our manhood from us as they try to steal our land! We must not allow them to set foot on our world!"

"The time for such foolishness is long past," Tammad answered coldly. "They wish to have the use of our world, and shall have that use whether *we* wish it or no. They have greater numbers than we, greater weapons, and greater knowledge. We may refuse to allow them entry this *Ratanan*; by the next, those of us who have not died shall see the deed done!"

"I had thought you spoke *for* the offworlders," Miggan put in from his spot. "Your words do not seem to agree with this."

"I speak only for our people!" Tammad said forcefully, rising to his feet. "The offworlders shall have what they covet, yet our people may still survive and prosper should this thing be done properly. Allow them their complex, yes, but with many sides to the agreement. The complex must be built in an area of our choosing; the laws of our people must be obeyed by all who walk among us; schooling in their knowledge must be made available to our young; much *dinga* must be available for our use. All these things and more they may be made to agree to *now!* Should they come in force for their complex, we shall be allowed only the right to die!"

"What of the life we have known!" Rommar shouted, also getting to his feet. "Think you our lives shall remain unchanged? That which we have always known shall be no more! Far better that we die than see the ways of our fathers fall to ashes before us!"

"Should we die, the ways of our fathers shall truly fall to ashes!" Tammad shouted back. "Only by living and growing with whatever comes may we preserve what there is to preserve. Our sons shall respect the words of living fathers; they may only mourn and forget the dead. We may die easily in righteousness, or we may live to struggle for our way of life. I am *l'lenda*! I cannot choose death over struggle!"

The roar of acclaim was deafening, and the other *dendayy* were also on their feet, shouting with the crowd. The agreement was there, so strong that nothing else came through. If the mood could be preserved, victory was inevitable.

"You do not hear my words!" Rommar screamed, his mind frothing with madness. "This man shall lead you all to destruction, yet I have never been one to follow blindly. I call this Tammad *darayse*, and spit on him! He does not dare to face me with sword in hand!"

The crowd quieted immediately, and Miggan stepped to Tammad. "It is not necessary to take notice of that one," he said quietly. "He speaks of the ways of our fathers, yet spurns the laws of the *Ratanan*. He may be sent from here in disgrace should that be your wish."

"The laws of the *Ratanan* are to be obeyed," Tammad said, his eyes on Rommar. "Yet, I, too, must spurn them for a greater purpose. I accept his challenge."

The crowd moved aside to let the *dendayy* off the pavilion platform, then formed a large ring. Tammad and Rommar stepped into the center of the ring and faced each other with drawn swords, fury filling Rommar, satisfaction in Tammad.

Rommar moved first, swinging his sword back, then bringing it forward two-handed. Tammad brought his own sword up and caught the blow, then swung in attack at Rommar. Metal clashed and rang, and it was obvious that Tammad faced a man who was his equal. The two giants swung at each other, but not blindly. Each handled his blade with skill and control, Rommar using his rage to add to his strength. He whipped his sword at Tammad, trying to open him wide, and Tammad jumped back out of the way just in time. Tammad avoided the back-swing as well, then chopped hard at Rommar, making him duck away from the vengeful edge that would have cut him in two.

Then, without any warning, the end came. Rommar swung his sword back for another furious assault, and Tammad's blade arched down, splitting Rommar's head. Rommar's mind was then beyond pain, and his body fell to the dust of Rimilia, having finally achieved the ultimate isolation.

The *l'lendaa* moved forward to voice their approval, and I turned silently and went back to our pavilion to sit myself among the cushions. I needed some time to think, to straighten out in my own mind what had happened.

Tammad had won his victory, but not along the lines we had discussed. He was supposed to have stressed the benefits of membership in the Amalgamation, instead he had used distrust and urgency to make his points. He intended to use the Amalgamation to get what he wanted for his people, just as he had used the information I had provided to sway the *dendayy*. His game was deep, and I finally understood why I hadn't been included in the talks with his allies. They, presumably, had been told his true plans. In spite of all of my previous decisions, I didn't know whether or not I completely approved of his intention to use the Amalgamation to achieve his ends. It didn't seem quite fair.

When Tammad finally got back to the pavilion, he was calmly pleased. He threw himself down on the pillows near me and grinned happily.

"The thing is done," he said, pulling me to him. "The *dendayy* support my suggestions, and shortly the offworlders shall be allowed their complex. My people have much to look forward to, but great care must be taken lest they lose all through innocence. I shall do all I may to see that such does not occur."

"Do you really think the Amalgamation will deliberately destroy your people?" I asked quietly. "Can you believe them such heartless monsters?"

He sighed and smoothed my hair. "It shall not be from conscienceless doing that such will occur, Terril mine. In the presence of new ways, the old must change or die completely. Many years ago, I traveled to the lands that lie far to the south. Two separate peoples dwell in that land, one with greater ability than the other. The two peoples had never fought, yet the people with lesser ability were nearly gone. They had clung to their old ways and attempted to make no changes, as they wished to preserve what their fathers had built. Their children looked about them, yearned for the greater knowledge to be had with the abler people, and left their homes never to return. These children took the ways of the abler people as well as their knowledge, and their fathers died alone, bitter and deserted. It was not the fault of the abler people, not that of the children. Should greater knowledge be available, it is part of a man to wish to possess it."

"And you don't want your people to die bitter and alone,"
I summed up, stroking his face. The courage it takes to force
people to survive! "You'll see that they change their ways so
that those ways may be preserved. Rapan was right when she
spoke of your wisdom. You will be *denday* of *dendayy* and
your people will flourish."

"I have little wisdom." He grinned. "Else I would not have
faced Rommar. Should he have bested me, my people would
soon have followed in my path. I took a boy's satisfaction,
and shall not do so again until my successor is chosen. Then
my death will be meaningless."

"Never will it be meaningless!" I gasped, holding him tight.
"You are foolish indeed to speak so!"

"Forgive me, *l'lenda wenda*," he laughed softly. "I shall
not speak so again. With one such as you, there is little need
to speak at all."

He spoke to me then without words, and I sang in re-
sponse. Never before had I known such a man, never again
will there be another.

After we had eaten together, he left to see to his business
and I stayed in the pavilion and dreamed. I was eager to get
back to our city so I could learn what Gilor had to teach me.
I wanted to do everything for Tammad and be everything to
him, and proudly bear his children. My gift would be a part
of every child I gave him, and I would give him as many as
he wished. I would be his to the end of my days.

There were still at least three hours to sundown when he
returned. I ran to greet him, but he drew me outside where
Loddar, Kennan, and a dozen other *l'lendaa* were waiting,
mounted on *seetarr* with pack *seetarr* as well. I stared at
them, not understanding, and Tammad put his arm around
my shoulders.

"You shall go with Loddar and Kennan," he said quietly.
"They are charged with your safety, and shall care for you."

"Go?" I echoed in confusion. "Go where? Where am I
being sent?"

"You go to the house of the offworlders," he answered.
"As it is a long journey, it is best you begin now. Fare you
well, Terril mine, and see that you mind Loddar. He shall
look upon you as one of his daughters."

He squeezed me briefly, then turned away and headed
back toward the *dendarsa camtah*. In deep shock I put my
hand out after him, wanting to call him back, wanting to beg

him to keep me. My mind went to his and my soul screamed in agony—because there was no sadness or regret in him, no sense of loss of any sort. He was sending me back because my job was done, and he would not miss the Prime he had used. My hand fell again to my side, the words unspoken, and my world was dead and gone.

"Come, Terrill," Loddar said gently. "You shall ride with me."

I walked woodenly to Loddar and let him lift me to the saddle fur behind him. I put my arms around his waist, feeling nothing, and we started for the road. Not once did I try to look back.

★ 17 ★

The trip was the dream of a nightmare. When we camped, I didn't care where we were and I spoke to no one. I ate what was given me, and if nothing was given I didn't miss it. In the beginning, Loddar tried to get me to cook the game that they caught, then he gave up. Kennan would stare at me worriedly and draw Loddar aside to speak to him, then they would both stare at me, shake their heads, and go away. It made no difference at all to the way I felt.

I kept asking myself how I could have been so wrong, how I could have made such an enormous mistake. He cared for me and he'd said so—but he'd also sent me away. He had called me *hama*—but *hama* translated as "sweetheart" as well as "beloved." It had been no more than wishful thinking on my part that I was his beloved, no more than my own blinding need for him that had convinced me that he wanted me, too. He cared for me, yes—but he didn't love me.

I sat on the bare ground outside the *camtah* that was mine, seeing nothing but my lap and the motionless hands that lay in it. He'd had so many women in his bands—everyone said so—but he'd tired of all of them, and had given them away. In all honesty it was hard understanding how he *wouldn't* tire of any single woman. With the variety he was constantly offered as *denday*, there was no need for him to look for one woman of his own. What in the world had made me think that *I* could do any more for him than the others had?

He had been attracted to me, he had cared for me, he had enjoyed having a Prime in his furs—but now it was over. He had other things to concern himself with, things of greater importance than an offworlder *wenda*. I didn't know the details of his plans, but I had no doubt that he was planning something he'd discussed with no one, something that neither the Amalgamation nor his own people had a hint about. He would unveil it at just the right moment, and it would be as successful as everything else he did. Everything else.

I lay alone in my furs, night after night, my hand on the only place any part of him remained with me. I had been honored with the child of a *denday*, when what I'd wanted was the *denday* himself. But he was *l'lenda*, and he'd made his choice, and I was too proud to crawl back on my knees to argue his choice. Not that it would have done any good—arguing with him had never done any good. His choice was made, and it was final.

Eventually the road went around the small village I remembered, and I knew we were almost to the embassy. I thought about how much I'd wanted to get back to the embassy, and I could have laughed. I was finally getting my wish.

We pulled up at the small back door of the embassy, and Loddar and Kennan dismounted, taking me with them. Loddar pounded on the door until it opened, then stepped aside. Denny stood there and gaped at me, then looked questioningly at Loddar.

"The *denday* Tammad sends his greetings and his *wenda*," Loddar said to him. "May your road be an easy one."

He and Kennan turned and left then, riding away with the other *l'lendaa*. Denny put his arm around me, drew me inside, and closed the door.

"Terry, what's happened?" he demanded. "Where's Tammad?"

"He's with his people," I answered tonelessly. "Making final arrangements for the complex."

"Then you did it!" He grinned, hugging me. "Come on, let's pass on the good word."

He took my hand and drew me after him, but not upramp. We went to the embassy's spacious visitors' room instead, which held five men. The men turned to us as we entered, and Denny laughed.

"Gentlemen, it was a success," he announced. "The complex will be allowed, and I think we owe a toast to our Prime for another excellent job."

The men murmured happy agreement, and Denny moved

toward the autobar that the room held, but my attention was caught by a motionless figure, my eyes meeting those of Murdock McKenzie. He was really there, right in the room, and he was staring at me.

"And what of Tammad, Terrillian?" he asked quietly. "Hasn't he come back with you?"

I shook my head from side to side, seeing Murdock McKenzie for the first time when I was awakened. His face was sourly emotionless and professionally calm, but his mind cared for me, worried about me, ached for me. He saw my pain as Denny hadn't, and he cried for my hurt.

"He doesn't want me, Father," I choked out. "I love him so, but he doesn't want me."

Murdock McKenzie's arm lifted and I ran to him, huddling against his twisted body, sobbing out the unbearable agony I was filled with. He didn't want me, and my life would be forever grey.

When I had no strength left to cry with, Denny helped me upramp to a room. He was silent as we walked, but his mind was grim with the hurt of disappointment. He put warm water in the bathroom's tub, then stopped short on his way to the door. He came back to stare at the bands I still wore, and I realized I'd forgotten all about them.

"Well, that's one thing you won't need anymore," he growled, reaching out to my wrist. His muscles bunched, and he had to strain, but the bands opened one after the other. When all five of them lay on the floor he left, but I stared at the heap of chain with the most desperate longing imaginable. By the time I got to the bath, the water was cold.

I slept for a long time, and when I woke I dressed in my own clothes and went downramp. Denny and Murdock and the others were in the embassy dining room, occupying only a small section of the formal dining table. I'd always had difficulty accepting the fact that diplomats were used to feeding their temporary guests and visitors, but right then it seemed the most natural thing in the world. Everyone's head turned toward me as I entered, and Denny rose quickly to come to me.

"Terry, how are you feeling?" he asked gently, his face and thoughts concerned. "Come and have something to eat."

"I'm all right, Denny," I answered, patting his arm. "The world hasn't really come to an end, and it's about time I got used to the idea."

"Terrillian, come sit with me," Murdock called, and I could feel his tender concern. I went to the table and took the chair next to his, and he stared into my eyes. "Terrillian, tell me about what went on between you and Tammad. I'd like to have the complete story."

I shrugged a little and told him everything, every stupid, foolish thing I had done since I reached Rimilia. I didn't tell him about being pregnant, as that was something I had to reassess myself before I would discuss it with anyone else. When he had it all, I finished up with, "I suppose I have no one but myself to blame. I *am* useless in his world, and I mistook gratitude and respect for my professional ability, for love and desire for me personally. He's a very special man, Murdock, and he deserves the best."

"As do you, my dear Terrillian," he answered in his stiff, sharp way. "You don't seem the same as you were, and the change enhances you. There is quite a lot I can do for you on Central now, and I will be pleased to see to it. Rathmore will be very grateful."

"There's no need for that," I said, feeling his desire to protect me. "It was just another job, and I did it. My hazard insurance will cover everything else."

"Hazards of that sort are never covered by insurance," he came back dryly. "Allow me to see to the matter."

He went back to eating and I turned to my own food, glad that Murdock was there. I rarely feel the need to be protected, but there are times when strong protection is the only thing that will let you rest. I was very tired, and I needed rest badly.

After the meal was over, we returned to the visitor's room. I hadn't enjoyed the food, and I was still trying to understand why. Stasis will keep food fresh forever, but every dish had somehow tasted flat and stale, as if it *had* been in stasis forever. I accepted the glass of wine Denny poured for me, and sat down to listen to the conversation of one of the Diplomacy Bureau people Murdock had brought with him. The man found me attractive, but he'd said nothing about it yet. Since the bruises were completely gone from my face, I wondered why he didn't say something, then briefly closed my eyes. It would be a long trip crossing back to my own world.

It didn't take long before I was ready to return to my room. I wasn't sleepy, but the diplomat had finally gotten around to discussing—not very diplomatically—the sex practices of the Ramilian people. He had asked with a snicker if it was true that they exchanged women all the time. When I told him that women were exchanged only under special circumstances, he laughed aloud and commented that that was as good an excuse as any other, then asked me if I was in the mood to be exchanged. I stood up without saying anything, and went to pour myself another glass of wine.

As soon as transportation was available, I would be on my way back to Central, back to a life I wasn't sure I could live any longer. I saw everyone differently now, and it would be no surprise to find that I no longer fit in. If that turned out to be the case, I would leave Central again, to find somewhere else to live. I had no idea where, but decided that it didn't really matter. I'd make a new beginning on a new planet, and try to forget something that would never let itself be forgotten. One day I might find myself able to accept it instead, and then I'd know that I was home.